By Janet Pywell

Masterpiece

ISBN: 978-0-9926686-7-9

Cover Art copyright © 2016 Candescent Press

Published by Richmond Heights Publishing

For more information visit: www.janetpywell.com

AUTHOR'S NOTE

In the early hours of March 18th 1990, two men dressed as Boston police officers duped security guards into letting them inside the Isabella Stewart Museum. The guards were tied up and the thieves stole thirteen pieces of artwork at an estimated total value of $500 million.

These original pieces of art have never been recovered and the case remains open and unsolved. *The Concert* was one of the stolen pieces.

I would like to thank Ariel Bruce a Registered Independent Social Worker who specialises in tracing people affected by adoption and, with her associates, has undertaken all of the research to trace and make contact with missing family members for every series of ITV's Long Lost Family. Jo Rzymowksa for sharing her extraordinary story that has no bearing on this novel but gave me an insight into 'relative' documents. Laurence Everitt and Kirsty Logan for their musical advice, which has helped bring Mikky's quirky character to life. The team at Cornerstones UK; Ayisha Malik, Alex Hammond and author Alison Taft for her invaluable feedback. Many thanks to author Joe McCoubrey for his advice and support.
Finally, a massive thank you to my family and friends.

Chapter One

'It is good to love many things, for therein lies the true strength,
and whosoever loves much performs much,
and can accomplish much, and what is done in love is well done.'
Vincent van Gogh

I begin work early and I am finished by mid-afternoon. I leave the museum and take the bus home, marvelling at the London scene around me; queues of traffic, road works, diversion signs, scaffolding and people – lots of them. A suited businessman talks animatedly into his phone, a young girl with a nose stud like mine stands laughing at a bus stop and a builder with a half–eaten sandwich dodges between motorcycles. It's that special time of the year and one of my favourites. It's nearly the end of November – and a perfect autumn afternoon. The day has been sunny with clear blue skies but a terse wind blows now as it begins to get dark and, as I leave the bus at Kew Bridge and walk along the towpath, headlights are switched on and there is a yellow glow across the river.

The air is cool on my face and I kick leaves watching them rise and fall revelling in their crunchy crispy sound. It reminds me of the north of Spain. I was young – probably seven or eight years old when we spent a winter in Pamplona. I remember walking through the romantic, French-styled, *Parque de la Taconera* filled with tropical trees, monuments, fountains and exotic flowers. I had watched amber and rusty red leaves falling from rows of solid chestnut trees. Most afternoons Mama left me in the Saint Nicholas church while she went to buy food in the supermarket or stopped at a café or bar and I wandered between dark timber pews, staring up at replicated biblical scenes carved in wood or stained on glass or painted in oils. The pungent smell of incense still lingered after Mass and it tickled my nose and made me sneeze. It's a smell that still comforts me. The church was my refuge. It was my sanctuary from a chaotic life; constantly moving home, moving on, accompanied by incessant rock music, discarded bottles of beer and the smell of black tobacco that clung to Papa's clothes and scraggy beard.

On the river two ducks chase, skim and glide across the water before braking, their wings outstretched, to land on their ski-like feet.

I shake my head as unwanted memories tumble together, confusing time and place, trying deliberately to block out my past. I decide to drop my camera bags at home and head out to start my Christmas shopping. Better get it over with. I might even buy a present for Papa – maybe a heavy metal CD or a book on motorbikes. Then there're the small gifts I will buy for Javier's family in Madrid, his parents and younger twin brothers.

I approach my flat and pause at the garden gate, my hand on the catch. Mrs Green's carton of milk and newspaper are still on her doorstep. I frown and walk up her path to the front door and ring her bell.

There is no answer so I slide my camera bags to the floor and bend over to peer through the letterbox. I take out my mobile and dial her home number. I hear it ringing inside. It continues to ring while I peer through the front window cupping my hand against the glass.

'Mrs Green?' I shout through the letterbox. I press my ear to the flap. I hear nothing. 'Mrs Green?'

There is no answer.

I open my front door, throw my bags onto the sofa and walk across the open plan lounge-diner to the kitchen.

My mobile rings and I fish it out of my pocket. Javier's normally soft voice is raised with excitement.

'Mikky – you're not going to believe it! I'm shortlisted.'

'Mrs Green hasn't taken her milk or newspaper inside.' I slide open the glass door that leads to a small paved patio area. 'And there's no answer from her landline.'

I pull a dining chair across the kitchen and drag it outside. A spider has nested, spinning the fence with an intricate patterned web that hangs with bulging, ripe drops of silver water. I place the spider to one side and push the chair up against the fence.

'What are you doing?' he asks.

'I'm standing on a chair looking over the fence into her house. I'm worried, Javier.'

'Maybe she's still in bed,' he says.

'You know she's always up by seven. It's the middle of the afternoon and it's almost dark. There's no movement in there,' I shout, 'Mrs Green?'

'Maybe she's gone out?' he says.

'Javier,' I say as if I am speaking to a wayward five-year-old instead of a thirty-two-year-old artist. 'Mrs Green is ninety. She never goes out. Besides she would have brought her milk and newspaper in first. It's still on the doorstep. There's something wrong.'

I lean forward on tiptoe for a better view of Mrs Green's house. The chair rocks, I slip and grab the fence. 'Ooops–'

'Mikky? What are you doing?

'Climbing over the fence.

'You mustn't. Call the police.'

'There's no time…'

'Mikky, my portfolio is shortlisted for the Italian commission…'

I pause with my arm resting on the fence and scan the layout before me.

'Mikky?'

When I don't reply he says, 'There are three finalists and I'm one of them.'

'Great.'

'But you haven't even asked me who I am going to paint. Ask me.'

'Javier, I don't have time–'

'Josephine La–'

'Good.'

'The opera singer.'

'Great.'

'You don't sound very excited for me.'

'I'm worried–'

'I may have to go and meet her. Imagine, Mikky, I might meet Josephine Lavelle – and guess what – if I do – you're coming with me.'

I pause mid-stride. My leg is in the air and I am about to straddle the fence but it begins wobbling.

'It says in the letter I can take a partner and so I'm taking you.'

'I'm not going to Italy. I haven't time. I've got to go, Javier – I think there's something seriously wrong…' I have my hand on top of the fence, testing its solidness, not doubting my courage only my technique. 'Got to go.'

'Mikky? What are you doing? Don't–'

I place the mobile in my pocket and pull my long skirt between my legs and lean forward to ease my right leg up onto the fence. My biker boots kick the wood and a rogue nail tears my leggings and cuts my thigh. I balance horizontally but when the fence begins to quiver I slide off my knees buckle and I tumble onto the patio, scraping skin from my palms, into my neighbour's garden.

Winded, I cough and bite on my lip to absorb the pain. 'Not very good spy material,' I mutter, brushing myself down. 'Not the next female James Bond that's for sure.' I spit on my hands, wipe my fingers onto my black skirt and hobble toward the nearest window.

'Mrs Green?' I rap on the pane. 'Are you in there?' I press my nose to the glass scanning the interior of the kitchen. I have never been inside her house. I don't know the layout. Her house hasn't been divided into two apartments like mine, one up and one down, so I guess she could be upstairs in one of the bedrooms. I go to the next window and cup my hand against the glass pane.

'Mrs Green?' I knock hard. Net curtains won't allow me to see in properly and the windows are all locked and secure. Downstairs all the rooms appear empty. I move away but then through the middle window I think I see a shadow on the floor illuminated by a yellow streetlight from the front window. It looks like is she lying in the hallway between the lounge and the kitchen. I hammer on the window but the figure doesn't move so I take off my duffle coat, wrap it around my fist and smash it against the glass. Nothing happens so I unzip my boot and smack it against the window. On the third attempt it fractures and I use my elbow to splinter it, smashing, pushing and pulling jagged shards of glass until there's a hole wide enough for me to scramble through. I ease myself inside but catch my calf and a slash rips open my skin and blood pours down my leg but I don't pause instead I heave myself harder through the gap and roll forward landing face down on the carpet.

'Oh my g–' I whisper, crawling over to her.

She's curled on her side, unmoving like a sleeping child, only a few meters from me.

'Mrs Green? Mrs Green, are you okay?' Her pulse is weak but she doesn't move. 'Mrs Green, can you hear me?' Instinct makes me pull out my mobile and with bloody fingers I dial 999.

The operator's voice is calm and I answer her questions but it's as though I am merely acting a role, watching myself from above – from somewhere in the corner – up near the ceiling and while I wait I smooth the old lady's thin white hair from her mask–like face. She murmurs as if in a deep and troubled sleep but she's alive. Very gently, I rub her arm and hold her fingers.

'Don't worry, Mrs Green. You'll be fine. The ambulance is on the way. You'll be okay.' It becomes my mantra that I repeat as I go into the kitchen. I wet a tea towel under the cold tap and press it against her forehead dabbing her temples and wiping her cheeks. I test her pulse then sit beside her on the floor and cradle her head in my lap willing the ambulance to hurry. It seems to take ages until I hear a siren then I lower her head onto my duffle coat so I can open the front door.

I stand aside for the ambulance crew.

The girl is dark and chubby. She has a colourful eagle tattoo on the back of her hand and when she sees me looking at it, she says. 'It fascinates everyone. It takes their mind off what's happening.'

I nod.

The boy is younger – early twenties. There's a gap between his teeth and he wears an earring with a diamond stud. He raises his voice to the old lady. 'We'll take you to A&E, Mrs Green. They'll probably keep you in for a while.'

They ask me questions as they place her on a stretcher. Once she is secure and an oxygen mask covers her face the boy turns to me.

'Let's have a look at your cuts while we're here. That one on your leg looks quite deep.'

'I'll be fine. It's only a scratch. Will Mrs Green, be okay?'

'It could be just a blackout. She seems to be coming round but they'll check her out at the hospital and make sure it's not a stroke or anything more serious,' he replies.

'Has she got any family?' asks the girl.

'I believe she has a son.'

'Right, we'd better get his contact details then. Where's her address book?' she asks.

'She probably keeps it beside the phone,' I reply.

I wait in the street.

'They are estranged,' I say, when the girl returns

clutching a tattered address book in her eagle-hand.

'What's that?' The boy frowns.

'They don't speak to each other – haven't done for years. She told me they don't get on,' I reply.

'Well, if he's next of kin they'll have to speak now, won't they?' He grins. 'No point in falling out with an old woman like that is there?'

'None at all,' I reply.

My mind is racing.

The ambulance doors slam shut like Mrs Green's eyes and I wait until it disappears around the corner then I call a glazier from her landline. As I wait in the hallway for the voice on the other end of the phone to confirm the time of his visit, I listen to the gentle tick of an old grandfather clock measuring seconds and counting minutes. It whirls and chimes the half hour and I drum the mahogany table with my nails to the rhythm of *Go With the Flow* my favourite track by Queen of the Stone Age that is carousing through my head.

My gaze travels over Mrs Green's unfamiliar home and I compare the layout to my flat next door. Her kitchen is at the back of the house where my bedroom is, it's modern and tidy with navy blue units and the walls are the colour of a dying daffodil. A comfortable rocking chair stuffed with knitted cushions has been placed at the window beside the back door where she sits and looks out at a bird table decked with multiple hanging feeders.

'This afternoon at six thirty,' the glazier confirms.

'Thank you.' I hang up the phone.

I walk to the front door thinking of my plan, weighing up my options and I slide the bolt shut. The lounge is cramped and dark, so different to my open plan and modern design, and I wonder how she navigates around the room. There's a chintz three-piece suite in the middle of the room and four mahogany glass cabinets along the right wall are filled with porcelain vases, snuffboxes and silver cigar cases.

When I flick on the table lamp a pair of blue reading glasses and a stack of folded, cryptic *Daily Telegraph* crosswords tumble to the floor. I pile them back up and walk to a waist-high shelf to admire a cut-glass fruit bowl, a decanter and matching glasses. I run my finger over a silver goblet, dust collects under my nail and I blow it away. I pick up a two-foot tall porcelain statue of a young naked woman reclining on a chaise longue with only a silk scarf covering her thighs and breasts. I examine its base deliberately delaying the moment. I know it's there waiting. It's calling me. Then very slowly, unable to delay the moment any longer, I look up. It hangs, where I thought it would, in a gilt ornate frame above the white marble mantelpiece. Although my heart is pumping rapidly I move very, very slowly and take a step closer.

It is striking. It is stunning. It's Vermeer's, *The Concert.*

With my hands on my hips I stare at the work of art. The rest of the world is moving but in this room time has stopped. I'm rooted to the spot caught in a breathless moment of excited anticipation and I want to savour it. I look at it from all angles, inspecting it from a distance then up close and from one side to the other. Then, when I am satisfied, I unhook the oil painting and for the first time hold the masterpiece in my hands.

The painting shows three musicians; a young woman seated at a harpsichord, a man with his back to the viewer playing a lute and a second woman to the right who is singing.

Unlike other artists, Vermeer allows the viewer the latitude to interpret the painting, to appreciate the girl's absorbed yet relaxed pose as she fingers the keys of the harpsichord. Little can be seen of the man playing the lute. Only a sash and a sword indicate his military status but the second woman is elegantly dressed and her gaze is focused on the sheet of music in her hands.

I tilt the painting toward the light. It appears that her bluish green jacket has faded with age and her once ultramarine blue gown has degraded with time.

I take a step back and hold the picture at arm's length. At the forefront of the painting, on the left, is an oriental carpet. Vermeer regularly depicted carpets from Iran and Turkey and the black and white patterned marble floor on the right was typically found in wealthy houses during the 17th century, and true to form, Vermeer has excluded any reflection that would normally have been evident.

The painting measures 69 centimetres high by 63 centimetres wide but the gilt-edged frame is a cheap replica. I turn it over in my hands noting the state of the canvas and the old stamps – evidence of its provenance.

I turn it to the front again and take a deep breath. The detail is exquisite. The two paintings hanging on the wall behind the trio are symbolic of the scene played out; a rough Arcadian landscape contrasts with the ladies' genteel beauty in the foreground and a resplendent tree represents Mother Nature, all typical themes of popular 17th century's songs and poems.

I frown and tilt the canvas to the light for a closer look. The second painting behind the trio is, *The Procuress* by Dirch van Baburen. It shows a young prostitute, a bearded client and an older procuress with an open palm who is soliciting payment. It is a work of art, typical of Utrecht Caravaggism. I smile. I am Caravaggio's greatest admirer.

The Concert is simply a work of genius and I've seen enough authentic pieces of art to spot a fake. This is genuine. It was one of the thirteen pieces stolen from the Isabella Stuart Museum in Boston and worth over $200 million only to turn up in a back street in Bruges two years ago.

Now it's in my hands and I have no intention of returning it to America or anywhere else but I must be patient. I hang the painting back on the wall. I never imagined I'd have to save her. That was never part of my plan but now I must wait – Mrs Green deserves that much.

I will move on and prepare for the next stage of my plan. I don't know how much time is left but I will be thorough and meticulous. With my heart beating wildly and my body racing with adrenalin, I return home to fetch my cameras and my props. My dream will come true. I will make sure of it. My future is about to change.

***

Less than a week later my head is throbbing – too much prosecco last night, my mouth is dry and I'm tired.

'You've been standing at that window for the past five minutes, Javier. What are you waiting for – a lover – or divine inspiration?' I finish adding blue mascara and then add pink lipstick.

'Neither. It's Salman.'

'Who?'

'Aaron's youngest boy from the shop – I didn't expect to see him delivering milk and *The Daily Telegraph* to Mrs Green this morning.' Javier checks his watch.

I slap my mirror shut and walk over to stand beside him. We both peer through the white wooden shutter that Javier tilts to disguise our spying.

Salman pushes open our neighbour's gate and takes four strides to the front door. He places the newspaper and milk on the ground and as he closes the latch gate behind him, he digs his hands in his pockets and whistles, Sam Smith's *Stay with me.*

'She must be back at home,' I say.

'We'll soon see,' Javier replies. 'Wait a minute.'

The Thames Road is misty. It's waking up slowly, stretching into life with early joggers and slow moving cars with yellow lights glowing like beacons at sea. A dog walker is dragged across the street by an excited terrier and they disappear down the small alleyway to the river. The buildings opposite are the back of the two story houses, mews and outhouses that face the Strand. In the late eighteenth and early nineteenth century, Strand-On-The-Green was a fishing village with fisherman's cottages and boat-building sheds. As the residence of the Court at Kew became more fashionable, riverside public houses became popular. Some of the best barley grew in the thriving Parish of

Chiswick and at one time there were five malt houses nearer the wharves where barley was loaded for transportation.

Sometimes when I walk along the towpath I close my eyes and imagine I'm transported back in time. I hear the workmen calling out and the banging of crates and boxes as they slam them onto the decks of the waiting boats.

'Look,' Javier whispers.

We both lean forward as our neighbour's door opens. A white head appears and a papery thin hand reaches out. Just as stealthily she is gone.

'I wonder if she is better,' I say.

Javier smiles triumphantly. 'She's back in her old routine. As regular as a clockwork mouse collecting the cheese.'

'You're turning into a stalker.' I walk over to the kitchen and toss the remains of my coffee into the sink. 'And it's quite worrying.'

'On the contrary, it's my meticulous attention to detail – a tribute to the powers of my observation and accuracy. It's why I'm such a great artist.'

'You're nosey.'

'No, merely a professional – I notice everything.'

'Yeah, a regular Inspector Clouseau – your talents are wasted Javier – you should have been a detective.'

'Did you notice her ring?'

'No,' I lie.

'It looks like a huge diamond. Do you think it is real?'

I shrug and he continues speaking.

'Are you going to call around to her? You saved her life.'

I ignore him and busy myself checking my bag for cameras and my light meter calibrated to match the sensitivity of my digital camera.

My head is thumping and it reminds me of my first job in the El Museo de arte Thyssen–Bornemisza where I worked cataloguing and documenting fine art. Javier and I regularly got stoned and drank copious amounts of alcohol. Once, we even ran out of a restaurant without paying the bill and legged it across the Plaza Mayor.

'I'm getting too old for hangovers,' I say.

'She never goes out. Never speaks to anyone.' Javier turns back to gaze out of the window. 'She reminds me of you.'

'I go out.'

'Only to work.'

'We went out last night.'

'That was only with Oscar and me for dinner. Mrs Green must have money to wear that ring. Was she ever married?'

I don't want to answer him.

'Was she?'

'We've been through all this before. Why are you so fascinated with her?' I zip the bag shut.

'I'd like to help. You know what it's like in Spain – families look after the older members – look at my grandmother. She practically lives with us–'

'She's old and she's frightened of falling, and besides, it takes all her energy to come round here for a cup of tea.'

'What's her house like inside?'

'Old and dusty.'

'Where are her friends and family?'

'I don't know. Old people get like that, Javier. They don't have many friends. Most of their peers have passed away. They lose confidence, they don't trust people – especially strangers.'

'That sounds like you,' he smiles. 'Old and crabby and you don't trust anyone either.'

I swing my bag onto my shoulder. It's heavy, stuffed with lights, small props and my cameras. Javier walks with me and opens the front door.

'I was thinking about this place,' he says. 'It could do with a good paint. The walls in this lounge are – well they look – simply terrible. Apart from my creative masterpiece on the wall.'

We both gaze over to the far wall near the kitchen counter that divides the open plan room. It's a dusky Argentinian street scene that he drew with charcoal one drunken evening a few months after he met Oscar in South America.

'Why?'

'If I get the portrait commission and if Josephine comes to London–'

'I'll think about it – *if* you get it.'

'She's a mega–'

'She's just an opera star, Javier. She's not the bloody Pope,' I interrupt.

'If it was the Pope then we would have to consider the ceilings and maybe replicate the Sistine Chapel,' he laughs.

'It's a rented flat. I might not be here that long.'

'What? We've moved three times in the last eighteen months. You were obsessed about finding a place in this area. We can't move out so soon. What do you think will happen – we'll win the Lottery – and live in Mayfair?' He casts his hands wide in a dramatic gesture. His eyes are rimmed with thick black lashes like mini sweeping brushes and I smile.

'Just open the door for me and get dressed. You've got work to finish just in case you get your famous commission.'

I hitch the bags further onto my shoulder. I'm used to carrying their weight but it's a decoy. I don't want him to see the look of excited anticipation on my face. Who needs the Lottery? Stealing the painting next door is a far bigger challenge and much more exhilarating.

'I was thinking ochre and pistachio green,' he persists.

'Feel free. Paint away, Picasso.'

'I don't do walls, my darling, only canvas.'

'Maybe you should–'

'What? Paint a portrait of your pretty wide mouth and bewitching grey green eyes on the wall?'

'Yup! That should do the trick. Should scare off any burglar.'

He laughs and my bag bangs against the doorframe on my way out.

'Don't be late home,' he calls. 'It's your turn to cook and you need all the practice you can get.'

I don't turn around and I don't look back. I just raise my middle finger as I walk away down the path.

***

I get as far as the corner shop then on impulse I turn back and walk up Mrs Green's pathway and press the doorbell.

I stand in the cold, humming Iron Maiden's *El*

Dorado, wondering if she heard the bell chimes when I hear the turn of her key and the door opens.

'Hello, Mrs Green, I saw Salman deliver your milk this morning. I'm so pleased you are home. Are you alright?' I smile.

'Mikky! Hello dear, will you come in?' She opens the door a fraction and her woolly yellow dressing gown flutters in the breeze. She pulls the collar to her throat and shivers. Her pale face and rheumy eyes make her look old and ill.

'I'm late for work. I just wanted to make sure you are okay. When did you get home?'

'Yesterday afternoon but I was so tired I went straight to bed.'

'Can you manage? Is there anything you need?'

'I telephoned Aaron yesterday and Salman is going to run some errands for me later today.'

'If you need anything, just call me.'

'Thank you. That's so kind of you, Mikky but my son, Roy, is coming home to look after me. He's moving in with his wife Annie and son Max.'

'Oh...that's good. Well, close the door, Mrs Green. Don't lose all the heat. I left my phone number beside the telephone for you – just in case.'

'I saw it my dear and I'll settle up for the window pane.'

'No worries, Mrs Green, I'll speak to you later.' I wave and walk away, anxious for her to go back inside the house and stay warm. I need to think.

My son, Roy, is coming home to look after me.

I am distracted gazing at my feet thinking about the implications that their arrival could have on my plan. I don't see the bus and it passes inches from my face. I jump back away from the road cursing London traffic and the arrival of my new neighbours.

Chapter Two

'A painter should begin every canvas with a wash of black, because
all things in nature are dark except where exposed by the light.'
Leonardo da Vinci

'*Landscape with an Obelisk* is being examined by Sotheby's for authenticity.' Phyllis Laverty's voice comes from over my shoulder. 'But I doubt the experts will agree. They rarely do.'

I bend my knees and lean forward focusing on the painting in front of me.

'Wasn't it stolen?' I ask.

I focus the 50mm lens of my Nikon D7000 digital SLR camera to give me a sharper image.

'Yes, it was in the haul of the largest art theft in history. You know, the one from the Isabella Stuart Museum in Boston, back in 1990. The thieves stole thirteen pieces that were collectively worth more than $300 million. Would you believe they found it in a garden shed somewhere in Kent?'

'I hope your security is better here.' I smile and lean closer to examine the painting on the easel. It's the latest painting by a new artist, Marcus Danning known for his flamboyant dress sense and wide girth.

'Do you like it?' she asks.

'He focuses on the exploration of illusion and has an exceptional eye for detail,' I reply, hiding my dislike.

'I think it's very theatrical,' Phyllis Laverty says. Her eyes squint from behind round tortoiseshell glasses and she holds a dangling string of pearls to her flat chest. Her voice is clipped and her vowel sounds are rounded. 'It's a style borrowed from the past – a productive kind of retrospection – lavish costume and a complex set design. I think his exhibition will be a great success.'

'Each figure has been sympathetically re-imagined,' I agree. 'It's interesting, although I prefer Old Masters and in particular Caravaggio.'

'You don't look the type for classical art.'

'Why?'

'Well, I suppose…your wild hair and the black–'

I continue taking photos. 'My early days as a Goth,' I interrupt.

'You could be very pretty with a little makeover. They could tone down your wide eyes and large mouth. I could get you a sitting as a model if you like?'

'No thanks.'

My mobile vibrates and Hosier's, *Take Me To Church* echoes through the gallery.

'Sorry, Phyllis.' I turn my back and answer irritably. 'What is it, Javier? I'm busy.'

'I got it, Mikky! Nico Vastrano just called. I got the commission. They want the portrait to hang in their gallery – in the theatre Il Domo on Lake Como.'

'That's fantastic but I'm working,' I whisper, watching Phyllis Laverty circle the painting, stepping over lights and cables, hoping she doesn't upset the balance of my re-creation.

'Do you know what this means?' Javier insists in my ear. 'The fact he's phoned me personally. This could be my big opportunity–'

'Tell me about it later?'

'This is the breakthrough I need. This could get my work noticed at last. I will be famous–'

I hold my breath. Phyllis Laverty totters on maroon high-heels and she reaches out to the stone wall for support. She regains her step. Her eyes never leave Marcus's painting and I exhale with slow control.

'The other sponsor of the Teatro Il Domo is Dino Scrugli. Do you know who he is? He's probably the most famous patron of art in the whole of Europe and he likes my portfolio.'

'Okay, so now I'm impressed. That's fantastic.'

'What if they don't like it?'

'Don't be crazy–'

'I was up against DiFusco from America and a Dutchman, Vanderflute who painted Caroline of Monaco.'

Phyllis Laverty looks over at me and waves a hand impatiently.

'I have to go.'

'I can't believe it,' he purrs.

'Well, you like opera and that crap music…'

'It's better than your rock rubbish. But why me, Mikky?' he asks. 'Why would they ask me? How did they hear of me? I know that my last portrait – *Lady Rushworth* – was reviewed in the *Sunday Times* but that was last year. They wouldn't have seen that, would they?'

I shake my head trying desperately to ignore the glassy tortoiseshell gaze from across the room. 'I have no idea, Javier. But it could be to do with the fact that you have an amazing talent and you're beginning to make a name for yourself in the art world.'

He groans. 'My hands are trembling, Mikky. I'll never be able to paint her. She's my idol. My talent will vanish at the very sight of her.'

Phyllis coughs and combines it with another irritable wave in my direction.

'Look, man-up, Javier. Stay focused,' I hiss into the phone. 'You *can* do it and you *will* do it. Listen, I really have to go now, Phyllis is waiting but I'll be home by seven and don't forget it's your turn to cook – I'll be starving – so get something decent for dinner unless you are taking me out. We'll celebrate.' I turn off my phone and toss it into my camera bag.

'Will you finish the work on time?' Phyllis Laverty's voice is crisp in the cavity of the empty gallery. Her purple lips move up and out, reminding me of the paper fortune–teller I made as a child.

'The programme will be finished a week before the exhibition.' I do not add that I am a perfectionist and plan meticulously.

If only she knew.

'Your reputation is excellent and your references from the National Gallery were exceptional.'

I smile.

'And, by the way, Mikky, I've been thinking while you were on the telephone and I want to reassure you that, unlike the Isabella Stuart Museum, neither our security guards nor our security system will be fooled so easily. I can confidently say nothing will be stolen from here.'

***

When I arrive home Javier is standing at the door. He has on his coat.

'Mrs Green, called in. She left this for you. ' He thrusts an envelope into my hand. 'She said, it's for the window.'

'Did you ask her in for tea?'

'Yes but she wouldn't stay without you.'

'Are you cooking or are we going out for dinner? It is Friday – are we celebrating?' I take the cash from the envelope and stuff it in my purse.

'Indian takeaway – come with me. We'll go and get it together and I'll tell you what Mrs Green said to me.'

'What did she say?' I close the door behind us.

He hooks his arm through mine and pulls me playfully into the street. 'She talked about Roy and the bait she's used to lure him back into her life.'

'What do you mean? He's coming to look after her, isn't he?' I match Javier's long stride and snuggle my nose under the collar of my coat.

'Yes, but not because he loves her – it's far more devious than that. It's because she's pretending she got an authentic Vermeer hanging in her house.'

'What?'

'It's so funny. He's moving in to get his hands on her money. He thinks her house is full of antiques. But she's a shrewd old woman, she knows exactly what he's like.'

'Is that what she told you?'

'I told her she had better keep an eye on that big old diamond ring she wears,' he laughs.

'Oh, my good–'

'And she replied, the first thing she'll do every morning is to count her fingers – I just love her sense of humour. She really is a gem.'

***

The following Sunday morning after we have return from a long walk in Chiswick Park, Javier is standing in the bay window at the front of the flat with a glass of chilled prosecco, a pre-lunch drink, in his hand.

'They're moving in,' he says.

'Stop stalking the neighbours.' I reprimand but I walk over to stand beside him. 'What are you gawping at?'

Through the slatted blinds and beyond my miniature front garden a powder blue BMW is parked crookedly on the pavement. A broad-shouldered blond man with a trim beard is talking animatedly to a woman in the passenger seat. He looks older than her probably late fifties. There is a deep crease between his eyebrows and his mouth is moving in angry sequence as he gesticulates wildly. Then he gets out of the car and carries a suitcase inside.

What will I do?

Javier tilts the blind. 'He doesn't look happy,' he murmurs.

'They never got on,' I say.

'You don't look happy either. You seem preoccupied the past few days.' His gaze is on me and his breath is sweet on my cheek.

'I'm fine,' I lie.

I walk over to the fridge and take out a chilled bottle of prosecco. Outside in the garden, Javier's friend Oscar is hammering my fence with nails. He is repairing the wooden slats I broke while climbing over it. His rhythmic tapping seems to accompany the pauses in our conversation.

'Maybe the painting is the original. She said, the painting would make him come back,' Javier says.

'Don't be ridiculous. She hardly has a stolen painting hanging in her house.'

'I think we should find out. I'd like to take a look at it. Maybe we should speak to him or Mrs Green? Maybe we could negotiate its safe return to the museum. Maybe we could–'

'No!'

'Come on, Mikky. They may not know it's the original especially if she bought it off some market in the Borough. I've heard of that sort of thing happening before. Think of the notoriety and the fame that we would receive if we returned it.'

'Let's not get involved. You have too much going on at the moment with your commission.'

'Let's find an excuse to go around there and check it out–'

'Mrs Green is only just out of hospital and I don't want to get involved in her family disputes.' I turn away from the window. 'Besides, it can't be the original. It was stolen from Boston almost twenty years ago and there's no way it's turned up on the wall of an old lady in Chiswick. Besides, it's nothing to do with us,' I add.

'Perhaps I should speak to her–'

'Javier, don't go worrying her. There have been rumours and newspaper articles on the Internet. *The Concert* is now in Eastern Europe they think it was swapped for drugs or something like that by the Real IRA. It will probably never be seen again,' I insist.

'A lot of artwork is traded for drugs or prostitution within the old Eastern bloc countries. It's a form of trading currency and talking of newspapers there was a small article in the *Evening Standard* about you rescuing Mrs Green.' He holds out his glass and I refill his glass.

'I don't know how they found out. The only person I can think of was the man who came to replace the glass in her window.' I sip my prosecco. 'I don't understand why it reached the evening paper.'

'Well, I would like an article in the *Evening Standard*. I would love someone to write about me. Especially if I was a hero.'

'Well you would. Therein lies the difference between us,' I reply.

In the kitchen I place parboiled potatoes into sizzling fat. A sprig of rosemary cut from my garden tub has fallen into the oil so I fork it back on top of the roasting lamb then turn the potatoes in the hot oil before shoving the dish back into the oven.

Oscar continues banging nails into the fence and when he looks up, I wave.

'Lunch smells delicious.' Javier continues to stare out of the front window. 'Look!'

I stand beside him and watch the scene in the street. In the rear of the car a small boy with masses of blond curls sits with his face pressed to the window. His eyes wander over the row of Victorian houses where we live and he appears remotely detached and disinterested. Annie, a delicate blond woman in her thirties, unfolds her legs from the passenger side and opens the back door for her son.

'She looks like a model,' I whisper.

'A stick insect,' Javier murmurs.

Max escapes the confines of the car and runs excitedly up and down the small path with his arms spread wide as if he is *Superman*. His outstretched wings cause him to lean precariously and he swoops back out into the street and straight into his mother's leg wrapping his arms around her thigh and she laughs.

She hands him a blue backpack and gives him an encouraging push toward the front door. He takes small steps carrying it carefully in his arms, his pink tongue poking out of the side of his mouth.

Annie calls out and Roy reappears. He bangs his fist on the bonnet of the car, slams the driver's door and guns the engine. Annie pulls away just as the car bounces off the curb and squealing tyres slice though the tranquil street.

'Oh, my God,' says Javier. He turns to me with a frown. 'What a brute! I hope he treats his mother better than that.'

On the pathway Annie's step falters. She levels a penetrating stare and the shutters seem to disintegrate between us. My breath catches in my throat and I remain motionless until I blink and the thin web is broken and she moves quickly into the house.

Oscar's voice comes from the patio at the back of my flat. 'Any chance of another beer before lunch?' he shouts. 'This worker needs some refreshment.'

I find a *Stella* for Oscar and return to Javier side. He is standing in the middle of the lounge staring at his charcoal drawing, lost in thought, until I refill his glass and then he smiles.

'Did I tell you that a freelance journalist phoned me? He wants to do an ongoing interview while I'm painting Josephine's portrait. He seems to know a lot about her. He's a big fan. He wants me to talk him through the process. A step-by-step portrait guide and there would be a series of interviews and the television might get involved – perhaps even a documentary or something...'

'Wouldn't you have to ask the Director?'

Javier frowns. 'I hadn't thought of that. Maybe I should mention it to Nico Vastano, he's the Theatre Director.'

'You can ask Josephine when we meet her in Italy,' I say.

'Italy? Who said anything about going to Italy? We're going to Germany – to Dresden, the home of Stöllen cake and Christmas markets.'

'Why?'

'It's where she lives now.'

'Well, I would have thought the theatre would have to supervise all the publicity and interviews. They must have a press agent or a publicity person who can advise you.'

'But he sounded so nice: funny and friendly. He's asked me to meet him for lunch in *Randall and Aubin*.'

'Wow – that's your favourite restaurant – does he know that?'

'The oysters are to die for–'

'Not to mention the champagne,' I add and he laughs.

'Why don't you tell Dino or Nico that he contacted you? Then they can decide what they want to do. They might be glad of the publicity or they may already have something lined up. If he knows Josephine Lavelle then he's probably her friend. What's his name?'

'Karl Blakey.'

I shrug. 'Never heard of him.'

'How would you? You don't like opera music anyway,' he laughs. 'You've always refused to come to the opera with me. Remember that time in Madrid? I bought tickets to see the *Barber of Seville* and you wouldn't come. You went to a *Foo Fighters* concert instead.'

'True. Wailing cats at the opera – not my thing. Can't stand it – it all too phoney and unnatural.'

'I hope you'll be more polite when you meet Josephine Lavelle, next week.'

'Only if I can educate her on the merits of rock music.' I take a few steps and play air guitar around the sofa twanging my imaginary electric strings to the sounds of Meat Loaf's *Bat Out of Hell*.

'You're a philistine.'

'That's true. But you would be too if you'd had hippy parents who rocked around Spain like gypsies blaring out *Rolling Stones*, *The Who* and *The Grateful Dead* at full blast from a campervan that reeked of stale beer and cannabis.'

'Well, I admit, my life was more conventional – much more boring.'

'You had stability. You had a home and security, and copious amounts of money and love. My parents barely remembered to enrol me in school.'

'I'm amazed you turned out so perfect.'

'I was determined not to end up like them.' I give him my best sarcastic smile.

'I still think you should contact your father.'

I raise my palm. 'Don't go there.'

Javier has no understanding. He finds my past funny and adventurous. He's never understood loneliness nor felt the exclusion of having no friends.

'You always celebrated birthdays. You had a proper home. You don't know what it was like to sing lullabies alone in the dark when a party was in full swing and the air was filled with a foggy haze. Your parents knew where you were. Not like mine who didn't bother to check that I had got back safely from the church before it was dark.'

'You have to get over your past, Mikky. I've told you before and I'll keep telling you. You must speak to your father. He's your only family. It will help–'

'I don't want to think about my past – and certainly not him.'

My mind is focused on my plan but as we eat our roast dinner my mind strays. My past, that I normally keep firmly boxed in the deep recess of my mind, has been set free and my resentment gathers speed stirring my emotions quicker than Macbeth's three witches can utter their doomed prophecies.

As a child we travelled all over the country. They promised I could make friends and have birthday parties at the next school. They said next Christmas we would be in a proper home and that there would be no more fiestas spent in the caravan, or on a beach or parked in a stranger's field. And they said next year there would be money for presents and we would have a proper meal cooked in a proper home with a proper stove.

But there never was. They lied.

And then it was all too late anyway.

Trust doesn't come easy to me and I don't believe anyone. I am different. I will not become attached to anyone or anything.

At the table Oscar and Javier joke and tease. They are completely at ease with each other and unaware of my inner turmoil. Javier's eyes brown eyes sparkle and his laugh is deep and happy. He is the longest friend I have ever had. But I saw how he betrayed Carmen. It was nine years ago but I will never forget the hurt and damage he caused when he broke her heart. Everyone is betrayed in the end.

I will keep him away from Mrs Green and from the painting. My immediate task is to find out what the set-up is next door. Then I will take action. I will be methodical. I will get what I want. I always do – eventually.

***

On Monday morning I'm working in a secured vault underneath London's busy streets in a room probably wedged between tube tracks, sewers and a multitude of other unknown quantities. But it is the silence I relish, the hushed reverence. It's almost church-like but without the spiritual emotion, more like a library but without muted coughs, scratching chairs and squeaky footsteps. As I work I am deliberating on the family next door. My planning and the detail must be faultless.

I am rearranging the spotlight, tilting it slightly to eradicate the finest shadow in the right-hand corner. Precision and detail are imperative. A fraction of a millimetre can make all the difference.

'Mikky?'

I turn at my name.

'The Caravaggio is almost restored. It should be here by the end of the month.'

'Before Christmas?' I ask.

'I do hope so.' Sandra Jupiter is the museum's curator. We have worked together several times and we have a close professional relationship. She is a few years older than me, mid-thirties, attractive and I think she is a tough woman who is used to getting what she wants. 'I would like to think it would be here by then.'

'Brilliant.' I have no doubt she will get it.

I roll up my sleeve and I see her looking at the vibrant ink tattoo wrapped along my inner arm.

'The exhibition is on the 4th February so we have lots of work to do. Make sure you're free. I will go over the schedule with you,' she says.

I smile and nod. It's more money and it's also my insurance just in case my plan is delayed. 'I'll put the date in my diary.' I tilt the light with my disposable gloves. I want to be left alone. I want to concentrate.

'How's Javier?' she asks.

She knows him through his exhibition last year in a gallery off Bond Street. She purchased his portrait of Paco de Lucía, the world-renowned Flamenco guitarist. It hangs over the hearth in her dining room and is admired by artists, exhibitors and curators worldwide.

'Concerned about his commission – that it won't be good enough.'

'Why is he always so insecure about his talent?'

'Do you know, Dino Scrugli?' I ask

'Dino, was in my house for dinner a few months ago.'

'Javier applied for a commission. Dino Scrugli is one of the patrons but Javier can't work out how Dino heard of him. Perhaps he saw the portrait in your house?'

'I don't think I had it then. Javier's exhibition was in May but Dino came to me just before Easter. I remember he brought with him a gift of a Faberge egg.'

'Very classy.'

'Dino has class. He's from one of the best Italian families. His grandfather began collecting art, his father continued the tradition and both of them have left everything to Dino who subsequently loans pieces to the Italian museums – for a small price – of course,' she laughs. 'He's only used to the best.'

'Then I hope he likes Javier's portrait.'

'Who is Javier painting?'

'It's a singer, some opera star. I think her name is La Velle, someone or other.'

She holds her fingers to her throat. 'Josephine Lavelle? Is she well enough? Wasn't she injured quite recently?'

'I don't know.'

'I read about her in the newspapers. She had many admirers and also a very bad reputation. My goodness – Javier has done well. I think she will be a very interesting portrait.'

'The Theatre Il Domo have commissioned it.'

'Perhaps I should speak to Dino?' Sandra likes to be well connected and I have no doubt she will be on the phone to him as soon as possible.

'That would be fantastic. I'll tell, Javier.'

'What an opportunity – he deserves to do well. He is a talented and – handsome man.'

I move as she speaks lining up the painting that I want to capture with my lens. I would like her to contact Dino but she wasn't invited to the opening night of the theatre last year and I wonder if they are as friendly as she pretends.

'Did you hear that Sotheby's declared *Landscape with an Obelisk* a fake?' I ask, changing the subject.

'Can art critics ever agree?'

'It's not so much up to them any more though, is it?' I say. 'So much of it is now down to forensic science and X-rays, and a forged painting is soon discovered.' I stand back and stretch my neck muscles flexing my arm muscles and wrist.

'Thank goodness for modern technology,' Sandra says, 'or we would be in a right mess.'

'And the Art Loss Register,' I add.

'Yes, that too, at least we can keep a track of who owns what now, although there are still a lot of missing paintings – and many that certain collectors and dealers don't want to come to light.'

'It's curtailed the acts of many shady art dealers,' I agree.

'But not enough, time and time again there's some unscrupulous art dealer somewhere who's willing to sell a stolen painting for less than it's market value. Think of the artwork that the Nazis stole that has been sold on for a fraction...'

'Some of them will never come to light.' A shiver of excitement runs through me and I flex my shoulders to ease my shaking hands.

'That's true or they turn up years later hanging on

the wall of some obscure person who brought it at an antiques market or who found it in a shed at the bottom of an ageing relative's garden or such like,' she adds. 'And they don't even know it's valuable.'

'So many stolen paintings are used as currency now for illegal drug trafficking or prostitution and we'll never see them again. They're probably hanging on the walls of some oligarchs' houses in Russia or somewhere and they wouldn't have any appreciation of their artistic value,' I add. 'It's just a possession.'

'I blame the unscrupulous art dealers. There are so many of them. They should be closed down.'

'There's no code of behaviour,' I agree. 'It makes it hard to establish a painting's origins and authenticity. It's no wonder the experts can never agree.'

'It's a moral-less way to earn money and it makes me so angry.' She paces in front of me and I wait until she stops before realigning the camera angle. 'And it ruins the reputation of art dealers in general. I blame the forgers,' she adds. 'They're just as bad. No wonder so many are sceptical of our judgement.'

'Indeed.'

'A reputation is the most important thing one can have and once it's tarnished you never get it back. You might as well give up or go into hiding.'

'A reputation is priceless,' I agree.

Hiding? Now that does seem like a good idea.

***

After lunch I go home and I wait until I see Annie and Max leave the house, and I'm singing, *The Pretender* like Dave Grohl and mimicking his guitar playing when Mrs Green answers her front door.

'Mrs Green? How are you feeling?' I give her my best smile.

'Mikky? Hello dear. What a lovely surprise. Come in – what a pretty plant.'

'I would have popped in before but I didn't want to get in the way of your family moving in.'

She doesn't seem to hear me. 'I do love a poinsettia – a beautiful colour and so warm – it cheers the house at Christmas. Thank you, dear.'

'How are you feeling?'

'It's lovely to be home.'

'I hope you haven't come home too soon?'

My neighbour seems smaller. There is more colour in her cheeks than when I last saw her but she still looks frail and tired. I follow her slow shuffling gait along the hallway looking at the spot on the floor where I found her lying and I risk a quick glance into the lounge. *The Concert* no longer hangs above the mantelpiece. The gilt-frame is gone.

My mouth is dry.

Where is it?

'Have a cup of tea. Sit there by the window.' She is wearing the big diamond ring on her bent wedding finger.

What she has done with the painting?

'Roy seemed quite pleased when I telephoned him and told him that I wanted to heal the rift between us. He managed to get a transfer with his company in the north as they have offices near Heathrow airport. He will still have to travel abroad quite a lot but Annie and Max are happy here. He's settled into the nursery school, you know, the one at the back here.' She waves in the direction of the nursery tucked behind our homes.

I nod. 'I often hear them in the playground from my bedroom.'

'It's lovely to have young people around me. I had forgotten how lonely I was.'

What's he done with it?

The teapot is heavy in her hand and I manage to grab the spout before it spills. She slumps into the rocking chair and spends a few minutes settling patchwork cushions around her hips.

She sighs. 'Oh, Mikky, I couldn't go into a home and be parted from all my things. I don't want to be with old people who are ill all the time or have nothing to say. I like to have all my little bits and pieces around me and I enjoy television. What would I do with all my things if I went into a home? I couldn't sell them. They're not worth much but they're mine.'

She glances through to the lounge and I follow the direction of her gaze. 'I've had to put some of my favourite things away, some of those things dear to me and also the Vermeer I had hanging in the living room. Just to keep it safe.'

'Good idea, Mrs Green but I hope you can still appreciate it?'

'I've moved into my bedroom. It's not an original of course but the art dealer told me it was a good fake. It cost enough but I couldn't resist it, besides I always dreamed of owning the real thing and this is the nearest I will ever get...'

'I hope Roy doesn't think it's the original,' I laugh.

'I've led him on a little but it's up to him what he wants to think. At least it might keep him interested in staying here – even if it is only for his inheritance.'

She screws up her eyes and peers at the blue tits on the feeders and even when they fly away she continues staring, lost in thought, while I stroke the ugly ragged scar on the back of my left hand and think of the trouble I've gone to.

In 1994 a letter had been written to the Isabella Stewart Museum promising the safe return of the paintings for $2.6 million but the FBI had failed to negotiate. All communication stopped and nothing had been heard since then but I knew the art dealer in Bruges who 'acquired' the Vermeer two years ago. He was a conduit for the Real IRA and he had been forced into getting rid of it for them. He was scared. He wanted it off his hands – and quickly.

I was working in the gallery when I overheard their arrangement. They agreed that after Mrs Green died the art dealer would inherit the painting legitimately. He could therefore claim the huge reward the museum was offering, alternatively he could hand it in to another museum in Belgium or even to the Tate in London. Or he could sell the painting. Sometimes when the painting has changed hands a good few times the buyer can plausibly claim that they thought it was a legitimate sale. A buyer would normally pay less than ten percent of the normal market value. A low price because both parties are at risk of getting caught.

It used to be that only about 5% of stolen artwork was ever returned but more recently and since the Art Loss Register was formed and the ownership of paintings can be more readily identified, it has risen to almost 20%.

But this convenient arrangement with Mrs Green meant that after her death, the art dealer's family in Bruges would be financially taken care of and this pleased Mrs Green as her husband and the art dealer had once been very good friends.

'You wouldn't sell the painting?' I ask, suddenly conscious of her gaze on me.

'Not in a million years, I will keep it until the day I die. I enjoy looking at it. My Albert always said it was one of his favourite paintings. I just wish he had been alive to share it with me. He would be very impressed to know I had a Vermeer on my bedroom wall – even if it is a fake.'

'Does Roy share the same passion for artwork?'

'Let's say, I have to be a little careful with Roy. He's still got an eye for making money. He went through a phase where nothing was important to him. He got into a lot of debt and he would have sold everything to the devil but now he has Annie and I think he might have changed. Annie is good for him. He works hard and he travels abroad and he seems happier…'

'What does he do?'

'Technology, computers or something like that, I don't really know but Annie and Max will stay here with me when he has to go away so I won't be on my own any more.'

I know loneliness. I'm its best friend.

Mrs Green continues speaking. 'He seems much calmer than he used to be and I believe he was quite pleased when I asked them to move in. We've healed the rift and the past is past. We must move on. I'll just have to learn to live with the change won't I, my dear? Now, tell me, what about you? Is there any news?'

'Javier won a portrait commission and so we have been invited to Germany to meet Josephine Lavelle.'

'My goodness, she's even better than Maria Callas. Josephine Lavelle, well I never, what an honour that will be for him. There's no one in the world that could sing like her – is there?'

'It's not my type of music,' I confess. 'I find it so boring.'

'But you must go with him. Poor Javier will need you. She has a bit of a reputation with men. She's a bit of a man-eater. Is that what you would call her?'

I laugh. 'Is she a bit of a tart?'

Mrs Green giggles revealing a row of even false teeth. 'Not any more I shouldn't think. Didn't you hear what happened last summer?'

I shrug and shake my head.

'It was the opening night of *Tosca* and it should have been Glorietta Bareldo, her rival, who sang but at the last minute she was ill so they asked Josephine Lavelle to take over. It must have been terribly awkward as they were both going out with the same man – and then she was shot on stage.'

'Was her singing that bad?' I joke.

Mrs Green smiles but shakes her head sadly. 'The boyfriend – he was an artist I think – he died. She was shot too. The bullet pierced her lung. They say she will never sing again.'

I stare at her.

Raffaelle Peverelli, my Italian art tutor and mentor under whom I studied one summer in Italy in my first year at University had been shot at an incident in a theatre. I had been in Morocco last August and Carmen had phoned to say he had been killed. I'm sure it was at an opera. Surely this could not be the same incident?

'Were they lovers Josephine and this artist?'

'Yes, presumably, he had lived with Glorietta Bareldo for years but then he met Josephine Lavelle. It caused a lot of scandal of course. Josephine had faded from the spotlight. This was to be her first performance in over four years.'

'Is she better now?'

'It would seem so, if she is ready to have her portrait painted. It's all the more reason for you to go and chaperone, Javier. He will need you. He will need protecting.'

We talk for half an hour or so but my mind is preoccupied with the death of Raffa. Old memories have surged forward jostling and pushing for pole position in my reticent memory but I take comfort in the company of this old lady and her calm tranquillity. Mrs Green is naturally positive and upbeat. She has a curious mind and I enjoy her lively conversation. Half an hour later when I am leaving her house I bend forward to kiss her cheek as I would to the grandma I never had and, as I pull away, she takes hold of my wrist and presses a key into the palm of my hand wrapping my fingers tightly shut around it.

'Take this with you, Mikky. You saved my life and I'll never forget that. Especially the way you climbed over the fence. I've written the alarm code on the tag so that you'll be able to let yourself in and you won't get covered in cuts and bruises again. You were so brave and I'm very grateful. I could have lain there for days. I might never have been found. I could have died. And I have you to thank for all this now. My new exciting life and reconciliation with my family after all these years.'

'You don't need to give me a key, Mrs Green. Your family are here now and they'll look after you.'

'Just in case,' she insists. Her bony fingers keep the key firmly in my fist. 'One just never knows. It will be our secret.'

As I let myself into my flat I can't believe my luck. She's given me the key to her front door and the alarm code. What a result! Perhaps somewhere out in the Universe my grand scheming plan has been endorsed and everything will fall neatly into place. I celebrate with my air guitar dancing around my lounge singing, *Good Girls Go to Heaven*.

Chapter Three

'Everything you can imagine is real.'
Pablo Picasso

The week before Christmas I go to Germany like a child metaphorically screaming, kicking and having a tantrum. The thought of this woman with my mentor, Raffaelle Peverelli and now making friends with Javier is too much for me to contemplate. I know I will not like her.

I imagine Josephine Lavelle on a golden throne. A diva Goddess reclining languorously, treating me dismissively and with contempt. I don't want to go. I don't even like opera.

'What am I doing?' I ask Javier, draining my third gin and tonic and looking around for the air hostess but he isn't listening. He is tuned into his iPod and his eyes are closed.

It was eight years ago that I studied with Raffa in Italy but it could be last year. Having spoken about him with Mrs Green it has made my memories stronger: his soft voice, musky cologne and even the acrid tobacco from his moustache seem more pungent and I remember one evening toward the end of my visit we were in the market square in Bergamo. It was early evening and the sun was hiding behind the Church spire so I lifted my sunglasses on top of my head. Along with the other art students we were discussing, arguing and debating the merits of the Old Masters, the success of the Romantics and the evolution of Modern

Art. I was rolling a cigarette listening to other art students and drinking wine from Lombardy, when Raffa leaned toward me and said.

You're not original, Mikky. You copy too faithfully. You must show more flair if you want to be a proper artist. Your work is too faithful for this world, bellissima. You must believe in your talent and trust your instinct. You are a perfectionist. You could become the world's best forger.

I had laughed but I was annoyed with his advice. I did not like his suggestion to imitate art and like so many times in my life certain words stick in the back of my mind and lurk there waiting to pounce just when you think them forgotten. The plan that I have for stealing Mrs Green's painting now makes perfect sense and as the plane circles to land in Dresden I go over the details once again in my head. My life has been filled with triggers that have had a domino effect leading to this moment. It hasn't been fate or destiny. It has been me who has lined up the opportunistic dominos with patient precision. Patience was the most important thing I learnt as my parents dragged me around Spain. I learnt the art of waiting in the confines of the church or under the shade of a tamarind tree as they finished another beer or rolled another joint, and I learned not to get my hopes up and how to keep myself amused with my thoughts, puzzling and reasoning – not just about religion and spirituality – but also about art and beauty and through them I wanted to decipher the truth.

What is the truth? Wherein lays a lie?

I decided by the age of fourteen that the truth is whatever one believes it to be. Whatever anyone decides upon – that is their truth and theirs alone and that it's all right to have a different truth from family or lovers. It is like owning a painting. It is okay to have a fake painting and if someone believes it is authentic – then so be it – why destroy that belief?

The plane tilts its wings and I raise my tray table and throw my bag at my feet. The dark and lumpy clouds rock the plane reminding me of a ride at the fair ground. Javier stirs then settles again. His long eyelashes rest upon his cheeks. His olive skin looks soft and there is a fashionable shadow of a beard on his chin.

When I returned from studying in Italy, Carmen was a mess. She was heartbroken. Javier was as frivolous with love as he was with his emotions. His passion lasted for as long as he drew a painting. Then like a soldier after battle he was spent; exhausted and drained from the intensity of his affair. Carmen was despondent, desolate and broken. I have seen enough sadness and experienced more than enough heartbreak and I had cared for her the best I could, cajoling her back to life, stimulating her interest and healing her heart.

The cabin bell dings. We are reminded we are coming into land. I leave Javier asleep and watch the ground below coming closer and closer while hearing Raffa's words. Words that haunt me now even after his death.

You could become the world's best forger.

***

A stark wind whips across my face as we follow the tall, thin and anaemic looking driver called Andreas, to the black Mercedes. He lifts my case not bothering to look at me. We drive past busy streets with festive lights festooned across Christmas market stalls where steam rises from makeshift fires and a pig roasts on a spit. The city appears to be filled with magnificent historical buildings, statues in all shapes and sizes and illuminated churches with spires that stretch into the night-sky.

Josephine's house is in the suburbs. Pots of red and white poinsettias line a flight of stairs leading to the front door. Javier reaches for my hand and squeezes my fingers just before we step wordlessly into a warm room and the aroma of roasting apples and cinnamon.

Josephine Lavelle is not a princess; she is more like a dowager. In her early fifties, she looks like a woman who has inherited wealth from her late husband and is used to a life of privilege and luxury. She looks fragile and vulnerable but when she smiles her eyes are sharp like bright diamonds. She radiates excited energy but not stamina.

Javier is focused on his muse and his model. She doesn't stand up and it causes him to bend over her hand like an awkward servant. He takes her proffered fingers and he brings them to his lips in a manner that is both European and chivalrous. She has cast a spell over him. His brown eyes travel appreciatively over her face taking in the tiny details that only an artist like him can see and I know I have lost him. His smile is benevolent like he has stepped into the aisle of a glorious church and he is overcome with awe basking in the light of her glory.

I shudder and take a deep breath.

She turns her eyes on me and absorbs each detail

of my appearance; my creased checked shirt, tight black jeans right down to my thick black socks. Her eyes travel over my face, my dark hair and the details of my large features. I am a brute in the presence of a vulnerable gazelle. She's like a predator and an invading sense of uncertainty washes over me, fearful that this fragile woman before me is about to wreak havoc on my life.

She beckons me like I am a street urchin who is meeting royalty for the first time. She is too perfect. The laughter lines at the corner of her penetrating eyes and her dark hair, cut too short, and wide smile are all staged – it is an act and I will not be bought by her transparent smile and her false exuberance. An invisible cloak like a shroud wraps itself over me like a cold, dark shadow on a summer's day. It begins suffocating and stifling the vibrant fire burning within me, damping my enthusiasm, my creativity and snuffing life out of my soul.

She appears speechless but eventually and very softly, she says. 'Mikky, it's lovely to meet you.' Her fingers are soft and firm, then suddenly, it's as if the atmosphere changes and Josephine is excited and nervous, almost childlike. She claps her palms, squares her shoulders, sits straighter and pulling a heavy shawl across her chest she speaks in a strong voice with a trace of an American accent.

'I hope you had a good journey. Please do sit down. You must be tired. Andreas will bring us some refreshment.'

It isn't a question or a statement. It's more an observation or a preference, as if she is ordering dinner from a room service menu. We are invited to sit on the white leather sofa opposite her and Andreas is dispatched from the room.

'Delightful.' Javier sits beside me and crosses his ankles. 'It's a pleasure to be here. Thank you for inviting us...'

She waves her hand as if his thanks are unnecessary but her eyes flick between us, as she absorbs minuscule details in our appearance, drinking us both with her gaze as if we are exotic cocktails to be quaffed and then disgorged with distaste and over indulgence.

We have nothing in common. We are from different worlds.

Had it not been for Javier painting her portrait our paths would never have crossed. My destiny would never be entwined with hers. Her mind is clearly focused on a hidden agenda and my fear for Javier rises. I wish he wasn't so handsome or strong. Years of training in the gym have given him broad shoulders and a tiny waist and by the way her eyes travel over him I see she appreciates his efforts. When she smiles it is as if she is using a taut and magnetic invisible thread to reel him, emotionally and mentally toward her.

Is this what she did on stage? Is this why she was so captivating and popular? Is this what they call stage presence?

'Thank you for coming to visit me in Dresden, I do hope the journey was not too tedious for you? I am so excited by your visit. I have been looking forward to it.' She purrs and moves purposely, arching her back like a cat stretching in the sun. I expect her to yawn but she simply pulls her shawl around her shoulders and tilts her head as if each movement has been carefully staged and rehearsed.

I imagine her practicing scales, singing and filled with self-discipline and pride. All the years of devotion and dedication, all the hours of training and the time when she may have felt ill or too tired. I think of her constantly striving for perfection. The anger and frustration she experienced as the chrysalis emerged and a diva was born, secure in her talent and assured of her place on the world stage.

Has she ever struggled through self-doubt and insecurity?

'I love your portfolio, Javier. You are so talented. Tell me about yourself.'

Javier blinks rapidly and speaks quickly, telling her of his desire and delight to be chosen to paint her portrait but my attention strays.

The living room is ultra-modern with oak floors and ivory white rugs. Three white leather sofas are arranged in a U-shape around a burning log fire. A baby white grand piano is in the far corner beside a massive floor-to-ceiling window that overlooks a large balcony and a terraced garden filled with fruit trees. The view of the orchard, decorated with bulbous festive lights gives way to a view of illuminated spires of Dresden's city centre on the horizon.

There is no evidence of Christmas only one week away, apart from a hand-carved rotating float with angels that turn, propelled by the heat of burning red candles like an invisible wind. The wooden angels bring peace and joy, and the warmth of the fire and the alcohol I consumed on the flight make my eyelids droop and the room fades into haziness.

Javier's melodic voice seeps into my soul. My eyelids are heavy and the angel with the wooden wings hums. I grunt at a sharp dig in my chest and sit up quickly snorting myself awake.

Josephine stares at me with a bewildered and incredulous look on her face. She arches her eyebrow and pulls back the sleeve of her cotton shirt and checks her watch. 'You must both be exhausted. We will have an early dinner.'

Andreas arrives with a chilled ice bucket and four fluted glasses.

'Do you prefer tea?' she asks looking at me.

'No, thank you.' I blink conscious of her scrutiny. She is probably wondering what the divine and gorgeous Javier could possibly see in me. If only she knew.

'How lovely – prosecco.' Javier smoothes his palms on his jeans as if he might contaminate the glass with his touch.

'I much prefer it to champagne,' Josephine says. 'Especially to celebrate.'

He leans forward eagerly like an energised and nervous puppy. I want to pull on his arm and make him lean back nearer to me. He is far too keen and enthusiastic. What is so great about this woman that brings Javier to an excited wreck?

'We must have a toast,' she says and we raise our glass with hers. 'To friendship and success – to our future.'

'Our future,' Javier agrees.

I sip and swallow a burp.

'I think we're going to have a lot in common, Javier. I'm looking forward to sitting for you. I shall have to ask you to be kind in your work and be gentle on your observations.' She raises her glass in a mock toast to him. 'Could I persuade you to air brush me?'

'It won't be necessary, Josephine. Believe me. You have an incredibly interesting face.'

Andreas sits beside her like a silent young fawn, folding his longs legs to one side, his head tilted as if listening for danger.

As Josephine continues playing a part in her own mini Dresden opera where she is the protagonist, Javier is her young protégée and Andreas is the jealous suitor, my attention wanders and I retreat into my own sphere. It's my own space that served me well as a child and like a crab in a shell I take refuge behind a tough veneer – my suit of armour until I can rally and come out again with pincers at the ready.

How does she speak like that?

Years of voice coaching and breathing must have given a distinct quality to her voice. Her movements are slow and precise. Her words are measured and clipped. She tilts her head, raises an eyebrow or nods at Javier's awkward replies but it's the smile that annoys me. It lingers like an unwanted houseguest on her lips. It's a Cinderella smile, full of wistful promise and the vessel of her gushing praise.

I want to shout. '*Stop it, Javier! She's only human. She's a nobody.*' I want to take him by the shoulders and shake him, dangle him upside down from the outside balcony that gives us panoramic views of the Dresden skyline but I can't. Instead I try to regulate my breathing and relax against the soft cushions at my back while my stomach crunches with anxiety.

Andreas refills amber liquid into our glasses. He

is subservient yet there is a confident quality about him. Is it bordering on arrogance? What relationship does Josephine have with him?

The conversation flutters around me but I won't meet her gaze. Instead I stare at the roaring log fire. When she asks Andreas to bring Javier's portfolio, he clears a space between ripe green olives, stuffed red peppers and mixed nuts on the coffee table and opens it out for us all to see.

'This piece in particular is my favourite. I love the way you have captured the sensuality in her eyes.' She taps the page with a ruby red fingernail, pointing to a sketch of the Madonna. Mary, mother of Jesus sits with eyes downcast. Her lashes are extraordinarily long and a small smile plays on her lips in a knowing and secretive manner. Her gown, painted in Vermeer's ultramarine blue, hangs loosely emphasising pert and rounded breasts. Her fingers are extended against her pale neck in mock protest. It's a provocative piece of work and the detail is so intimate I can almost feel the softness of the Virgin's flesh.

'It is one of Javier's finer pieces and one of my favourite drawings,' I say.

When I look up Josephine is staring at me. It's a frank appraisal and her scrutiny causes me to sit back but she quickly averts her gaze. She looks at Javier and studies him with the same fascination as she does me but when he glances up, she smiles back at him with wistful uncertainty.

We drink the first bottle quickly and Andreas returns from the kitchen with another. I yawn loudly remembering to cover my mouth and I sit up straight wishing my eyes hadn't filled with tired watery tears.

'I hope you're hungry? Andreas is a wonderful cook. I have put on so much weight since I've been here.'

'I can't believe that,' Javier protests.

She is like a delicate and fragile skeleton. Is she looking for compliments?

The conversation returns to art and to exhibitions and then the theatre and audiences and finally to art galleries. She is articulate and well informed. She is interested in our opinions and the prosecco loosens my tongue and gives me confidence.

'Vermeer's, *Girl Reading a Letter by an Open Window,* is exhibited here in the Dresden National Gallery. I would like to see it – if I can?' I say.

'You like Vermeer?'

'Perhaps when you are busy with Javier, I can go there?' I don't say that it is the only way Javier could persuade me to come with him to Dresden.

'Do you paint?'

'I like Caravaggio,' I reply.

'Caravaggio?' She raises an eyebrow and I nod disconcerted by her stare but this time I refuse to look away.

I imagine her with my old tutor Raffa with his fiery and passionate arguments and her patient and calm persistence. Had they been happy?

'A friend of mine also liked Caravaggio–' Josephine appears distracted and she is lost for words.

'Raffaelle Peverelli?' I ask.

'Yes?' She raises an eyebrow.

'I studied with him one summer.' I sit forward, square my shoulders and clasp my hands together.

'You are an artist?'

'Javier and I studied together but now I prefer the medium of the camera.'

I wait for her to say something but she simply stares at me. I cannot fathom her expression but to my dismay it is one I would like to capture on camera. It is interesting yet elusive. Her eyes are sad and there is a registering of – what – sadness or pain?

'What made you want to paint?' I think the question is for me but Josephine Lavelle turns to Javier.

She compliments him on each sketch and painting, turning the pages of his portfolio, marvelling over each tiny detail as if she is playing to an audience, stroking his ego and as he basks in pleasure, it's as if Josephine is gauging my reaction to her over-effusive compliments. Javier is not perfect and a niggling feeling of annoyance grows in me.

Twenty minutes later Andreas calls us for dinner and when Josephine rises to her feet, she clutches her chest and her face grimaces in pain. She leans on Javier for support and walks with caution and her gait is slow. She clearly revels in being surrounded by men and she behaves like a glorious old-fashioned diva used to having people at her beck and call.

The dining room is illuminated with soft lamps, red candles and an assortment of white and red Christmas poinsettias. Framed pictures along the wall are prints of original paintings. I recognise two of them: Gerhard Richter's *Cathedral Square in Milan* and Anselm Kiefer's *To the Unknown Painter*.

At the table the men are placed between us like referees and when Josephine's eyes meet mine but I'm not quick enough to disguise my exasperation and a flash of surprise crosses her face.

Two nights I remind myself.

'They're beautiful,' I say, unfolding my red napkin and diverting attention to the wooden cherubic ornaments on the table.

'They're hand–made here in Dresden. You can pick some up at the Christmas markets. Perhaps tomorrow there will be time – no? Andreas?'

He nods but doesn't look up. He places a large tray of roasted pork, crunchy vegetables and mashed potatoes threaded with chives in the middle of the table. We praise his culinary skills and I wonder if his talents or duties for Josephine go beyond the kitchen.

He has yet to smile.

He serves red wine in large goblets with a gold rim. I need a drink – anything to get me through the next few hours but I wait for her toast.

'It is from Saxony – as is the lovely Andreas.' She raises her glass. 'You have probably wondered about our relationship…but Andreas is my protégée. He is my inspiration for opera and he keeps my passion alive.'

It is my turn to raise my eyebrow. I smile sweetly and begin to serve myself.

Andreas addresses us in perfect English. 'Ms Lavelle has been kind enough to support my career. She is my mentor and she is instructing and coaching me. She has taken me under her wing and is giving me the benefit of her experience–'

'Andreas is extremely talented. He has already performed in Berlin and Hamburg,' Josephine interjects.

'Only since we are working together – I have

been fortunate enough to be considered for such important roles.' He appears relieved to explain his position. There is even a hint of a smile on his lips.

'Very few tenors can sing up to two Fs above middle C. Andreas has this talent. He is simply a dream student.' She smiles indulgently at him and he flushes under her gaze.

Javier raises his glass to Andreas. 'That's a true gift and to find such a wonderful tutor must be a blessing for you.'

He holds Andreas' gaze just a fraction too long and I wonder if Josephine notices the burning competition between them.

'Music is an art. It's in here.' Javier clutches his fist and holds it to his heart. 'It's my passion and my soul.'

Josephine helps herself to a meagre portion. 'I am the same, Javier. Music was my life and singing was my passion. But I too, feel it in my heart. Many people go through their lives without recognising or developing their talents and I was fortunate to do both although it wasn't without sacrifice or sadness.' She holds her hand delicately to her chest in a classical acting pose. She locks her gaze with Andreas and they all appear to be joined by an invisible bond except for me.

I shift uncomfortably in my seat then take a mouthful of pork and as I chew I wash it down with a large gulp of wine. It is tender, tasty and delicious.

Throughout the meal I watch her intimate display toward the two men carefully balancing her attention like the Scales of Justice. Her behaviour doesn't seem entirely natural. It is as if she is playing a part, a role in the theatre and I don't know why she can't just be herself.

To my annoyance I find her as fascinating and as elusive as a ghostly presence at the table and my head fills with unanswered questions. Who is the real Josephine Lavelle? Where is your family? Why have you settled here in Dresden? Her interesting face becomes familiar to me. I imagine taking her photograph. How I would have her pose and what would I say to relax her and to make her laugh. What would I ask to bring the two different people out from inside her? When caught unaware the real Josephine appears excited and nervous but the other more formal Josephine seems to be acting the role of a diva – why two such different characters?

Is she excited or afraid? Is it because of the portrait? Is her ego really so big that she is scared Javier won't paint her in a favourable light?

Mrs Green is right. This woman is trouble. Josephine watches me but she can't interact with me. I sip my wine quickly. I want to antagonise her. I want to annoy her. I want to be back in London.

'Tomorrow morning Andreas will take you both on a tour of Dresden then in the afternoon we can have some time together to discuss the portrait.' She looks at Javier then eventually at me. 'And, during this time you may visit your Vermeer painting. We have several interesting museums and Andreas will arrange tickets for you. Tomorrow evening there is a special performance of *The Nutcracker Suite* in the Semperoper, the Dresden Opera House, which I am sure you will enjoy. It is the Philharmonic Orchestra from Berlin and they are delightful. It will be an experience for you both.'

'Fantastic,' Javier grins like a schoolboy and runs the palms of his hands excitedly together. 'That's so kind of you.'

'Unfortunately I will not be joining you. I have developed complications in my lungs and as a result I am unable to do certain things. Nor do I have the same stamina I once had. I think that after our meeting tomorrow afternoon I will rest but I shall wait up for you.'

'I am so looking forward to painting your portrait.' Javier gushes. The wine glass lists in his hand like a tilted sail in the wind.

Josephine nods her head in acquiescence and a smile of satisfaction crosses her face.

'And I am very pleased that you were the man chosen to paint my portrait. I'm so very pleased that you, and Mikky…' She nods at me, 'could join us here in my home. It's a very special time of year and to share it with such delightful, young companions makes me feel incredibly lucky. It is only through family and friends that I can now find true happiness and I do hope that one day you will come to regard me with special affection.'

How desperate she must be for company. To befriend us so quickly and to want everlasting friendship, she must want something else – but what? What could we possibly have that she would want?

One by one, they turn to look at me. I know that my life has changed irrevocably. My heart is heavy like a solid weight and it drags me down and I am sinking to the bottom of a deep dark well, struggling uselessly for survival under her watchful gaze.

'I hope so too,' I lie and I raise my glass for a toast with theirs.

***

I am stepping out of my jeans when Javier appears unceremoniously in the bedroom we are sharing.

'What are you playing at?' He hisses at me. 'What's wrong with you?'

'She doesn't like me.'

'She doesn't know you. Besides, you have been behaving like an idiot since you got here. You've been rude and hostile and completely unfriendly. Apart from falling asleep on the sofa and drinking too much, you have rebuffed any attempt from her to make you comfortable or be a friend. What's your problem, Mikky?'

'She's a….she's a–'

'What?'

'Man-eater,' I say repeating Mrs Green's observation of the once famous opera diva. It's the only thing I can think of to say.

'Don't be ridiculous – as if I would be interested in a fifty-something-year-old woman.'

'It's not that–'

'You're being crazy. She has invited us here so she can get to know me, so that I will paint a better portrait of her. She is trying to make us welcome but you are being awful. What is wrong with you?'

'I don't trust her.'

'You don't trust anyone.'

'That's not the point.'

'Yes, it is.'

'That's not fair–'

'You can have friends you know. Sometime there is no ulterior motive. Some people are kind and nice. Just give her the opportunity, Mikky. Stop being so hostile.'

I turn away but he grabs me by the shoulders.

'I know you had a rough time growing up. I know how hard you find it to make friends and to trust people but please give Josephine a chance. She is a kind woman and we are her guests. Please be decent in return.'

'She's only interested in you. I'm a tagged on appendage, part of the package.' I push him away but my mood has softened.

'You're wrong. She needs friends, Mikky. We all do. It's a big lonely world out there as you well know. She's probably been surrounded by insincere hangers-on and social climbers that want to bask in her famous status, money and the perks that go with it.'

'Like you?'

He frowns. 'That's not fair and it's not true.'

'I'm sorry. It's just that–'

'This is important to me, Mikky. Think about what is important to you. What would you like more than anything?'

I think of *The Concert* hanging on Mrs Green's wall.

'Well, this is just as important to me.'

He hasn't read my mind. He hasn't got a clue what I am thinking.

'Have you not noticed how much she's changed?' he asks. He turns his back and removes his shirt.

'Changed?'

'Yes – since her final performance – since *Tosca*, she's a shadow of her former self. She is weak and ill. You can see that she is struggling with her health. She has dark circles under her eyes that she covers with makeup and there is pain on her face whenever she moves. If you paid more attention to others and not just to yourself you will see that her left hand shakes, she also drags her left foot and her breathing is shallow, not to mention the perspiration constantly on her forehead.'

'You sound like a doctor.'

'And you are acting like a spoilt child.'

We glare at each other.

'Sort yourself out, Mikky. This is my big opportunity. You are here to support me, not to rattle and upset the woman I am to paint – a woman who has had the most amazing career and is revered around the world. She–'

There are footsteps outside in the hallway and we wait while they walk away until they finally fade.

'Andreas?' I whisper.

Javier nods. 'He's harmless.'

'I can't wait to get back to London.'

Chapter Four

Every time I paint a portrait I lose a friend.
John Singer Sargent

After breakfast Andreas drives us to the city centre. He stops outside a domed and historic building adorned with statues, overlooking the river Elbe.

'This is the Semperoper, our concert hall, and home to the Semperoper Ballet. This is where we will go tonight,' he says proudly. He eases the car away from the kerb in front of a yellow tram. 'And this is the magnificent Zwinger Museum in the Postplatz.' Andreas slows the car past the government buildings. 'And the Kongresszentrum here, is on the river Elbe. We will follow it to the Albertinum.' Andreas recites fact and figures. He knows his history and Javier nods encouragingly, like me, he is interested in history. I sit with my head resting against the leather and gaze out of the window – hearing the jackboots, bombs and shouts – imaging the fear.

'On the 13th February 1945 the British bombed Dresden and over 25,000 people were killed. In the initial years after the war the city centre was cleared of the enormous masses of rubble by tens of thousands of volunteer helpers,' Andreas explains. 'The reconstruction of selected architectural monuments was determined from the very beginning and the reconstruction of the Zwinger was completed in 1964. You will enjoy your visit there this afternoon, Mikky.'

I don't reply.

'The Elbe divides Dresden. This is the Court Church, Johanneum, Albertinum and the Royal Mews, rebuilt and restored in 1985. However not everything could be saved from the devastation of the war and sometimes valuable remains or monuments were demolished instead.'

'So many lives were lost so much waste and destruction,' Javier says.

'All the cultural buildings were obliterated and the lives of ordinary people were damaged and destroyed,' Andreas agrees.

'Did we learn anything from the war?' I mumble. I think of Caravaggio and his dark paintings and Christ suffering on the cross. Did we learn nothing from 2000 years ago?

'After the war the construction and rebuilding replenished pride in the people here,' Andreas says. 'This is the Blue Wonder. When we cross it you will see it offers a view of the Elbe valley. If Josephine is well enough we're having brunch up there tomorrow morning before your flight back to London.' Andreas points a finger, beyond the blue suspension bridge, to a castle on the hill on the bank of the river.

'The view should be amazing,' Javier's enthusiasm is endless and exhausting.

I yawn but I can't take my eyes from the streets wondering what life was like before the Wall came down.

'This is the Albertplatz – King Albert was the King of Saxony. His reign wasn't very exciting and he was a terrible fighter. In fact he lost nearly all the battles and then he lost the war. But, in his favour, he did spend all our money on collecting art.' Andreas grins at Javier and stops at the traffic lights. 'We have many Christmas markets all over the city. You must buy our famous Dresden Christmas Stöllen – it's delicious.'

I think about returning to England and my life after Christmas. A New Year begins and I have a growing feeling that these weeks will be my last with Javier.

In the city centre Andreas pulls the car to the kerb. 'One of the busiest markets is in Frauenkirche Square. Walk through it. You will enjoy the atmosphere and you can buy some German gifts or decorations for your home.'

I don't tell him, I hate Christmas.

'Don't forget, Javier. We have one hour and thirty minutes precisely,' I say, as we watch Andreas drive off. I breathe deeply and link my arm through his enjoying a flash of sunshine that appears from behind a dark cloud. Its brightness momentarily dazzles us and sends a welcome beam of heat to my cheeks. We are muffled up in hats and gloves but after five minutes I pull off my beanie and shake my mane free.

We browse market stalls, order mulled wine and savour the hint of cinnamon and lemon on our tongues. Fifteen minutes later we are sitting on the first floor of an Italian restaurant overlooking the old market square and the rebuilt Church of Our Lady. According to the guidebook that Javier reads from, the protestant church was only rebuilt after the reunification of Germany. Construction work began in1994 and it was consecrated again in 2005. I sip my beer and watch tourists, schoolchildren and Asians queue in an orderly line waiting to get inside.

We order plates of steaming pasta with garlic and mushrooms and sip more iced beer. Javier has integrated himself into the affections of Josephine Lavelle and even the aloof Andreas but I am sulky, uncommunicative and unable to maintain a proper conversation.

After lunch Andreas is waiting for us beside the car. The thought of getting inside and going back to Josephine's house fills me with dreariness.

'Don't worry about me. I'll find my own way back.' I wink at Javier and pat Andreas on the shoulder then I disappear into the Christmas crowds before they can stop me.

Overhead dark clouds cluster, a storm circles in the east and thunder rolls in rumbling like a troubled giant. I raise my face to the sky and walk with purpose enjoying the majesty of the buildings each one more magnificent than the last – all breathtakingly stunning and adorned with statues, drawings and paintings. I pass cafes and inhale baked apple strudel, strong dark coffee, roasting onions with potatoes and sometimes a whiff of cigar smoke.

I release my camera from the case and begin to snap with wild enthusiasm absorbing myself in colours, shapes and movement. I hear the sound of my own boots on cobbles then I imagine the city as a mass of rubble.

Posters advertise classical and pop concerts, individual artists, choirs, plays, operas, museums and exhibitions – this is the new Dresden. I take countless photographs and immerse myself in another culture, revelling in the sounds of foreign voices, the whine of trams and jolly, festive music. The Lutheran church of the Holy Cross is just another victim of the Dresden bombing and I am drawn to the starkness of its columns and its sober interior marvelling at the replicated detail.

Does a building or a city lose its value if it's a forgery?

The whole town is a beautiful and elaborate sham. It's just as stunning as the original, just as pleasing to the eye with just as much attention to detail to each of the crafts but nevertheless it's not the original city. Some may call it a fraud, imposter or a charlatan but I understand the skill in making an exact replica. A painting is challenging enough but a whole city inspires me and gives me hope. Do tourists marvel at the sheer beauty or at the sheer pretence?

The deception is exquisite.

I click photo after photo.

The city is a fake.

Perhaps one can accept beauty without knowing all the facts. So long as one believes it is true – therein lays the beauty. We admire what has been painstakingly rebuilt in the exact style of centuries before. There is no lie involved. If one did not pick up a guidebook it would not detract from the visual beauty of the city and the visitor who does not know the historical details would remain ignorant. They would bask solely in the pleasure of exquisiteness – thinking and believing it to be the original.

With my conscience cleansed I leave the sanctuary of the church and I make my way to the Gemädegalerie Alte Meister Art Gallery where I shake rain from my hair, wipe my face dry and blow my nose.

I am exhilarated; my heart is racing, my soul is pumping.

The brochure tells me of its excellent collection of masterpieces from fifteenth to eighteenth–century; paintings that were acquired during the reign of Augustus Strong and his son between the years, 1694 to 1763. As Andreas said – he was not a fighter but a collector.

I walk slowly absorbing the atmosphere of the building and upstairs I find a leather bench where I sit and stare at Vermeer's *Girl Reading a Letter at an Open Window* and I compare the similarities in the painting to *The Concert*. In this painting a lady reads from a letter similarly, in *The Concert,* the singer reads from a sheet of music, both women show the same gentle scrutiny and intensity on their faces at what they read. Even the Oriental rug in the foreground on the left makes me believe the similarities are unquestionable.

Afterwards I stroll through the rooms taking a particular interest in the Italian master painters; Caravaggio and Raphael's *Sistine Madonna*, known for the depiction of two little angels that appears on books and posters all around Dresden city and in Bellotto's paintings of historic Dresden.

I think of my art master and mentor Raffaelle Peverelli and how he mixed techniques of the Old Masters with surrealism. In his most recent exhibition he had copied Rembrandt and Michaelangelo and he painted iPods and iPads onto the canvas mixing oil painting skills with modern technology. The exhibition had been called *Juxtaposed Evolution* and the critics had slated it until his death. Now his work is hailed as innovative and creative, and Raffaelle, an art master and hero.

There had been a strange look on Josephine's face when I told her I studied with Raffa. Had it been jealousy? Had she believed me?

It was difficult for me to believe that such a passionate and gifted man could be dead but it must be harder for Josephine – she had loved him.

I wander through the galleries from one floor to the next, each one more splendid than the last, immersing myself in a time gone by with Old Masters, and I look to the future through the eyes of new artists with equal enthusiasm wishing I could capture their work with my lens but my camera along with my bag and coat is shut firmly away in a locker behind the foyer on the ground floor.

I return for one last look at the Flemish master painters: Rubens, Van Dyck and Rembrandt but once again it is Vermeer's painting that draws me. Captivated I stand back gazing at it from different angles then I sit for a while lost in thought until I sense someone move close to me.

I turn. 'What are you doing here?'

'Ms Lavelle didn't want you to be alone.'

'You mean, she wanted to be alone with Javier and they threw you out.'

Andreas shakes his head. 'She is concerned about you. You have been missing a long time.'

'Missing?' I stand up. Having Andreas with me is like having a chain attached to a heavy boulder around my ankle. My sense of freedom as well as my good humour evaporates like a fading rainbow as we stroll through the gallery and by the time I collect my belongings from the locker my mood is as dark and as cold as the evening outside.

Andreas guides me toward the car through the illuminated Christmas market where rich cheeses and roasting meats chase me and my stomach rumbles.

'Have you tried mulled wine with anise?'

I shake my head and he takes my elbow and steers me through the crowd. He orders two glasses from a woman dressed in a thick fur hat and a traditional dirndl dress and we stand quietly watching the bustle of people listening to snatches of their conversation.

'This is my favourite time of year,' Andreas says, looking at a man who grips his daughter's hand as he steers her toward a small stage.

When I don't reply he asks.

'What do you do for Christmas?'

'Nothing.'

He laughs.

'I hate Christmas,' I add.

His eyes widen in surprise. 'How can you hate all this?'

The anise and hot wine is warm in my stomach.

'What about you parents? Don't you celebrate with your family?' he insists.

'My parents never needed Christmas – every night was a celebration.'

'Wow, lucky you – happy parents,' he smiles in misunderstanding.

The rain has stopped and the sky is filled with smoke and the smell of freshly baking bread curls around us. The aniseed is sharp and sweet on the back of my throat.

'She's not well. You know that don't you? The

bullet punctured her lung and she still hasn't recovered. She had a series of complications and an infection that almost killed her. She is lucky to be alive.'

'Opera's not my thing.'

'But you knew, Raffaelle?'

'We weren't in touch,' I reply.

'Where have you been living? Where were you last August?'

'I was travelling through the Atlas Mountains – in Morocco. I'm a photographer.'

'That explains it.' He turns away distracted by a traditionally dressed trio with an accordion who climb onto the stage.

'I did some work for The Matisse Art Gallery in Marrakech for a few months. It was showcasing Ari Mashood's work and other local Moroccans and international artists. My friend Carmen told me but I never knew what…' my voice loses momentum as the singing from the stage begins.

Andreas looks directly into my eyes. 'She was shot on stage during her final performance of *Tosca*? She moved to stand in front of him but he died – lying on the floor beside her. She will never sing again.'

'She must be–'

'Devastated? She is. But she understands the passion of opera and that is why she wants to help me.'

'How did you meet her?'

'Glorietta Bareldo introduced us. She saw me sing in *La Traviata* and she suggested that Josephine tutor me. I think she saw it as a solution for us both. I needed a tutor and Josephine needs to know that she is still, how would you say, worthwhile?'

'Valued.'

'Exactly. Valued. But she should not travel. She should rest. She shouldn't be pushing herself like this. She said she is going to London so that Javier can paint her.'

'What? Can't Javier paint her here?'

'She is insisting. She is determined. There is something else, too…'

'What?'

He shrugs. 'I don't know. It is like she has something she must do. Something that she must find – I'm not sure what or who it is.'

'Have you asked her?'

'She won't speak about it. I think there is a man who is helping her. She has been different these past few weeks, excited, worried, nervous – I'm not sure.'

'She can't travel if she is not well.'

'I think that is why she wants to return to London. It is as if she must make amends for her past.' He shakes his head.

'She can't go to London!'

He smiles thinking that I actually care about her. 'That's what I say to her but she has her own mind. She will do as she pleases. I think it is the only way that she will find inner peace…'

I shake my head. Around us the crowd are laughing at the trio singing in exaggerated pantomime voices.

'I doubt she will let me go with her.' He leans closer to my ear. 'I would like to help her. But if she won't let me, I want to ask you a favour.'

'Favour?' The anise is welcoming and I finish the glass in one gulp and look around needing another.

'I want you to look after her. If she needs anything then you must let me know. You must keep an eye on her. I am worried that she will overdo things–'

'Why should I look after her?'

'Because you are a kind woman.'

I shake my head. I think that Andreas has led a very sheltered life. 'Josephine Lavelle is able to look after herself. I know her type of woman,' I reply with my best smile.

'You do?'

'Absolutely.'

It is true. I have known women like Josephine. They have this knack of keeping men at their beck and call. I see the way Josephine has them hovering around her. Weak men who bend to her whims and desire, and grown men who have turned into ingratiating servants like *Stepford Men* who have had their personalities erased, their only aim to please her like Javier. He has put her on a pedestal and he treats her with undiluted adoration and I am filled with loathing and rising anger. It brings back memories and feelings I had as a child. Papa was constantly at Mama's side, doing her bidding, always fetching and carrying, attending to her every need while I was neglected and cast aside. She manipulated his feelings with practised skill and it was no wonder I had spent vast chunks of my childhood in the sanctuary of churches trying to convince myself that I was loved and wanted.

I brush a tear from my eye and focus on the neatly tended stalls of soaps, jewellery, decorations and candles. Sweet, heady and nauseating scents like the cannabis of my childhood home invade my senses. I look down at my hand and I trace the deep white scar running along the back of my hand to my wrist then Andreas rests his fingers on the sleeve of my coat.

'Please, be compassionate, Mikky. She needs someone to care for her–'

'Then she had better bring her own nursemaid. I'm a very busy woman.'

***

Javier is waiting for us. I barely have time to change out of my *Queen of Stone* T–shirt. I would much prefer to go to a rock concert and play air guitar with passion to get rid of this pent–up frustration and anger that circulates my soul.

But once at the Opera I am captivated with the atmosphere, the audience and the stage production of *The Nutcracker Suite* and surprisingly, I lose myself in the ballet, the movements, the lifts and the music.

On our way home Andreas says, 'Ms Lavelle has overdone everything since you arrived. She is very tired this evening.'

'We spoke endlessly about the type of portrait that would be suitable and she was shattered afterwards,' Javier replies.

'She would find London exhausting if she's tired after today,' I add.

However when we arrive back to her home she is awake and sitting beside a dwindling fire with a shawl around her shoulders. In the candlelight her cheeks are hollow. Dark circles accentuate her eyes making her look pale and interesting and I realise I would like to capture the look she gives me on my camera.

They fuss around her but she looks over their

shoulder at me with reproach so I turn away and absorb myself in the titles of the books along the shelf.

Andreas produces a light supper of sliced melon, blue cheese, dates, nuts and olives then he pours red wine. We sit in our places on the white sofas and Javier heaps praise on the artistic performance and the beauty of the Semperoper.

'Thank you so much for arranging the ballet we loved it, didn't we, Mikky?' He nudges me with his knee.

'It was very special. The building is stunning,' I smile.

'And did you have champagne? Andreas did you arrange champagne?'

He finishes chewing an olive before replying. 'They did.'

'It was a wonderful evening,' I say before Javier can prod or provoke me again.

'I'm so pleased you enjoyed the ballet perhaps I may get you interested in opera next?' Her smile is slow and her gaze captivating.

'I doubt it,' I grin back.

Javier pushes his knee against mine. 'She's not really a Philistine – she prefers rock music – her parents were bikers.'

I move my leg away from his and drink my wine quickly.

'Really?' Josephine leans forward. 'How interesting.'

Javier continues but this time about himself. 'When I was young my parents always took us to the opera in Madrid. I remember once I saw you on stage in the Teatro Real.' Javier's cheeks flush crimson.

Josephine looks thoughtful as if he has reminded her of her age and then the moment passes.

'Yes, I sang there many times. I once sang with Montserrat Caballé – you must know her?' She raises an eyebrow.

'Of course, she sang *Barcelona* with Freddy Mercury,' Javier replies and then a conversation begins about operas and classically trained singers who have become international stars like Katherine Jenkins and Sara Brightman.

I smother a yawn.

'They are not proper opera singers,' she says. 'They have lowered themselves to the genre of pop music. Now take Glorietta Bareldo – she *is* a star. She is in *Norma* at Covent Garden early next year and has offered me a box. You must come and be my guest – both of you,' Josephine says looking at me. 'I would be delighted to show you real opera, Mikky. I think until you have witnessed a performance and have been moved by it you will have no comprehension of the emotion involved. I would like the opportunity, if you would allow me?'

Her request hangs in the air like a floating bubble.

'That would be fantastic,' Javier replies for me rubbing his palms. If he had a tail he would be wagging it. 'I would love to see her. They say she is amazing – well, not as good as you but–'

Josephine holds up her hand. 'Please, Javier, she is every bit as good as me. In fact, I believe, she is better. She has a quality and tone that has added timbre to her voice in the past few months and it supersedes any range I may once have had.'

'Impossible. I cannot agree with you,' he protests.

'You will when you hear her voice.'

'I cannot believe you are friends. Is there no competition between you?' I ask.

Javier stares at me. Andreas looks away.

The logs hiss and one falls in the grate causing a burst of orange flames.

I cut a sliver of cheese, chew slowly then sip the red wine from Saxony that Josephine has assured us is the best in the region and I wait for her to answer.

'We were rivals for many years but in the past months we have become very good friends. It is surprising, I know. It was an enormous lesson for me to learn. That someone you once resented or don't like, or of whom you may have been jealous, may very well turn out to become a very special friend.' Josephine regards me before continuing. 'She once gave me this.'

She reaches into her pocket then holds a clenched palm across the table and when she unfurls her fingers a small golden ingot gleams in the lamplight.

It is a two inch golden icon of the Madonna.

'It's beautiful.' I take it and turn it in my fingers examining it carefully with a practised eye. 'She is absolutely exquisite.'

'She saved my life,' Josephine whispers. 'I had nothing left to live for but now – I do.'

When I return it, her hand is shaking and the intimacy is over.

Javier talks about Rafael's, *La Madonna dei Garofani*, hanging in the National Gallery and I slug back the Saxony wine.

The room is warm so I pull my black jumper over my head forgetting my thin, worn out T–shirt, with *Guns and Roses* emblazoned across my chest but it is not my old and creased shirt that attracts Josephine's gaze. It is the elaborate and shocking tattoo that I have on my right forearm.

Her eyes widen and she gasps unable to hide her surprise and shock.

I wait. I want her to say something. I want her to challenge me. I would welcome confrontation. I have so much pent–up emotion inside that I want to leap to my feet, jump on the white pristine sofas and play air guitar with high energy and attitude. But instead I pick up an olive and chew it deliberately with my mouth open.

'Perhaps when you are in London we can go together,' Javier asks. He looks from Josephine to me and then to Josephine.

Andreas talks about a visit he once made to the Tate Modern and the conversation turns to her visit, the opera, the Royal Albert hall and random words that suddenly don't make sense and float around me like airborne dust motes.

'Mikky,' Javier whispers, 'don't drink any more'

I shake my head. I want to be back in London. I want my painting.

Josephine asks where we will eat supper after the performance of *Norma* then she frowns and adds.

'You know, there is one condition attached to you painting my portrait.'

Javier's shoulders stiffen and I trace the scar on the back of my hand.

'You will gain a lot of publicity and Nico Vastano will want you at the unveiling in Lake Como next year but there is one thing that I must insist upon. Has Nico mentioned it to you?'

'No…why, no…' Javier appears confused.

'No? But I have insisted. I told him – I told Nico.' She looks at Andreas but he remains impassive.

'There is one journalist that you must never speak to, Javier. Never invite him to any press gatherings and certainly there should be no private interviews. Do not mention anything about me to him. In fact, you must never speak to him – ever.'

Javier's body relaxes and he grins. 'You had me worried. I thought–'

'His name is Karl Blakey. You must never speak to this man or I will cancel everything. There will be no commission – no painting.'

Javier scratches his chin.

I bite my lower lip. I remember the journalist's name. There was a vague promise of a television documentary – and lunch – in Javier's favourite restaurant: champagne and oysters?

'Agreed.' Javier raises his glass with a determined smile. 'No problem.'

Josephine smiles. 'Thank you.'

'Why?' I ask.

But one nudge from Javier tells me not to say another word and my question is swallowed up in a flurry of movement as Josephine decides she is exhausted and is going to bed.

Javier holds out his arm like a chivalrous knight in an old black and white B movie and escorts her to the door.

'Thank you Javier, perhaps you will help me just to the end of the corridor. I can manage the stairs. Goodnight, Mikky. I do hope that you will feel in a better humour tomorrow. Perhaps if you come to

Dresden again I may interest you in a trip to the New Green Vault – our Museum of Treasury Art. It might stir your enthusiasm for this beautiful country. Or perhaps I should think of a better way to please you?'

'It's a beautiful city. I enjoyed my visit–' I reply.

'Perhaps you did.' She doesn't look at me. 'Goodnight.'

'Goodnight, Josephine.' I watch her slow gait until she leaves the room then I smile at Andreas as if he is my new best friend.

'I am going home tomorrow.' I punch the air with my fist and play air guitar to the Foo Fighters, *Learn to Fly.*

***

The following morning I slide into the seat across the table from Javier. He hasn't touched his breakfast but he is nursing a mug of coffee. He doesn't smile and he shakes his head at me.

'Don't be angry. It's you she loves,' I say.

'No thanks to you – we are guests here. And your behaviour was–'

'Do you think she heard?'

'I think you woke the whole house. You tripped and you screamed – remember?'

'I thought there were giant cobwebs attacking me–'

'You pulled down the Christmas decoration.'

I giggle. 'I have a hangover if that's any consolation.'

'Not to me.'

I cannot remember a time in our friendship when

he was this angry.

'What about Karl Blakey? What was that all about?' I ask.

'Shush!' He looks over his shoulder just as Andreas appears.

'Morning,' I say with false cheerfulness. 'I'm sorry if I was a little …loud last night.'

He doesn't smile and I am subdued by his coldness. He places heated croissants on the table and when he leaves the room I whisper, 'He's like something out of the Addams family.'

'You're not funny.'

'Sorry. It's just that, well, come on, this place – have you noticed there's a wooden swing and a rope ladder hanging from the tree in the garden? Is this her home? Or is this Andreas's family home? Is it rented?'

Javier shrugs.

'Where is her family?' I persist. 'She must have one. What about that journalist – Karl Blakey? Did you meet him for lunch? She will cancel the commission if she finds out.'

There are quick footsteps.

'Shush.'

Andreas stands in the doorway.

'Ms Lavelle sends her apologies but she feels unwell this morning and is unable to join you in the castle. She wishes you both a pleasant journey home.'

Javier scowls and his face tells me that it's all my fault.

Chapter Five

'Only when he no longer knows what he is doing does the
painter do good things.'
Edgar Degas

It's three days after the New Year, I have finished my
own masterpiece and I am cleaning up the flat. It smells
like an art studio: oils, varnish and turpentine. The
dank canvas clings to me and I am transported back to
my childhood when I would hide in the dark recess of
Spanish churches, behind sketchpads, surrounded by
pencils, oils and paintings, staring at miniscule biblical
scenes carved intricately into wood and recreated in
stained glass.

I feigned the pressure of work as an excuse not to
go to Madrid with Javier for Christmas telling him
Sandra Jupiter's pre exhibition schedule is demanding
and I'm pleased to get him out of the flat so I can paint
without the smell causing suspicion. I think he was also
pleased I stayed behind in London. My visit to Dresden
has caused him anguish and concern – he still hasn't
forgiven me – even when I kissed him on his cheek,
gave him presents for his family and wished him
Happy Christmas.

The quality and detailed photographs that I took
of the painting when Mrs Green went into hospital has
allowed me to paint slowly and with consideration. I
was confident I could do a good job and now as I step
back from the canvas admiring my work and clean my
fingers with a paint-stained rag, I smile. Remarkably, I

haven't lost my touch.

Raffa would be proud of me. I had been one of the first students to arrive in his studio and I remember our conversation early one morning with the warm Italian sun shining through the circular window. He had leaned over me, his breath filled with tobacco and warm coffee as he steadied my hand pointing to the detail and finally leaning back he said:

'Han van Meergeren, a Dutchman, was most probably the most prominent and successful art forger. He forged old masters including several by Vermeer and was possibly most famous for his forgery of Johannes Vermeer's *The Supper at Emmaus*. He sold it to the Director of the Museum Boymans in 1937 for 540,000 guilders. I don't know what that would be worth today – but believe me Mikky – it's a lot!' His laugh was throaty and warm.

'He wouldn't get away with it now,' I had replied.

'In his lifetime he amassed over half a billion dollars by painting fakes. Unfortunately for him this particular painting ended up in the possession of Nazi minister, Hermann Göring who, as I'm sure you know, was stealing and collecting artwork across Europe for Hitler's museum in Lintz.' His dark passionate eyes reflected the excitement in his voice and he leaned forward, analysing my replica of *The Astromomer*.

'Van Meergeren was put on trial and forced to demonstrate his forgery techniques and he became known as, *the man who swindled Göring*. The secret is not to get caught, Mikky. Don't get greedy.'

I smile remembering his words. He would be proud of my work today. Now all I have to do is to swindle Roy and I am happy to spend Christmas alone in order to do this. My makeshift table is covered in old newspapers, paints, brushes, varnish pots and soiled rags and like an art studio the room has plenty of light. Two easels are side by side; one to hold the Vermeer photographs stuck around the wood; countless close-up images revealing intricate details of faces, hands and background – all equally important – that I will dispose of with care. The other easel contains my recently finished canvas. It is drying now and I am pleased that I trawled London markets looking for the right canvas. *The Concert* was painted in 1664 so wanted to find an old painting from around that time. I plugged wormholes created by beetles and silverfish and added fox marks and rusty looking spots for authenticity. Having seen the original next door I was confident I could replicate it quite adequately.

Vermeer would grind his pigments. He used lead white paint and blue ultramarine known as *lapiz azul*. It was extracted from a semi-precious stone found in 1600 in Afghanistan but paint takes a long time to dry – time that I don't have. I need my canvas to look authentically old and once the paint is hardened I will crack the oils and fill the fissures with Vaseline and dust from the vacuum.

For his fake masterpieces, Van Meegeren used genuine seventeenth-century canvases and to seal the pigments he used Bakelite which when heated, hardened to produce a surface similar to that of a seventeenth-century painting. This convinced the so-called experts of the authenticity of his works but I would not presume to be in the same category as him nor would I go to so much trouble. My painting needs to appear hardened and weathered with age like the one next door and I only need a temporary illusion – not an exact replica – I only have to fool Roy then make my escape.

I sip coffee and stand gazing at my painting.

Forgery is a performance and I am simply the magician. It is an art in itself to suppress a natural artistic inclination or creativity and although I'm copying a Vermeer I have not found the process as hard as I had anticipated. I only have to create a painting that looks convincingly old. I do not have to prove where the painting has been or who has owned it. I have no need to produce a fake provenance. The Vermeer is after all – and as the whole world knows – a stolen masterpiece.

My forgery wouldn't pass the scrutiny and chemical tests that van Meergeren's painting had been subjected to and it wouldn't fool many of the world's 'so called' experts but it would be adequate, if not perfect, for the untrained eye.

My initial plan had been simple. I would just duck into Mrs Green's house at the appropriate moment – straight after her death – and make the switch, stealing the painting now hanging on her bedroom wall. I would substitute it with a photograph of the painting that I would varnish over. She had no visitors and no friends and there was no one who could prove I had replaced it. Timing was crucial, observation paramount and my plan – perfect.

But two things changed: Mrs Green became ill and Roy moved in. Now my plan is understandably flawed because Mrs Green and Roy would spot a varnished photograph immediately and know the painting had been switched. Since my visit to Dresden

I realise I must replace the original with a forgery. Now my plan is to sneak into the house next door and switch the original painting for my fake – easy.

The fact that Mrs Green has left the painting in her Will to the art dealer in Bruges does not faze me. Although Roy might not know an authentic Vermeer the art dealer would be harder to fool. But I'm hoping that he will assume that Roy is the culprit. And if Roy tries to sell the painting he'd be told it was a fake and as long as he could never implicate me or suspect me I would be long gone and free with my treasure.

I ponder every single scenario planning how things can go wrong at the moment of the swap. Now I have her key and the alarm code my job will be easy but I still run the risk of getting caught.

And in the meantime, if Javier returns and walks in to the smell of oil paint it will arouse suspicion. So I throw open windows and patio doors allowing damp, cold January air to circulate the room. I pull my woolly hat over my ears, place my boots on the coffee table and hug myself. Cold is transient. Soon I would have all the money to go wherever I wanted – Spain, the Caribbean even South America.

Getting rid of the masterpiece afterwards would be a delicate process and I close my eyes and consider my options: return the painting to the Isabella Stewart Museum and claim the reward or use someone in Spain who would attest to finding the painting in a dusty attic. I could place it in the hands of an art dealer who would broker the negotiations of the sale – probably to an unscrupulous collector who would then provide me with a very generous commission.

This is a chance in a lifetime but the problem with

stealing an already stolen masterpiece is that not many people would touch it – only the greedy and unscrupulous – and they are understandably dangerous.

I wipe down the surfaces in the kitchen as rain begins to drum against the window and dark clouds gather and a storm rumbles overhead. I turn up the volume to Foo Fighters – *Congregation* and play air guitar pretending I am Dave Grohl then I pour a glass of iced vodka, raising it to the chaotic storm and down it quickly before refilling my shot glass again.

Some forgers are bitter and self-centred. They are romantic or misunderstood and sometimes they are angry. They are unrecognized as geniuses but they are skilled and talented craftsmen. I believe I am a well-balanced combination of all these attributes.

Forgery is a craft. It is a technique that has become harder because there are more tools now to discover a fake. Chemicals, scientists and even X-rays will reveal the truth but sometimes forgers are careless. They go to the effort to paint a masterpiece then use modern tacks to attach it to the frame. It's the small detail that gets them caught. Forgery is also dangerous. I have known men who would kill for a painting and sometimes stolen paintings create more greed and unnecessary violence.

But this is a one off opportunity – it's a lifetime chance and a simple scam that will give me security for life. I won't need anyone - ever. I will buy my own villa. Travel. Live life to the full and I will never be beholden to anyone. I will be free.

But my dreams are a long way off. First, I have to steal the painting and get away with it. I cannot fail. I must not make a mistake. I go over the details again – what if Roy finds out it is a fake? Nothing ever slots neatly into place and things always go wrong and just when you least expect it.

I was in essence waiting for Mrs Green to die but I'm not in any hurry for her life to end. I have become fond of her and I would save her again. Like me, she has been alone and she knows what it's like to have no one. I want her to enjoy this time that she has with her family. I will wait until the painting dries or until natural causes or God decides on Mrs Green's demise. I will know when the moment is right and I will take the opportunity.

On Christmas Eve when I knew she was alone I had popped in with a card and chocolates and it was as if I had plucked a brilliant jewel from the night sky and given it to her as a gift. Her blue eyes had glistened as brightly as the diamond on her finger.

'Come and have Christmas lunch with us, Mikky. Please don't be alone.'

'I hate Christmas, Mrs Green, all the gaiety and joviality doesn't suit me.'

We had chatted for an hour before I made an excuse to pop upstairs to the bathroom and I made a quick detour to her bedroom reassured that the painting was still safe on her bedroom wall.

I pour another vodka and glance out of the front window where darkness was settling like a silk curtain. I had been happy to spend Christmas alone. As a child the tassels, tinsel and gold trimmings each year seduced me into happy anticipation but it was quickly replaced by snide comments, jealousy and drunken arguments. Each year I hid in a church, finding sanctuary in the calmness of Mass. Incense became my regular fix, filling me with comfort and joy and inner calm and a stranger's smile was the nicest gift.

Birthdays were no better.

On my twelfth birthday Papa was so drunk he fell down the steps of the caravan. He cried out and held his ankle. I placed his arm around my shoulder to help him stand. The stale alcohol from his mouth made me recoil but I held my breath but then Mama staggered down the caravan steps with a meat knife. She leaped at me, her face contorted in a blaze of fury. Holding Papa I was slow to react but I managed to cover my face with my hand but not before I saw jealously flashing from her eyes as she ripped my skin with its blade. Blood gushed down my arm, I screamed and Papa fell to the floor.

When my hand was being stitched in the local hospital she had laughingly told the doctor I was careless, always having minor scrapes, burns and incidents while she flirted shamelessly.

I was subdued. Shocked by her deceit and betrayal, and afterwards when we got back to the caravan we were greeted by Papa's drunken snoring, and she had shoved me inside with a poke in the back and said, *let this be a lesson to you.*

There was no remorse or compassion so I developed it into a game, deliberately laughing louder, acting bolder, taunting, teasing and testing. When she saw Papa and me laughing she would pretend to ignore us both then she would get one of us to do a chore to break us up. At first Papa would tease me back and make me laugh, but we both paid a heavy price at the hands of her temper and her violent anger.

Sometimes she would banish me from the caravan and I would take refuge in a local church while she took Papa to the nearest bar where they would drink until they could barely stand and when they came home I was forced to listen to their rows and their love making.

It didn't take me long to realise he was a weak man and it was easier for him to please her than to suffer her constant mood swings. Why hadn't I been more compliant?

There is a crack of thunder overhead. I stand at the patio door and I am reminded of another storm, in another country, a long time ago when I was a child trapped helplessly in a life where I didn't belong.

That night after a violent argument and in a blind drunk and jealous rage she had taken Papa's motorcycle. I had watched her drive manically and erratically down the dirt path from our caravan to the coast road a few kilometres away bouncing into puddles and skidding at the corner.

Later that night the Guardia Civil told us she had wrapped Papa's favourite *Yamaha* around a tree. She had never woken from her coma and after a week I stood with Papa, beside her bed, as the life support was switched off.

I was fourteen years old.

In my grief, I hoped that her death would bring us closer together and we could shake off the shroud of her constant jealousy but in the years that Papa and I lived alone we rarely laughed. He trod on eggshells around me, politely, formally and distantly as if Mama was watching us from above.

And that was when I missed my Mama most and

the games we had played to annoy her. The flicker of laughter Papa created in me was a light that had illuminated my life but like the hiss of a burning candle it died and was snuffed out. Papa no longer smiled.

Even though she was gone from our lives she had scarred us forever. Papa withdrew into himself and I was left to fend for myself and I soon discovered the only way out of my life was education and money.

A cracking explosion fills the London sky and the heavens are ripped open. Rain drums on the patio and I stand mesmerized watching the wild storm, thunderous and rumbling like an angry giant. I trace my ugly, ragged wound on the back of my left hand that runs from my middle finger beyond my wrist, listening as thunder rolls, rumbles and roars overhead. The eight-inch scar is as jagged and as resplendent as the white forked lightening that splits the black sky above my head, and as vivid as my childhood memory.

Enough! The past is over. I slam the patio door. I must plan the future.

***

On the following Saturday Javier, Oscar and I have just returned home from a long walk through Chiswick Park. The house is aired, the easels and paintings are hidden and my brushes are cleaned and put away.

I flick on the kettle focusing on my task ahead and the exhibition for Sandra Jupiter at the beginning of February. A forgotten Caravaggio from a private collection is to be loaned to the Knightsbridge Museum. Caravaggio's *The Cardsharps* became an immediate sensation and will be the focal point for the Baroque Exhibition.

Javier's mobile rings and his cheeks flush with excitement. He paces the lounge: tilts the blinds, walks to the breakfast bar and lifts an orange then replaces it. He sits on the sofa and crosses his legs, stands up goes to the window and tilts the blind again.

'Josephine is coming to London next week.' He tells us when he hangs up. 'We are invited to the opera to see *Norma* with Glorietta Bareldo. It's opening at the end of the month in Covent Garden. It's like a dream – to meet two opera singers – and for them to want to know me. Can you believe it?' Javier takes the mug of coffee from me and stands at the window absorbing the details of her visit.

Oscar claps his hands. 'I hope I'm here but I think I will be away on business. That is when I go to–'

'I hope you are here, Oscar. You can take my place. I don't like opera. I don't understand it and it won't bother me if I don't have to go,' I say.

'Thank you, Mikky, I–'

'But Josephine has invited you,' Javier says turning around. 'She said specifically...'

I shrug. 'I don't need friends and I certainly don't need Josephine Lavelle in my life.'

In the lounge I put a match to the hearth and the twigs and logs stir into a flame burning and flickering like the ardent light in Javier's eyes; dancing in rhythm with the eagerness of his voice.

'Glorietta Bareldo would like to meet me,' he says. 'I don't know all the details yet but she will be hosting a drinks reception. There will be interviews and other events and I must make sure I will be available. It's all about raising my profile and speaking about Josephine's portrait.'

'Can't you go to Dresden to paint her?'

'No, Mikky! Besides, she has made great progress in the past few weeks. Her health has improved and she is stronger. She is looking forward to returning to England.' Javier rubs his hands as he conveys each detail of Josephine's plan but only Oscar pays attention. I am wrapped up in the thought of seeing her again and knowing that she will be so important to Javier that he becomes obsessed with pleasing her.

It fills me with déjà vu. I witnessed her jealousy. I know she will wield her power over Javier just as Mama did with Papa and just like my father, I know Javier is a weak man. He adores the attention she lavishes upon him. He will bask in her affection and her praise just as Papa had bathed in Mama's adoration as she stroked away his insecurities boosting his ego and his confidence.

Javier and Papa share many similarities.

But I'm different. I have developed resilience. This woman will not interfere with my plans. She's nothing to do with me. She's Javier's muse. She will not affect my life. I will not let her.

Javier's voice interrupts my thoughts.

'I will arrange to use Sandra Jupiter's art studio. You know the one she has above the museum – on the top floor? Marcus Danning has used it many times, and I think Josephine will find it comfortable.'

'How long is she here?'

'Two weeks perhaps three.'

'But that's when the Caravaggio is being exhibited,' I complain.

'Fantastic. We will invite her – and Glorietta Bareldo.'

'No–'

'Why not? Sandra will be delighted – two famous opera divas at the exhibition will be amazing. Think of the media coverage, Mikky. Think how prestigious it will be for us.'

'I don't want either of them there.' It is my work and my exhibition.

'Don't be so negative, Mikky. It will be a good endorsement for you. Come on, get your diary out, I think we should check our schedules and arrange Josephine's visit. We must plan something nice for her.'

Oscar nods enthusiastically. 'Perhaps a trip to the country – Windsor?'

'What for?' I say.

'She said in Dresden that she wants to form a friendship with us. I like her, Mikky. She's interesting company and I want you to get to like her too. There is something deep about her; sadness or tragedy – something so concealed that I can see the pain hidden in her eyes.'

I raise my eyes to the ceiling and shake my head. 'There are lots of people who are sad inside, Javier. She's not the only one hiding her emotions.'

He ignores me. 'Perhaps she can come here for dinner or lunch or both?'

'No!'

'I want to welcome her to London…'

I groan.

'It's the least we can do.' He glares at me. 'The least you can do…'

'To make amends for my behaviour in Dresden?'

'I want her to get to know you.'

'Well, I don't.'

'Why?'

'It's you she likes. It's you she wants in her life – not me.'

'You would need to spruce this place up a bit,' Oscar says, ignoring the tension between us. 'It doesn't look fit for a diva at the moment.'

'Let's just go out to eat?' I say

'She wants to get to know us, Mikky. She has taken a great amount of interest in knowing who I am, where I'm from, and about my family and my life. She's interested. She wants us to become friends.'

'How delightful,' I reply with my best sarcastic smile.

'Give her a chance. I think that's the reason she wants to do the sitting here in London. She doesn't want it to be formal and awkward. She wants us all to be friends.'

'I have all the friends I need–'

'Decorating is the best idea.' Oscar interjects trying to placate us both. He places a hand on mine not taking his eyes from Javier's face. 'A new look, a new image, that's what this place needs. I know it's a rented apartment but a coat of paint wouldn't be too expensive. But don't paint over our mural. It always reminds me of our holiday, Javier and when we met.'

We all glance at the charcoal drawing. I have also become attached to the mural, the Argentinian dusky street that fills the gap on the wall, disguising the flaky paint, between the hearth and the kitchen worktop. It's a life size sketch of crooked houses, wooden doors and street urchins that demonstrate Javier's artistic talents and I know it will impress Josephine.

This clever diversion leads them to remember how they met in South America so I head to the kitchen and dump my dirty mug in the sink, leaving them debating the merits of the charcoal drawing and what had inspired it.

I venture outside onto the patio where the air is cold and fresh. The early morning blue sky has been replaced with large white cumulous clouds with pearly, silver edges. I'm distracted by their changing shapes; changing patterns in continuous flowing movements, from a dog to an elephant before fragmenting to become a giant mouse with a long wispy vapour tail. It's rather like friendship, never the same, constantly changing and completely unreliable.

I pick up a discarded trowel and bend my knees to inspect the terracotta pots where clusters of lilac crocuses and white snowdrops are ripening and about to burst but voices next–door cause my body to freeze.

'You'll be away again all week?' Annie's husky tone drifts over the fence. 'Do they not realise you have a sick mother? I've uprooted my life to accommodate you and her. It's me that has made all the changes. And what's it all for?'

Roy must be standing near the back door so I only hear the end of his sentence. 'It'll be worth it – you'll see.'

'It's me that sacrificed my job to move here. Your life hasn't changed at all.'

I don't hear his reply.

'You promised me! Now you're telling me you're going to Berlin… You've conveniently forgotten the successful business I gave up... I'll go mad all day… at home with your bloody mother–'

'She's worth a fortune… It won't be for long–'

I hear footsteps and when I look up Oscar is standing in the doorway. I put my finger to my lips.

'Mikky? What on earth are you doing grovelling on the floor? You look like you're practising for the Territorial Army,' he laughs.

I shake my head but he continues. 'It's going to rain. Come inside and I'll make some coffee.'

Roy's voice comes clearly from over the fence. 'That nosy bloody bitch can hear everything we say.'

***

Mrs Green's blue eyes are twinkling when she opens the front door. There is colour in her cheeks and she seems sprightly and happy.

'Snow is forecast,' she says.

'I hope you're keeping warm,' I reply.

She ushers me along the hallway to the kitchen. Her house is unusual in as much as it hasn't been remodelled or updated since it was built. I follow her down the dark corridor glancing into the front living room. Her old three-piece chintz suite has been replaced with a modern leather armchair and a beige L-shaped sofa. The display cases have been replaced by flat pack units and are now filled with DVDs and framed family photographs of Roy, Annie and Max on holiday in various locations: snorkelling, skiing and diving. But there is still an empty space above the mantelpiece.

I stumble on an assortment of shoes in all sizes, shapes and colours and the grandfather clock ticks, whirls and then chimes.

'They have rather taken over,' she says. 'They've only been here a few weeks but I do enjoy their company especially young, Max. He really is such a good child and I'm not just saying that because he's my only grandchild.' She waggles a finger at me and laughs.

The smell of fresh coffee still lingers in the kitchen and with the large diamond ring on her finger that catches the light she indicates an empty chair where I sit and gaze out at the garden. It was once a sanctuary for birds but now the feeders are empty and a flat football, small bicycle and plastic truck lay abandoned on the worn, muddy grass.

Her armchair now filled with a pile of unfolded washing has been moved away from the window, and an assortment of jackets and coats hang on the back of the kitchen door. Toy cars and plastic people are strewn across the floor so I gather them up and place them in a basket under the table.

'I had to pack up most of my own things. Max was hiding them everywhere – things went missing. But Roy has put them in boxes for me and he's put them in the attic. He says I can get them down any time I like. He says there's no problem,' she says this as if repeating her son's reassuring words.

What's he done with the painting?

She fills the kettle. Beside her Max's drawings are stuck haphazardly on the fridge door: a scribbled yellow sun, a tree with matchstick figures and a white owl.

Is it still in her bedroom?

'Annie and Max have popped down to enrol at the local library. Max loves to read. He likes the sound of animals. He roars like a lion and barks like a dog. They're his favourites.' She rinses hot water into the teapot before throwing it down the sink then she adds fresh tea leaves then more hot water. It's a ritual and she places in on the table between us leaving it to brew and she sits opposite me.

Where is it?

Her papery-thin hands move briskly pouring milk. 'I don't understand these modern marriages. Roy travels all the time. I hardly see him. Annie is kind although sometimes, I shouldn't really say it but she is impatient. She can be quite stern. Max is only young and she's very strict. I would hate to cross her or get on the wrong side of her.'

'Really?'

'She tells me some strange stories and she has a peculiar sense of humour – it's almost as if she wants to scare me – stories of old people in homes and places...' She bites into a biscuit and it snaps spreading crumbs over her lap. She pokes a piece into the corner of her mouth and sipping her tea noisily she continues:

'Roy was born in Germany. My Arnold was stationed over there after the war. He was in the army and we lived there for twelve years...' She reminisces about her husband Arnold and what a fine man he was and although he didn't fight in the war there were a lot of operational tasks that he was involved in after it ended.

She speaks about Roy as a child and I imagine him running around just as I have seen Max do with his arms spread wide as if he is an aeroplane.

'At least you're friends again with your son. It must be lovely to have him back in your life,' I say.

How can I get upstairs?

'I will admit that it was difficult. I had to make my stand at the time and say what I thought. It was a matter of principle. He spent money that wasn't his and I had to bail him out on several occasions but he was young then. Now I've put the past behind and we have both move on. He is the only family I have.'

'You need family around you and people who you can *trust*.'

'That's what I say.'

'Have you kept the painting–'

'Did you phone your family at Christmas?' she asks.

'My father lives in Malaga.' I don't tell her that we haven't spoken since I left University.

'That's where Picasso was born,' she replies.

'I worked in the Picasso museum for about a year taking photographs for their brochure and website and all their exhibition materials. The family donated hundreds of paintings and they all had to be photographed and catalogued.'

'How interesting, Mikky. I do like Picasso but he's not my favourite artist.'

'Nor mine.' I lean forward. 'Who do you like?'

'There is only one artist for me – Vermeer.'

'Vermeer is very special probably because he painted so few. Do you still have yours?'

'One of the best forgeries,' she says with satisfaction, nodding and reaching for another biscuit.

'Did you ever get it… valued?'

'No dear, it isn't worth much although I did pay quite a lot for it at the time. I suppose at the back of your mind you hope it maybe the original although you know it isn't.'

'If it is, the Isabella Stewart Museum would want it back,' I chuckle.

'Well, they can't have it,' she says. 'It's mine and I paid good money for it. Anyway I don't want to get it looked at or valued by anyone. That's what Roy keeps going on about but what good would it do? Money is no good to me when I'm dead. It's family that's important. Besides I have an agreement with the art dealer that he can have it back when I die.'

'Why have you agreed that?' I probe.

'Because he was a friend of Albert's and it is the right thing to do.' She sips her tea and gazes out of the window not meeting my gaze.

'Won't Roy mind?'

'Roy won't find out until I'm gone.'

A robin hops onto the fence and chirps.

'He's pretty,' I say.

Mrs Green leans forward trying hard to see the bird. He regards us momentarily before flying off but she still peers outside not realising he has flown away and in the silence I listen to the ticking grandfather clock, formulating an idea.

'You're right, Mrs Green. Say nothing. Just enjoy the painting. There are very few people that appreciate something for its beauty rather than wondering about the cost all the time.'

'Oh dear, well Roy has been nagging at me to get it looked at. He wants me to take it to Sotheby's or somewhere but I don't want all that fuss…beside I promised…I don't want to go to all that trouble. I trust my friend – the art dealer. He and Albert knew each other for years and if my Albert were alive he wouldn't let Roy anywhere near my things and they certainly wouldn't have ended up in the attic.' She continues to stare out of the window.

The painting will be no good to her when she is dead. She said it herself. So in effect it is Roy that I am steal the painting from or the art dealer.

'You do still have it, don't you?' I ask.

'Of course.'

'It is a shame to keep it hidden away.'

'It's in my bedroom. I keep it up there because I like to look at it and it makes me happy. It's the one thing I wouldn't let him take away from me and put in the attic.'

'Good for you, Mrs Green.' I stand up. 'You keep it safe in there – where no one can get to it – and enjoy it!'

'I will. No one is getting their hands on it,' she adds.

At the front door I lean down and peck her cheek. The irony of Judas planting a kiss on Jesus' cheek doesn't escape me but we are both distracted by tiny footsteps running up the pathway.

'I got you a book, Granny.' Max gathers Mrs Green's skirt around her legs in a big hug and she laughs and places her gnarled old hand on his young head.

The introductions are over in seconds, Annie's grip is firm and she watches me with the skill and grace of a predatory owl.

'Annie's looking for some work. I think she's bored at home with me every day. She used to have her own business. Didn't you, dear?'

'I'm an interior decorator. I may put a card in the

window of the corner shop. I can't go far because Max is at the nursery,' she explains.

'Really? I'm thinking about getting my apartment painted,' I say.

Her eyes light up and I return her smile.

Know thy enemy.

***

A few days later I arrive home from a meeting with Sandra Jupiter. It is mid-afternoon and I am unpacking my camera bag when I see a note in Javier's handwriting on the counter.

Mrs Green wanted to speak to you. I made her tea and we had a chat. Javier X

I need to download the last images of Caravaggio's *Boy Bitten by a Lizard*. It is one of two versions that normally hangs in the National Gallery, the second one hangs in Fondazione Roberto Longhi in Florence, and I am eager to look at the images. This painting of a young boy recoiling as a lizard, hidden among fruit, bites his finger is enthralling and captivating. It's a painting in motion – the equivalent of a sixteenth century snapshot.

The thrill of being with the original all day has filled me with excitement and I still have the smell of the oil and canvas inside my nostrils. Now I need to be alone to remember the memory and absorb the intricate details of a canvas painted by a man who was also accused of murder.

I am setting up my laptop when the doorbell rings.

'Sorry to bother you but I really need your help. My mother-in-law, you know – Mrs Green, isn't feeling very well.' Annie waves a finger in the direction of the house next door. 'And I have to go to the nursery to pick up Max and I'm already late. I wonder if you could stay with her for a few minutes. Just until I get back. I won't be long.' She casts an imploring look. 'It was Gran who said that you wouldn't mind. Would you? I really must go or Max will be upset...'

'Yes, of course.' I follow Annie down the path 'Take as long as you like,' I call.

'I won't be long – promise.' Her footsteps splash in the puddles as she hurries out of the gate.

'Mrs Green?' I call out. I venture inside and glance up the staircase before heading for the kitchen. She is propped up in her chair with soft cushions beside the window. Her diamond ring glistens in the light and she waves for me to sit beside her.

'Thank you, Mikky.'

'Are you all right?'

'I'm fine. Annie does panic. I'm sure that she thinks I'll be pushing up the daisies soon but there's life in the old girl yet,' she laughs. 'She's a good girl is Annie. She means well but she does get things wrong sometimes. She does talk a lot. She's full of stories and she can be very gloomy but she's given up a lot to look after me. I often wonder if Roy deserves a woman like that. Is that a dreadful thing to say?'

'No.' I pull out a chair and sit beside her.

We sit watching a pair of goldfinches eating Niger seed from the birdfeeders and I wonder who refilled them.

'You popped in this morning and spoke to Javier?' I say.

'I wanted to know, do you still need your flat painting?' she asks.

'I do. I'm going to have a very important guest but you must not tell anyone... It's Josephine Lavelle.' When I see her face ignite with interest I go on to explain about her imminent visit to London.

'My dear, how exciting – Javier did tell me about the portrait and your trip to Dresden. She was always one of my favourite opera singers. I saw her once, years ago, in Covent Garden. She was simply wonderful. Albert loved her...'

'So I think it might be a good idea to get the flat painted.' I don't add that it will also help me know what is going on in her house and give me the opportunity to switch the paintings.

'I do like the mural Javier painted. He's such a good boy and so handsome. He insisted on making me coffee and he gave me a biscuit. We talked about art and paintings and I wouldn't have mentioned it but he's so knowledgeable and so I told him about the Vermeer, you know, the one upstairs.'

What?

'And he has given me such good advice–'

The front door bangs.

Advice?

Running feet pound along the hallway and Max hangs on the door handle eying us both silently. I am lost for words.

I stand up.

'You're so kind,' she says. 'Imagine... Josephine Lavelle...next door.'

'I'll make sure that you meet her.'

'That would be so exciting. How kind you are, Mikky.' She grips my fingers and tries to stand but I place my hand firmly on her shoulder and insist she sits back.

I ruffle Max's hair. 'Bye, bye, terror!'

He eyes me with concern and I leave him clambering onto his Grandma's knee and Annie walks with me to the front door.

'I may finally get some peace and quiet,' she says. 'With them both asleep in the afternoon I often get an hour to myself. Not that I have much to do but it's nice not to be at someone's beck and call the whole time. Thanks for coming in and sitting with Gran, I mean Mrs Green. Roy was in Germany last week – this week it's Poland so it's nice to have a proper adult to speak to for a change...' her voice trails off.

'It can't be easy coping with them both.'

'Conversation with a three-year-old and a ninety-year-old isn't always the most stimulating,' she lowers her voice. 'I know I shouldn't say it and I love them both very much but it is not always... satisfying.' She leans forward and speaks earnestly. 'You see, I need to do something for *me*. I need fulfilment. Does that sound very selfish?'

'No.'

'I suppose it does and you're probably too polite to say anything,' Annie's laugh is a deep, friendly chuckle. 'I told Roy I was going to look for work. I can't stand doing nothing.'

My hand rests on the front door. 'Perhaps you could paint my flat. Like I said, I am thinking of decorating the place.'

'That sounds great. Can I call in and we can discuss it?' she asks.

***

Two days later I'm spending the afternoon working from home and my quiet time absorbed in Caravaggio's painting has been ruined with nagging doubts that Javier knows about the painting and has spoken to Mrs Green.

What advice did he give her?

I'm still lost in thought when the doorbell rings.

'I hope I'm not too late? I've dropped Max off at a friend's house and Gran's all settled with the re-runs of Antique Road Show.' Annie shakes rain from a quilted maroon jacket and places it over the arm of the blue sofa. 'Goodness – this is so different from next door. These houses are fabulous inside when they're modernised. Look at that charcoal mural and these paintings – are they all originals? What a wonderful fireplace…'

'It's black marble. It was popular six years ago but I'm not sure about it now.'

'It's not exactly unattractive though, is it?' Annie runs her hand over the mantelpiece. 'I do like the floor. Oak is so warm looking and much more practical than a carpet – more hygienic – but we just need to do something about these walls. Certainly not wallpaper but maybe some rag rolling in rustic shades – get rid of the green in the kitchen which is quite bright, don't you think?'

I follow her eyes to where she looks over my shoulder. 'Whatever you think.'

'And the mural?'

'Javier painted that for Oscar. It's symbolic of where they met.'

'It must go.'

'Javier would never forgive me.'

She stands back and gazes at it analytically as if gaining perspective. Her hands are poised on her hips as she moves backwards and forwards.

'Would you like coffee?'

As I busy myself in the kitchen she is examining, touching and appraising the room. She strokes picture frames, scan-reads book covers and flicks through art magazines then settles her gaze on me.

'The existing bold colours will go. I'll replace them with tranquil tones; sage green for the lounge which will be comforting and relaxing, and I think beige and rust for the kitchen.'

I wonder if Annie's combination of pale skin and streaky blond hair comes from a distant Scandinavian descent. Her slim straight back and narrow shoulders give her an aura of vulnerability and I can't imagine her climbing a stepladder. Only thin laughter lines around her mouth betray her youthful body and I think she is slightly older than me, and at least fifteen years younger than her husband.

She slides her thin arms into the bulky jacket. 'I hope you'll trust me to do a good job? We'll think about the mural. Are you sure that you don't want me to paint over it?

'Definitely.'

'Can I say something to you?' Her eyes turn serious. 'I know that we don't know each other well but Gran speaks very highly of you. You even saved her life. But I am worried. You know he came over to see Gran last night.'

'Who?'

'Javier.'

'Really?' I can only shake my head.

'I worry because of the painting. She has it in her bedroom. I know it isn't the original Vermeer but he does seem very interested in it.'

***

Javier has been working late in the studio and I'm still formulating what I will say to him. My plan is going to unravel and it will be because of him. I'm in a hurry to make my swap but the painting, hidden in my bedroom, is still not dry.

On Saturday night I am asleep on the sofa when the doorbell rings. I rise groggily and flick off the television assuming he has forgotten his key but the door is pulled from my grasp. Roy pushes me, sending me reeling against the wall and I bang my head. He stands over me and the sweet alcohol coming from his breath makes me nauseous.

'Home alone?' he spits.

'What do you want?'

'This.' He waves a bottle of wine wrapped in gold mesh. 'Is a present for you.'

'I don't want it.' I try to block his way into my home by keeping my hand on the open door handle and a chill wind whisks around my ankles.

'Let's not play games. You know who I am and I know who you are.' He is a taller than me. He looks older close up and there are ingrained lines at the corner of his mouth and furrows on his forehead – he's mid-fifties. His arms are muscled and I try to push him away.

'Nice flat.' He whistles. 'It doesn't look like it needs decorating to me. It looks perfectly all right. I mean the paintings are a bit…weird…nudist crap but then again, everyone can't have the same taste can they?' He waves the bottle in my face. 'Don't even need a corkscrew. Get some glasses.' He moves further into the room.

'I want you to leave.' I block his path but he's light on his feet and he dodges, thrusting the bottle into my chest and with his free hand he slams the front door shut. 'You're letting all the heat out,' he hisses.

My back is against the wall. 'What do you want?'

'It's a present.'

'What for?'

He bounces on his heels then scratches his trimmed beard and contemplates. 'It's a gift for looking after my mother and …for being such a wonderful neighbour.' He doesn't slur but he speaks cautiously and when he leans toward me his spittle lands on my cheek. I wipe it off with the back of my hand.

'I never thanked you for looking after Mum when she had her fall. Then Annie tells me that you came in and sat with her when she wasn't well this week so it seems I am in debt to your… kindness. And I don't like to be in debt. It makes me feel uncomfortable.'

'I don't want this. I like your Mother.' I push the wine bottle firmly against his chest.

'Umm.' He scratches his beard with his index finger.

'I thought it was your boyfriend who likes my mother.' His eyes are flat and lifeless. He waves his arms expansively. 'I'm also in debt to you because you're offering my wife a job. You want her to paint and decorate for you – in here. Don't you have time to do it yourself? Why do you want *my* wife in here?'

I slide along the wall changing my grip to hold the bottle by its neck.

'Let me explain things to you, shall I? Let me make things perfectly clear. I will spell it out slowly, so–you–will–understand–me. My wife doesn't need the work. She's a–very–busy–woman. So, it would be better for everyone if you tell her that you–don't–need–your–flat–decorating. Tell her you have–changed–your–mind.' His lips are close to mine. 'Understand?'

'Annie offered.' I stare him in the eye. I have been in worse situations.

His breath is hot on my cheek, my nose and then my ear. His lips are close to my skin. I think he may kiss me or perhaps try to kill me. I turn away and hold my breath. My grip tightens on the bottle.

'I don't want you near my wife. Is that clear? Stay away from her or you will...'

I close my eyes.

'And tell you boyfriend to stay away too.'

The front door slams.

When I open my eyes Roy is gone.

***

The following morning I'm at home trying to concentrate on my work for the art exhibition in

Knightsbridge in just ten days' time but my mind is wandering. Roy's visit hasn't unnerved me as much as the fact that Javier might have seen the painting.

Did Mrs Green show it to him?

He texted me but he stayed at his studio working last night as he has done for most of the past fortnight. He is finishing a canvas so that he can devote all his time to Josephine Lavelle when she arrives here at the end of the week.

The doorbell rings.

It couldn't be Roy.

Couldn't the postman just put the bills through the box?

On the second ring I sigh and stretch, straighten my baggy black shirt and open the door.

'Give me a hand will you?' I stare down at the top of Annie's dusky blond hair. 'God, it's been a nightmare finding the right paint. I wanted to get the perfect colours.'

There are six large tins, several smaller ones, two rollers and half a dozen paintbrushes of various sizes. With a grunt she lifts a couple of heavy cans across the threshold.

'I've time for a quick coffee if you ask me nicely but I have to collect Max in half an hour. I'll start painting tomorrow morning. I've got some wonderful shades. Look at this lilac. Isn't it perfect for the bedroom? And this sage green is ideal for the living room. I asked them to mix a special tone – I think it will look fabulous.' Annie pushes me toward the kitchen. 'Come on, Mikky. Chop, chop! Haven't got all day you know. Heaven's you look busy.' She nods at my computer and my notes scattered across the table. 'I promise not to disturb you while you're working. I'll be very quiet. No singing or whistling.' She talks about the paint; texture and contrasts, and in the end I say.

'Annie, is it okay, you know, you decorating for me?'

'Of course it is.'

'What about, Roy?'

'Roy's in Slovenia, he left this morning.'

'He came around here last night.'

'Yes. I know. With a bottle of wine.'

'He threatened me.'

'Roy?'

'He said he didn't want you painting my flat. He said that it would be better for me if I told you that I didn't need the flat painting.'

Her eyes are like two dark grey puddles and she bites the corner of her bottom lip. 'He doesn't have to know, does he?' she says. 'We don't have to tell him.'

'And what if he finds out?'

'I won't say a word,' she says. 'Will you?'

***

I look sideways at Javier's handsome profile. We're eating in the local French restaurant around the corner from our flat near the river. He hasn't shaved and his eyes are red and bloodshot – he has been working day and night finishing a canvas. It is the first time that we have had chance to talk together and enjoy a tasty meal.

Over his fresh lobster and my chicken in cream sauce I tell him about Roy's threatening visit and how Annie turned up the next morning with paints.

'She's got balls! Especially if you say Roy was so angry.'

'I had the wine bottle in my hand ready to smack him with it.'

'He wouldn't want to mess with you. I've seen you – you're like a tiger when you get angry.'

'It only happened once. Don't exaggerate.'

'Yes, and the guy never bothered you after that.'

I shake my head remembering the incident at University. Javier, Carmen and I had been at a Spanish rock band concert, I don't remember the name of the group now but as we were leaving the venue a guy roughly pushed Carmen smacking her temple against a wall.

I tried to grab him but he escaped in the medley of people. We knew him. He was a cocky student with wealthy parents from Bilbao. He was loud, often drunk and brash.

When we got to the bar where the student's hung out – he was there. I showed him Carmen's bruised and bleeding face but he had laughed, worse still, he refused to apologise and in the end Javier had to pull me away.

But I waited and watched then I followed him down the dimly lit passageway to the toilet, taking him alone and by surprise with my biker boot kicking him in the middle of his spine. He crashed against the wall and I spun him around and raised my knee hard into his balls. He doubled over and I chopped the middle of his back with my elbow. Winded he slumped to the floor where I kicked him hard in the gut a few times and left him lying with pee seeping through his trousers and crying out in pain.

'I'm sure you'll sort out Roy if he turns up again.' Javier refills our glasses. Our empty dinner plates are removed and we order coffee and whiskey.

'He also told me to tell you not to bother Mrs Green again,' I say.

He looks surprised and his cheeks flush.

'I didn't know that you had gone into see her,' I add.

'Ah, I was going to leave it as a surprise.'

'Surprise?'

'Well, you know the morning Mrs Green called in to see you? We talked a lot about paintings and she mentioned that she had an excellent forgery of a Vermeer and I wanted to take a look at it.'

'Why?'

'Well, think about it. Paintings turn up all the time – out of the blue – out of nowhere. If it is the original the museum would pay a fortune to get it back.'

'It's not the original.'

'It might be.'

'Have you seen it?' I ask holding my breath.

'Not yet – she didn't want to risk showing it to me or having the discussion with her family around. Annie was there.'

'She's teasing you,' I say. 'Mrs Green is playing.'

'Do you think so?'

'I've seen it.'

'And it couldn't possibly be the–'

'No.'

'But just supposing it is. We could give–'

'It's not.'

'But–'

'It wouldn't be ours to give–'

'I know but just supposing we persuaded Mrs Green to give it back I'm sure we could get some reward. We could negotiate–'

'You always said you weren't interested in money and that it was more important to be a good artist.'

'Think of the fame and the recognition we would get.'

I stare at him.

'It's true, Mikky. What if we found the world's most expensive stolen painting and returned it? Look what happened to Josephine Lavelle – she found the Golden Icon. She is revered and famous.'

'She was famous already.'

'And now she's a hero for returning a piece of national treasure.'

I shake my head. My mind is leaping at the thought of Javier taking my Vermeer and returning it to Boston – it just isn't going to happen.

'It's Mrs Green's painting. Let her enjoy it.' My voice sounds harsher than I intended. 'It's not the original. It's a fake. I've seen it, remember?'

'I told her she should get it valued.'

'What?'

'She should.'

'She can't.'

'Why?'

'She doesn't want to make a fuss and she doesn't want Roy to get his hands on it. She doesn't want him to get ideas about the painting. He's had a gambling problem before and she's still wary of him.'

My plan is unravelling. I never wanted Javier to know about the painting. If only I had been home when Mrs Green called in.

'Then it makes me all the more determined to do the right thing.' He stirs sugar into his coffee.

'If it is the original, I would agree with you, Javier,' I lie. 'But it isn't. Let an old lady enjoy the last remaining years she has with the painting. Be kind, Javier. Don't cause a fuss. She doesn't need that.'

'So you think Mrs Green's painting is a fake, do you? I wish she had shown it to me.' He sips the last of his whiskey and stretches his legs. 'Where did she get it?'

'From an art dealer in Paris, I think.'

Javier yawns. 'Don't you know anyone who might know someone who could check it out? You know–'

'I checked. My dealer told me the original is somewhere in Kazakhstan. It was once valued at $500 million. He heard through a reliable source that it's in the hands of a businessman and a collector.' I don't elaborate fearing my lie will lead me further from the truth and seem implausible.

Javier chuckles. 'Collector – that's a joke – he probably stole it in the first place, although wasn't there a rumour the real IRA stole it?'

'How do they find out about these things?' I say matching his smile.

'Journalists and investigators, I suppose.'

'They're not always reliable or even honest.'

'So much information is subterfuge,' he agrees. 'The value of any valuable art possession depends on the ability to demonstrate clear title and evidence of its undisputed ownership.' He smiles and seems absorbed watching the waitress clearing the empty table in the corner of the room and I study him and wonder about his motive. Javier is a clever and gentle man:

captivating, entertaining, caring and sincere. Can anyone be that perfect?

'And what about Roy?' he asks.

'He won't get his hands on it while Mrs Green is alive,' I say.

'We'll have to make sure of that.' Javier asks for the bill.

I finish my whiskey and sit back mulling over our conversation. Time is critical and like an hour–glass I wonder how much I have left.

When will be a good time for me to make the swap?

'You remember the journalist, Karl Blakey, the one Josephine told us not to speak to…' he says.

'I'd forgotten about him besides she asked *you* not to speak to him,' I correct him.

'He's been following me.' Javier looks out of the window and scans the dark and empty street.

'Did you have lunch with him?'

'We had a drink,' he says.

'And?'

'I told him I wouldn't speak to him but he won't take no for an answer. He was actually very good company. He's knowledgeable and well informed and he's also got amazing contacts in the art world.'

Javier pays with his credit card. He taps his secret number into the machine and although the waitress looks at him with a flirty smile he is oblivious of her good looks.

Outside I button my duffel coat against the cold and we walk down to the river and along the towpath. Javier links his arm through mine. 'Karl Blakey has written a lot about Josephine. He seems very interested in her career but it's as if he doesn't like her. He reported on her cocaine use that shocked her fans–'

'Josephine took cocaine?' I say.

'Didn't you know? Her career went into decline when the public found out.'

'So, it turns out he isn't such a nice guy.' I push my nose under my collar. 'Why is he following you?' I ask.

'I assume it's because he got lucky reporting on her coke habit and he made a name for himself as an investigative reporter. He pretends he's interested in her portrait but I think he's trying to get me to reveal things I know about her. He wants to know when she is arriving in London and where she's staying.'

'An investigative journalist? I'll sort him out for you, Javier. I'll protect you.' I tug on his arm and pull him closer to me.

The last thing I need is a nosey journalist sniffing around and I feel the sand shifting and draining away from under my toes.

***

In the last week of January three events happen simultaneously: Josephine arrives and checks into the Savoy Hotel. An article about Javier and his new portrait commission appears in The Sunday Times Supplement and thirdly, in the same newspaper there's an interview with a wealthy Romanian businessman by Karl Blakey. The event that interests me most is the article on the Romanian Alexandru Negrescu presumably he has important information leading to the recovery of a stolen Vermeer painting and the curator from the Isabella Stewart Museum from Boston is also flying over from America for a meeting with Christie's Auction House.

To clear my head I head for Chiswick Park looking for evidence that spring could be on its way but it is still January and a covering of snow has melted on the paths and muffled-up dog walkers and joggers whose breath comes out like plumes of smoke from a steam engine, hurry with purpose keen to get home.

I pass the pond and at the small bridge I pause to admire nesting ducks while pondering the implications of stealing the painting while Mrs Green is still alive. I can't wait. The noose is tightening. There is suddenly too much interest in this lost masterpiece.

It couldn't be the same Vermeer. The coincidence seems implausible. I sit for a while on a bench watching ducks glide across the water seemingly effortlessly while their feet paddle frantically underneath and I know how they feel.

A black Cockerpoo chases a Dalmatian and it sniffs snootily before turning dismissively and runs away.

'Mikky Dos Santos?' I turn at the sound of my name.

His face has been splashed on all the media outlets for the past few days under the heading of 'Talented Investigative Journalist' but it still takes me a few seconds to recognise him.

'My name is Karl Blakey.' He takes a card from his pocket and holds out his arm to stop me from moving away. 'It's important.' His small rodent eyes are watchful and wary.

Josephine Lavelle is not here – does her rule apply

to me? Besides I'm curious about the newspaper article and the Vermeer.

What does he want from me?

'Nothing you say to me has an importance,' I reply and walk away.

'Come and have a coffee with me. I think we could help each other,' he urges.

I continue walking. The black Cockerpoo runs toward me, his coat shines electric blue and I bend to pat his head, stalling and waiting for Karl Blakey to follow.

'It can't be a coincidence that you're living with an artist who has been commissioned to paint a portrait of Josephine Lavelle, an ex–cocaine user, and a serial liar with a dubious past.'

I look up. It's the first time I've heard anyone speak negatively about Josephine Lavelle and in spite of myself I smile.

He speaks quickly. 'You must know the story of the Golden Icon and I believe she stole more from Dieter Guzman's apartment when she collected it in Munich.'

'What?'

'And it's no coincidence that a Romanian businessman has information leading to the recovery of a stolen painting. A painting that she reported seeing in that apartment in Munich last August. She was the last person ever to see it.'

I have no idea what he is talking about.

Karl's small pink eyes regard me unblinkingly. He is about my age or slightly older perhaps thirty-five but his jowls wobble when he speaks. 'Wait, Mikky, come back! Do you also know that your boyfriend is dealing with some well know art crooks? Ah? I can see from your face that you don't. Be careful. Don't trust him. Don't trust what Javier says.'

I throw my head back, laugh in his face and turn away.

'Call me anytime. You may need me,' he shouts.

Drops of rain begin to splash on my cheek then my forehead. I know Karl continues to stand rooted to the spot, the heat of his eyes are on my back and as the storm breaks overhead rain falls in torrents and I run with my hands in my pockets. I take cover under a fir tree and shake water from my hair. Karl hasn't followed me nor is he still standing in the rain. He has disappeared.

On the way out of the park I drop his business card into the bin with the doggy poo bags and head home.

***

We are sitting in a taxi on our way to the ballet at the Royal Opera House.

'She's excited to be here,' Javier says. 'She wouldn't come tonight. She wanted to rest after her journey. It seems she spent quite a lot of time here when she was performing. She tells me London holds a very special place in her heart – for personal reasons. I didn't know what she meant but I'm looking forward to spending time with her, Mikky. She is so interesting… she's an amazing woman.'

The collar of his trench coat is pulled up in a fashionable manner, his manicured hands are clasped in his lap and *Armani* aftershave lingers in the black cab.

'Is she excited about her portrait?' I imagine it hanging on the wall of the theatre along with her contemporaries, famous in the world of music and opera. I don't tell him that I spent the best part of last night Googling her and I found newspaper reports about the Golden Icon and an account of the events during Josephine's final performance as *Tosca*, and interestingly the events leading to Raffa's death.

'She can't wait to get started tomorrow.

'She's certainly had a chequered past,' I say, glancing out of the window at Parliament Square and the illuminated face of Big Ben as we head along the embankment. 'What do you think about Karl Blakey's article and Alexandru Negrescu's account of the missing Vermeer?' I ask. 'Karl hinted that Josephine stole a painting from an apartment in Germany. The newspaper articles say her ex-husband blackmailed her to go to Munich to recover a stolen Golden Icon. He wanted to use it to pay off the debts in his failing construction business in Dublin.'

'She told me in Dresden that as soon as she saw the Golden Icon she knew she must return it to Italy,' Javier says. 'She had no intention of keeping it.'

'It took her a few weeks before she returned it. Do you think she thought about stealing it?'

'She's not like that.'

Well, at least if they think the Vermeer in Munich was the original then the painting in Mrs Green's house must be a forgery. You can rest easy now, Javier.'

'Mrs Green told Roy it *is* the original and if anything happens to Mrs Green the painting shouldn't belong to him – or to an art dealer. If it is the original Vermeer it belongs to the Isabella Stewart Museum. It was stolen from there,' he insists.

'She was only saying that to get Roy to move in. It's just a good forgery.' I squeeze his arm and the taxi pulls to the kerb. 'Forget about it. Trust me.'

Javier pays the fare and as we walk toward the theatre in Covent Garden he links his arm though mine. 'After I've finished painting Josephine's portrait I've been offered work back in Spain. There's some restoration work in a church near Toledo and I am thinking of taking it – just for a few months...'

'Restoration work?'

'Yes.'

I know artists can augment their income by preserving and renovating artwork, paintings, buildings and statues. It all depends on what their interest is and their experience or artistic background. This would be perfect for Javier but I don't want him to leave England or me. Not just yet. Not until the time is right.

'And your portrait work?'

'I don't know.'

'You may get another commission after Josephine.'

'Perhaps I may but I don't have to live in London to do it.'

We mix with the remaining stragglers heading into the foyer. We are late and I am aware of my rapidly beating heart and my growing fear. I have a sense that my life is about to change and that events are happening in our world that neither Javier nor I can control. It is as if destiny is taking a hold of our lives and the period of calm that we have known is preceding a tempest that is about to be unleashed upon us. Change would normally excite me but for some reason a shiver of fear causes me to falter and Javier steadies my step.

In the auditorium I pull my black hat from my head and take a bulldog clip from my pocket to secure my hair, careful of my pearl necklace and drop earrings. I straighten my black and red giant poppies print dress and black leggings and Javier places his hand in the middle of my back and escorts me to the front row of the Stalls.

Javier's recent interviews have increased his celebrity status and his profile with the media has escalated. He is aware of his public image and he has enlisted my help. Attending the ballet is all part of his increasing high profile; paid for and organised by Nico Vastano, thoroughly enjoyed by Javier and hated by me.

He scans the seats around us and just as the lights dim he raises a hand to wave. I marvel at how quickly he is adapting to life in the limelight and how much he might miss all the adoration and attention in Spain.

During the first Act of *Swan Lake* my mind wanders. Josephine was never a dancer but I think of the live performances on stage, the grease paint, the lights, the anticipation and the glory of an acclaimed performance. A yawn wells up from inside and I cover my mouth.

In profile Javier's face is engrossed with appreciation, rapt in concentration and I think perhaps had he not been an artist a life on stage would have suited him. I imagine him taking a bow, his smile wide and his eyes shining with delight. He would revel in the fame and glory not unlike Josephine Lavelle.

Another yawn. My eyelids are heavy.

Maybe he has more in common with her that I thought. He would also like to be revered and known for the recovery of stolen artwork as much as he would for painting the portrait of a once loved opera star. He is strong in his ambition but fickle in emotion and I would not trust him with my life or my feelings. He wants the Vermeer for different reasons. I must stay alert and guard against his inquisitiveness. I want this sorted out and over with.

I sigh and return my attention to the stage. Josephine Lavelle is in London. Annie should finish painting soon and I will invite Mrs Green and Josephine Lavelle to dinner and keep an old lady happy. We could persuade Javier that it isn't an original and just a good forgery – and what a big joke it has all been – especially if I have already made the switch.

At the interval I applaud and return Javier's enthusiastic smile. His grey suit and pale lilac shirt accentuates his olive skin and his fingers are firm when he reaches over and squeezes my fingers.

'Look! Up there,' he whispers, nodding at the box. 'It's Alexandru Negrescu, I recognise him from the newspaper article.'

The Romanian has black eyebrows, a hooked nose and thin lips. Beside him are two young girls. Their hair and makeup are perfect and their bodies stick-thin like teenage models.

'His daughters?' Javier asks, as if reading my mind.

Along the rows of the audience I see a familiar face and I nudge him. 'Karl Blakey.'

'He's a friend of the Romanian. We'll just have to avoid him.'

'Not such a friend that he's invited to sit in the box with them.' I return my attention, once again to the stage thinking of Josephine. All her years of training, hard work, dedication and devotion are over, all those years of practise and perfection are finished. Now she is an ordinary mortal with only Andreas for company as her protégée. Why did she never have a family? Was she too busy?

Perhaps she is lonely? I understand sadness and isolation and I am curious about those people like me. Mrs Green lived alone and saw no one until we became friends and I understand her, as I may perhaps understand Josephine Lavelle. My dinner party for lonely people – it will be a great distraction. Josephine is a challenge but I will not let Javier go easily.

The audience is hushed and lights dim for Act Two. I look along the row at the rapt faces all caught up in the anticipation of the performance. It would make a great photograph and I remember Josephine's voice over dinner in Dresden, tinged with a hint of an American accent, her tone crisp and factual.

The stage is a place where I will no longer walk and a place where I will no longer perform. Gone are the cheers and applause they have all died. All I have are memories. But they are mine. I have known the power of true glory but now everything is over. Gone in the blink of an eye.'

***

Early the next morning Javier is excited. He is meeting

Josephine.

'Andreas is with her,' he says.

'She brought him with her? What is he going to do – watch you?' I ask.

'I have no idea but he's not welcome in the studio. He can go sightseeing.'

'Maybe she wants a chaperone?' I smile.

'I thought I'm the one who needs protecting?' His kiss is soft on my cheek.

'I think she likes her men young and virile. You're a perfect stud muffin. Behave!' I call out as he slams the front door.

Annie arrives a little later and although she is quiet as she paints I am aware of her presence in the room and the soft scraping and slushing of the wet roller as it glides across the wall.

It's hard to concentrate. She's in the lounge stretching over the fireplace and moving resolutely toward the dusky Argentinean scene.

I want to say, *be careful – Javier's drawing is important.* But she is lost in thought – focused on another world.

After percolating fresh coffee I go to my bedroom. It's my haven. I am taking a risk with Annie in the house but I have to formulate my plan. I have been in a vortex of confusion but now I am determined. I must be prepared. I must swap it this week. With careful and quiet movements, I remove my forgery from the wardrobe and check it carefully. It looks cracked and old. I have been diligent in choosing the right sized canvas and I cannot help but stand back and admire my work, and even though I know it wouldn't pass a chemical test it was impressive. It was ready.

Raffa would approve and so too would Dolores my art teacher from the University in Madrid. She's retired now. I remember the look of disbelief when I told her I was giving up art in favour of photography. The long cheroot had fallen from her lips but her dark eyes had not wavered and she had nodded curtly. She knew me well enough not to argue.

I sit on my bed, edgy and nervous. The more I think about the Vermeer the more unsettled I become. The implications of its theft are becoming complicated – until recently it was a relatively simple plan but the odds are stacking up against me. Roy, Javier and Karl Blakey are all chasing it and now my mission is urgent.

Josephine saw a Vermeer in a flat in Munich. *How is that possible?* It must have been a fake but Karl Blakey believes it was the original, which means the one hanging in Mrs Green's house couldn't possibly be.

Josephine must be mistaken.

I cannot lose focus. I will succeed. I wrap the forgery in hessian and place it carefully back in my wardrobe.

Last week Mrs Green couldn't see the robin in the garden. Could she be fooled so easily with her favourite artist?

I consider the possibilities of swapping it while Roy is away and I think it's the best idea. I cannot wait for her to die – she could live a long time besides – if she suspected anything she would accuse Roy of cheating her and stealing it from her – not me.

She trusts me.

I should test her eyesight one last time. Suddenly, excited by the idea I jump up. I need some fresh air.

Why wait?

Why didn't I think of this before?

I can make the swap today. Tonight?

I have a key. I could wait until Mrs Green was sleeping – this afternoon – and sneak into her house. Would she notice? Would Annie?

I grab my jacket and call out. 'I'm going to get some milk from the corner shop, do you want anything?'

My plan is already formulating in my mind. It would be easy. I could be gone by next week.

'No thanks, although a doughnut would be lovely, I'll have to collect Max in twenty minutes but I'll look in on Gran before I go.' She doesn't stop painting.

'Okay. I won't be long.' I slam the front door shut behind me and outside I inhale deeply.

Freedom.

It is fresh, cold and damp and I welcome the elements on my skin. A strong wind runs through my hair and through my thin jumper and black leather jacket. On impulse I cross the road and skip through the small alley to the river, playing air guitar to Dire Straits, *Money for Nothing.*

Why wait?

The brown current is flowing briskly and a few ducks quack in greeting, flapping their wings, waddling on the embankment searching for food in the muddy tide. I twang a few invisible chords at them and shout aloud: 'Yey!'

Further along the tow path a man walks a white terrier and in the distance a familiar figure is striding away from me.

Javier? He's wearing his brown jacket with the

collar pulled up around his ears. He disappears around the bend in the river. I'm sure it's him. Wasn't he meeting Josephine today? I walk quickly. He moves out of sight so I run, hoping to catch him cutting through the alley. But on the road the stranger in the brown jacket has disappeared.

I check both directions but the street is empty. I turn toward Chiswick peering into passing cars knowing Javier doesn't drive in England but checking anyway.

A Land Rover cruises past. The woman at the wheel is wearing sunglasses and she stares back at me.

Overhead a white jet rumbles making its descent to Heathrow. It drones in the sky and I turn to see it tilt its wings. Then forgetting Javier I head into the corner shop and my body is filled with adrenaline.

Tonight.

I choose a newspaper, fresh milk, a bag of jam doughnuts and a packet of chocolate biscuits. My conversation with Aaron is the same as usual. He talks about Salman's school work then about the laziness of his eldest son who is at Leeds University.

'He says he studies as many hours a day as I work here, in this shop. But he doesn't know what hard work is. They have it too easy now.' Aaron's bloodshot eyes sparkle and he hands me my change.

My mind is a cacophony of ideas and jumbled thoughts but I mumble a suitable reply and take my shopping. Next week I could be in South America. I am crossing the small road that leads behind my apartment to Max's nursery when I see a metallic powder blue Mercedes parked up on the kerb.

Didn't Annie say Roy is working in Slovenia this

week?

Still uneasy at his recent threat and with Annie decorating my home my pulse races and I quicken my pace, my heart thumping wildly and in time with my heavy step. I fling open my front door and pause with my hand still on the handle. Annie is washing brushes at the sink with her back toward me. The tap is gushing water and when she turns around she appears breathless and her face is flushed.

'Is Roy here?'

Her grey eyes darken. 'No. Why?'

'I thought I saw his car parked in the road leading to the nursery.'

'He's not due back until Friday – tomorrow night.'

Annie scrapes paint from the thick brush with an expert's ease. Her long fingers stroke the brush against the tin, almost lovingly. There is something in the slow ease of her wrist and the slight tremor in her hand. She seems out of breath and perhaps a little nervous. Was it because I mentioned Roy?

She looks questioningly at me. Her eyes shine brightly and when I say nothing she lays the brush down on an old newspaper. 'I'm going to pop home. Gran wasn't feeling too well this morning. I'll just check and see how she is. I'll only be a few minutes. I'll still have a time for a donut before I collect Max. Pop the kettle on.' She grins and rubs my arm as she passes me on her way out.

I dump my shopping on top of the counter and regulate my breathing, forcing my lungs to move slowly and rhythmically and my hands to stop shaking. Is it the thought of the swap making me unsettled?

Javier has an interview with a prestigious art magazine on Saturday and I have agreed to meet Josephine for lunch beside the river. Could this be what is making me nervous?

I shake my head. The room looks different. I stare hard concentrating and then it dawns on me. Annie has painted over Javier's mural. It's gone. I stare at the spot where it had been. No! How could she have painted over it?

I have a sudden urge to speak to Javier. I need to hear his voice I dial his number and it clicks to voicemail but I don't leave a message.

Was he walking along the river just now?

Impossible.

I fill the kettle. I am placing mugs on the counter when the door bangs open.

'Come, quickly! Oh my God, Mikky, I think she's dead.'

I run. I jump the wall between our pathways and stumble on a plastic car in the hallway. The grandfather clock clicks, whines and chimes three. My senses are heightened: stale cheese, burnt toast and aftershave. She is asleep in her chair at the kitchen window.

'Mrs Green?'

Annie kneels beside her. 'I don't think she's asleep,' she whispers.

Mrs Green's mouth sags open and her eyes are closed in a dreamless and eternal sleep. Her fingers are limp and cold.

'Gran...Gran,' Annie calls softly.

'Call an ambulance,' I whisper but I know it's too late.

Annie doesn't move so I pull my mobile from my

pocket and as I speak I watch Annie pick a discarded cushion up from the floor. She hugs it tightly to her chest while shaking her head from side to side. Her bewildered grey eyes are wide with disbelief. 'Roy will never forgive me. He will kill me.'

A sense of loss washes over me and I cannot believe the old lady's life is over. In my mind I see blinking red lights from a pinball machine, flashing vividly and repeatedly: Game Over.

I lean against the kitchen table. My legs feel weak and a pocket of tears wait at the base of my throat. Outside in the garden goldfinches feed happily and the chirping robin perches on the fence. Now it is time, the moment I have waited and planned. I must grab my opportunity. There's not a moment to lose.

***

The rest of the day passes in timeless slow motion. The doctor is called, the police arrive and an autopsy will be performed. It has to be tonight that I make the switch.

By eleven o'clock I am exhausted. Javier returns home and we discuss the events of the day. I am sad but wired. 'Were you on the towpath this morning? I called out and ran after you.'

'It wasn't me,' he replies. He yawns. He is tired. He has started a new project and his mind is elsewhere – probably with Josephine.

'Did it go okay?'

'Yes.'

He's too tired to speak. He hugs me goodnight and I wait, sitting in the lounge, staring out into the street then my patio. I wander and pace and I realise Javier didn't notice his mural has gone.

It is past three o'clock when I check his room. He is curled on his side and snoring. I take Mrs Green's key from its hiding place, swing my bag over my shoulder and let myself out of the front door. Carrying my small torch I swing my legs over the low wall and peer through my neighbour's letterbox.

I know Roy came home earlier this evening and my plan is risky but I can't take a chance. He is unscrupulous. He could have it on the market by the morning.

When I let myself into the house each miniscule click of the lock and the hinge seems to echo loudly. I am hoping they are all asleep. I don't know what I will say if I get caught. I stand for a few seconds until my eyes are accustomed to the dark remembering how Mrs Green lay on the floor a few feet from me. I was able to save her then – but today I was too late.

I shake my head to clear the memory and swallow the knot in my throat. I check there is no alarm set downstairs and move forward. My foot kicks a boot carelessly strewn on the floor and I pause with only my beating heart for company.

Silence.

My flashlight precedes me up the stairs one very slow creaking step at a time. The house is cold and I shiver. The bedroom door at the back of the house is ajar and I tiptoe far enough inside to see an outline of someone asleep tucked under a thick duvet. Annie is curled like a crescent shaped moon and snoring lightly. Against the wall a child's single bed lays empty.

I ease myself slowly along the landing past the

second bedroom that lays empty and I pause to check the bathroom then I head to the front of the house to the last bedroom. The door squeaks as I push it gently open.

Roy is turned away from me, asleep on his side with his arms curled protectively around Max and I am caught out and surprised by the tenderness of his pose.

On the right-hand side, on the wall beside the wardrobe and opposite the bed, hangs the Vermeer.

Behind me there is a cough and bedsprings groan so I move quickly, ducking inside the bedroom as soft footsteps pad along the landing toward me. I hold my breath as the click of the light illuminates the corridor and the bathroom door half closes.

Annie pees long and hard and I crouch down behind the door waiting for her to finish. The toilet flushes, the tap gushes, the light clicks off.

Her footsteps come closer so I hunch down, lower toward the floor. She pushes open the bedroom door and stands gazing at her husband and son. We are inches away from each other with only the door separating us and I hold my breath.

If she turns around she will see me.

Finally she backs away and only when I hear her soft footfall recede down the corridor and the squeak of the bed do I breathe slowly out.

So many plans fail because of impatience, carelessness and over confidence. I will not fail so I wait.

The carpet is soft under my black trainers. I reach up and lift the painting down, tilting my torch to examine it further. The picture depicts a man and two women playing music. It is the reason I moved here.

On the landing I crouch down ready to run if necessary. I cut the canvas carefully with my scalpel and roll the painting into my rucksack. Occasionally I am distracted by a night-time sigh from the bedroom and I pause to glance around, listening intently, hoping they won't stir. I pull out my forgery unroll it and tape it securely back into the frame. It is 69 centimetres high by 63 centimetres wide – the exact measurements as the original.

Any expert, and also the art dealer in Bruges would know it has been tampered with but to Roy's untrained eye I am hoping he will not notice. I have memorised how to match the tape on to the frame from the photographs and I work quickly. I'm a professional. In my capacity as a restorer I have done this many times. But it is not a quick or an easy job. Several times Roy murmurs in his sleep or Max sighs and I pause. My body tenses. After I replace the forgery on its hook I glance down at the bed and Max's eyelids flutter in sleep.

I tip toe down the stairs and I close and lock the front door softly behind me feeling an increasing sense of euphoria and by the time I am inside my flat my breathing is calm, my hands are steady and my head is clear.

The masterpiece is mine.

Chapter Six

'Art is what you can get away with.'
Andy Warhol

I check my watch cursing the London trains. The photo shoot for the pre-exhibition took longer than I expected and I hate to be late. I quicken my pace to keep up with the assortment of travellers, commuters, tourists and students who spew out of Victoria underground like a heard of wildebeests. A man bumps my shoulder knocking my bag of photography equipment and it falls to the floor. I swear and turn around but he doesn't stop or even notice. But in that flicker of an instance, in that small second of time, I glimpse a face in the crowd behind me. His features are clear amid a backdrop of blurred and colourful kiosks selling fast foods and drinks and it's as if I am clicking his image with the eye of my camera.

I miss my footing and stumble forward tripping down the steps. A stranger – a girl – grabs my arm and steadies me with annoyance but doesn't stop.

He is following me. He is like a chameleon in my wake and when I turn he has already disappeared. I weave and dodge past busy commuters in the underground tunnels. I can't let him follow me. He must not know where I am going.

At the bottom of the escalator I turn right and dip through the narrow subway onto the platform. It's packed tight so I squeeze and jostle through the crowd, holding my bag like a shield in front of me, moving along the platform and when the train breezes past I turn around.

Karl Blakey continues to follow me. The collar of his dull green jacket is pulled around his neck and secured with a checked scarf. He has obviously given up following Javier and now he is tailing me. I read his scathing reports depicting Josephine's descent into drugs and his more lurid articles on her affairs. It seems he has a personal vendetta toward her. He has written unflinchingly and with exaggerated detail charting every wrong movement of her life. He wrote about the discovery of the Golden Icon and her final performance. He also reported that Josephine's ex-husband had been murdered in his home in Ireland and it had been a surprise to me to know that she had once been married. It seems he wants to damage her and I guess he will use Javier or me to help him.

The crowds surge forward to board the tube but I hold back. I wait. I dip my head low onto my chest and mingle with the disembarking passengers walking in their herd back toward the steep escalator I have just descended.

My heart is thumping rapidly and perspiration forms on my forehead and when I am half way up the rising steps I turn to look down. He is standing at the bottom gazing up at me. My pursuer has detected my ruse so I begin walking the giant staircase as if I am striding toward heaven followed by the devil himself. He moves quickly taking long strides up the escalator in my wake, chasing me.

At the top I consider all the exits. A noisy group of American tourists come toward me so I slip off my burgundy duffel coat, wrap it inside out and push it under my arm, and I join their group. They babble excitedly and don't notice me as I duck between them as they head to the down escalator. I keep my back turned and my face averted and when I risk a quick glance over to the up escalator Karl Blakey is taking long, confident strides toward the top. He doesn't look to his right. He doesn't see me.

At the bottom of the escalator, on the opposite platform, tube train doors are open. I turn sideways and slip through the closing gap conscious that my whole body is trembling and my mouth is dry. Karl Blakey is following me and I have the Vermeer tucked in the back of my wardrobe.

To the surprise of the people in the carriage I punch the air with my fist, strum my air guitar and begin to laugh loudly.

***

The winter sun is warm on my cheeks and I squint at the rowing crew as they pass by, the Cox shouting orders like a Sergeant Major on parade. A plane flies overhead and I shield my eyes to watch its gradual descent wondering how soon I can escape from lunch. I have arranged to meet Josephine in The Bell on the river near my flat where the food is good and the place is busy enough to be distracting. But because of my decoy manoeuvre I'm twenty minutes late.

Through the window I see a group of diners with chilled glasses of Sauvignon Blanc talking animatedly. The thought of seeing Josephine doesn't excite me but I mustn't raise suspicion. I must develop a valid reason for leaving this city – and soon.

'Mikky, you look lovely.' Josephine stands up banging her leg on the table. She winces, bends over and grips the table. Her face is etched with tiredness – or is it grief?

'Are you okay?'

'Thank you for coming.' She forces a wide smile and holds out her hand formally.

My touch is impersonal, hard and cool. I will not be fooled by her fragility. 'Couldn't find a bloody taxi,' I lie, slinging my pack of equipment onto the floor. I remove my jacket, revealing a creased *Iron Maiden* T-shirt with a faded logo and when I look up she is gazing at the tattoo wrapped along the length of my right forearm.

'My goodness,' she says. 'That's amazing.'

It is a three dimensional elongated picture of a figure with hands clapped to its cheek in an agonised cry. The background is a lush deep red, orange and crimson landscape and my arm is suffused in colour.

'It's *Scream*.' I hold it out for her to admire.

'Edvard Munch,' she says. 'It's amazing.'

'Do you like it?'

'Why this painting?' she asks.

'Because it was painted by a man who knew what madness and horror was really like.'

'And you can relate to that?'

'I have known madness and insanity.'

'But you are so young…' Her forehead creases and a flash of sadness flickers across her eyes.

I don't want her pity so I pull my arm away. 'Age has no hold over your mind or your suffering.'

'Haven't you been happy, Mikky?'

I don't reply.

'Javier told me that his family love you,' she insists.

'This all happened before I met them.' I lean my elbows on the table and pick up a menu. 'God, I'm starving.'

'Me too,' she says, and I know it is a lie. She has lost more weight and her face is gaunt. I remember she hardly ate in Dresden.

'What would you like?' I ask.

'What do you recommend?'

'Everything.' I say.

The waitress arrives.

'Would you like wine?' she asks.

'No. I'll have a pint of cold *Stella* and the burger.' I close the menu decisively and look at the people around us while Josephine orders plain fish and white wine.

'Thank you for meeting me,' she says, when we are alone. 'I thought it would be nice if we met up and got to know each other. Javier is busy – another big interview – besides I'm sure he's sick of the sight of me.'

'How is Andreas?'

'He's never been to London before. This afternoon he has gone to the National Gallery,' she pauses and stares at me.

'How did your session with Javier go?' I ask.

'It was extremely interesting. We talked about what I would wear and how I would wear my hair and things like that. He has a real eye for detail. Nothing escapes him.'

'He's extremely talented,' I agree.

'You have a very close relationship.'

'Yes.'

'You met at University in Madrid.'

'Yes.'

'I have become very…very, fond of him.'

I shift in my seat. 'He's a professional. You chose the right man to paint your portrait.'

'He's very special, extremely understanding and easy to talk to,' she smiles. 'I would like to think that we have formed a lasting friendship and he is so obviously fond of you.'

My smile is tight. 'He's the best.'

Why did they speak about me? I don't need more friends. I don't want this woman in my life. Mrs Green had been different. She had been caring – not invasive. She had been interesting and she did not pry. I would miss her. My mouth quivers and tugs at the corner and I try to smile but it seems to turn into a frown.

'Tell me about you, Mikky – about your work. Do you like photography?' She leans across the table and smiles graciously with all the ease and charm learned from a career on the stage.

My ringless hands lay on the table and I am aware of the new Madonna tattoo on my left index finger. It was a Christmas gift to myself while on a trip to Camden scouring for canvasses and paintings. The tattooist was recommended and the tattoo was a welcome respite from copying the Vermeer.

'I like this,' she says, she takes my hand.

The Madonna's covered head is tilted forward and her eyes appear closed.

'Thank you.' I pull away.

'Does this have anything to do with who you are?'

I shake my head.

'Are you religious?' she persists.

'Do I look like a Christian?'

'Is there such a thing?'

'You?'

'Me?' she laughs.

'I am not like you, Josephine. I Googled you – Raffaelle Peverelli was your lover.' The words are out and they seem to still her. She doesn't move and I continue speaking. 'You know I studied with him. That is where I got my love for Caravaggio and my interest for religious paintings but I am not a believer. It was only when I studied with him that I learned so much. He taught me the influence of light and dark, good versus evil and the struggle we all have within ourselves. It is easy to slip over to the dark side. It's easy to become bad…'

The waitress interrupts my flow with the delivery of our drinks and cutlery wrapped in a napkin. I take advantage of the distraction to calm myself and to assess the situation. I am babbling. I must regain control of my emotions.

'When did you study with Raffaelle?' she asks, after the waitress disappears.

'It was during my first year at University – eight or nine years ago.'

'Before I went to Lake Como. Before I knew him. He slept with lots of his students. Did you… did you have an affair with him?'

I am tempted to lie but instead I shake my head. 'No.'

She drops her shoulders, breathes more easily and colour comes back to her cheeks.

'He wasn't my type. Besides he was too old for

me but he was talented. He mixed techniques. He taught me how to do that. He copied Old Masters then painted headphones, microwaves and lawnmowers into the scene. The juxtaposition was brilliant. He was amazing. It was modernism and surrealism. So original…' my voice trails off and I am lost in another time and place.

'You remember all this about his work?'

'Of course, he taught me how to copy Old Masters. I prefer to use my imagination but I used biblical references and scenes in my own work. Did he ever speak to you about his ideas?' I ask.

'I remember a conversation we once had when I was leaving his villa.' Her eyes stray to look out of the window and I know she is not here with me but has been transported to the past. 'We were standing by the garden gate and he said he would make a great forger. He said that it would be easier instead of trying to do something original each time and I had replied that he would miss the creativity. I remember it well. I placed my hand on his cheek and it was soft. He had shaved and he smelled of tobacco and cologne. *You don't think forgers are creative,* he said.' Her smile is filled with his memory. She looks younger and more alive. Conscious I am watching her she raises her glass and sips wine. 'Tell me about your art and your paintings.'

It is, as if by changing the subject from Raffa the memory will belong to her alone and she won't have to share it with me. She is as vulnerable as I am and like me, she doesn't share her feelings.

The waitress places my burger on the table and Josephine orders more wine and another beer for me.

I move the bun to one side and add mayonnaise to

my chips.

'What are you painting now?' she asks.

'I don't paint now,' I lie.

'Never?'

'No.'

'Don't you miss it?'

I shrug.

'So you photograph artwork for museums?'

It's probably to keep Javier happy that she wants to know about me and I remember his warning to me this morning when we were eating cereal.

Be kind to her, Mikky. She's an ill woman. She has no one. No family and very few friends. It can't harm you to be civil and nice. Make an effort for me. I have a feeling that she will be in my life for a very long time.

So determined to make up for my bad manners in Dresden I speak candidly over lunch about art, restoration and my photography; its pitfalls and its challenges. 'After University I spent a long time supplementing my income by restoring old paintings.'

'Just as Javier did?'

'Yes, we worked together some of the time. Then we worked on different projects–'

'But you always lived together?'

'Not always.'

'He must have lots of girlfriends.' She pushes her fish around the plate.

I shrug.

She can barely take her eyes from my face as I explain the details of my craft, determined not to speak about Javier or our friendship. Instead I tell her about the monasteries, churches and museums where worked.

'I did cleaning and restoration around Andalusia for a long time. One year I painted a special canvas of Christ ascending into Heaven. A priest wanted it but he wasn't allowed to accept it and I wouldn't sell it to him – so I gave it to the church as a gift. They couldn't afford an Old Master and they were delighted. It made their church look more original and authentic. The painting would never bear up under scrutiny but it looked good hanging on the wall of the monastery. I have Raffa to thank for this – he gave me his passion. He gave me life as an artist.'

A child totters over to our table and we both glance at her blue eyes and blond hair. We don't move or speak until the mother comes and leads her away by her pudgy arm. 'Come on, Libby. Don't disturb these nice ladies.'

The thread of my conversation is sliced with finality like a guillotine separating a head from its body and I sit wondering what to say but it is Josephine who speaks next.

'He was living with Glorietta Bareldo when I met him. Glorietta and I were rivals in every sense of the word and that was the final straw for us both.' A frown creases her forehead giving her a slightly puzzled air and she sighs. 'It's not a secret. It's all on the Internet.'

'Karl Blakey wrote about you. You have an injunction against him.'

'If he comes near me again I would be capable of killing him,' she replies. She looks fragile and far too ill to murder anyone but I contemplate the extent of her hatred for this man as I take deep gulps of my pint.

I deliberately smack my glass on the table and wipe my mouth on the back of my arm willing her to squirm at my uncouth manners. 'I read about your career and your rise to fame and how you turned to cocaine. Then you went to Italy to make your comeback for the role of *Tosca*. I even listened to you singing…'

'You bought the CD?'

'I listened on iTunes…'

'Did you like it?'

'Can't bear it.'

'Why?'

'I don't understand it.' I pick dismissively at my burger. Why does she make me feel as if I need her approval?

'I Googled you, too,' she smiles. 'You are well known in the art world. You have a very good reputation.' She hides her fish under mashed potato. She has barely eaten a thing.

'You don't strike me as a woman who spends a lot of time on the computer.'

'I don't have much else to do these days.' She stares defiantly at me and any sympathy I have for her instantly disappears.

'You have, Andreas.'

'Thankfully yes. He is a diligent student. Remarkably well educated and extremely polite – all the qualities I admire in a person.'

I don't reply and we order coffee from the hovering waitress.

Outside it begins to drizzle and the Thames rises, lapping in small swells and I remember sitting outside in the summer and when it was high tide how the water came up beyond our seats.

'I do love London. I have been here many times. I

have an affinity for this city.' She tells me how she sang in the Royal Albert Hall, the Royal Opera House in Covent Garden and at the London Coliseum in St Martin's lane. We talk about London, the West End, the markets and the museums. She seems reticent and thoughtful and I wonder if she misses the fame and adoration of her past.

As we leave the restaurant I indicate the old tidemark on the wall. 'The Thames rises to here at high tide.'

'I never knew that.'

I point to the tables and benches. 'We have to move inside and all the footpath gets flooded too. I'm surprised you don't know this. You seem to know London so well.'

'It was a different time. I was always working, rehearsing, training and practising. There was no time for enjoyment.'

'I thought that had been your downfall – wasn't that the problem?' Her head turns away but not before I see a flash of stark regret in her eyes and I am ashamed. 'Javier tells me that you have an emotional attachment to the city,' I add to make amends.

She looks around as if considering this statement and her eyes travel along the river. She walks carefully carrying her right arm across her stomach as if protecting herself and I consider taking her arm but she walks on ahead of me.

'You know Javier's family well?' she asks, when I catch her up.

'I haven't seen them for a few years. He has two younger brothers who are very different.'

'He's lucky to have a kind family.'

'They don't always get on.'

'Why?'

'His father remarried and the boys are from his second wife.'

She seems to consider this. 'And your family?'

'My parents were bikers. They travelled around Europe. They had no roots. I was just extra baggage. Mama wasn't the maternal type. Why they had me is a mystery. Papa says she was jealous of me but I don't know why. She was young and beautiful and she had everything.'

'Do you see them often.'

'My mother died when I was fourteen.'

Her step falters and she touches my arm. 'I'm sorry–'

'It is a time that I don't talk about.' I walk on ahead. I am not interested in her pity but I rub my fingers across *Scream* on my forearm.

'You must have loved her a lot.' She catches me up.

'I hated her.'

We walk in silence with only the clipping of her heels, the rowing Cox and a tired Jumbo for company until she says. 'And your father?'

'He's a mechanic.'

'Here?'

'In Malaga – he has a garage – he repairs motorbikes. Javier will be home soon,' I say, glancing at my watch and I have a feeling that, like me, she can't wait to see him.

I have done my best. I have been friendly and I have revealed more of me than I had intended – purely to make amends for Dresden. I have tried but we have nothing in common. She clearly adores Javier and if she befriends me then she is a step closer to him and I feel a sudden surge of loathing and revulsion toward her just as I did toward Mama and I suddenly want to be on my own.

***

As we come out of Ship Alley a white van is parked in front of my flat. Its back doors are open and Roy is carrying one of Mrs Green's cabinet display cases. I slow down and wait for him to go back inside. I want to avoid him but I also want to know what he is doing with her furniture and where he is going. She's barely been dead twenty-four hours.

'Is everything alright?' Josephine asks.

I'm unlocking the front door when Annie appears in the doorway. She stops abruptly at the sight of me and is about to speak but Roy's voice shouts out from inside. She places a finger to her lips and disappears inside toward the direction of his voice.

Josephine witnesses our exchange and raises an eyebrow but I ignore her and inside the flat I throw open the patio doors. Cool air rushes in and I turn up the heating.

'It smells of paint. Are you decorating?' she asks.

'Annie, the girl next door has been painting.'

'Nice colour.'

'Her mother-in-law lived next door and she passed away yesterday. So now I don't know if the rest of the apartment will get painted. She was supposed to do the hallway and the two bedrooms but now…well, I don't know what will happen.'

'I'm sorry.'

'Wait a second.' I leave her while I go to my bedroom. I open the wardrobe and I am still smiling when I return to the living room a few minutes later.

'Mrs Green was an adorable old lady – almost ninety. She wanted to meet you.'

'Me?'

'She liked opera music. She was a fan of yours. I was going to invite her for dinner so that she could meet you.'

'That would have been …kind of you.'

'I liked her.'

'She lived alone?'

'She didn't speak to her son until she became ill just before Christmas. Then they moved in to look after her – her son is after her money.'

'You don't like him?'

I shrug. 'She was lonely – they didn't get on. She hadn't seen him in years but they made it up in the end. There's a difference between loneliness and being solitary.'

'Which are you?' Josephine asks.

'Solitary. And you?'

'Like you, I have learned to be alone.'

'Drink? Tea? Wine?' I ask.

'Wine would be lovely.'

I open a bottle and pour two glasses. Josephine wanders around my living room reading book spines, picking out art books and flicking though pages before replacing them on the shelves. I whistle The Killers, *The Way it Was*, as she walks around the room studying the artwork.

Where is Javier?

'Is this an original Byrones?'

'A copy.'

'And this one an original Frampton?'

'A print.'

'You like modern art?'

'My religious paintings would look out of place hanging up in here. I painted one of Christ on the cross with the tide of the Thames rising around him and the disciples at his feet trying to hold back the waves.' I don't know why I am telling her this.

'Like Moses and the parting of the sea?' she asks.

I smile. 'Light from a plane flying into Heathrow illuminates Christ's face. It is distorted and twisted with sadness – not at his fate – he was more concerned that his followers would drown so he implored them with his eyes to leave him alone. There was Peter the fisherman and Joseph – Jesus' father, no one really knows what happened to him but he was there with Judas who I painted like Neptune. Judas the traitor – the murderer – the instigator, so I called it *Betrayer*.' I pause and tilt my head to one side contemplating the empty space on the wall where Javier's mural had once been. He had been upset and angry this morning but because we were both dealing with Mrs Green's death it didn't seem the right time to argue about his charcoal drawing.

'What happened to it?' Josephine asks.

I look blankly then remember that she is asking about *Betrayer*.

'It's hanging on a wall in Spain.'

'Is it for sale?'

'No.' I look at the Virgin tattooed on my finger.

'Are there no women in the painting?'

'No.'

'Why not paint the Madonna?'

'I never paint her. She is like my mother. Beyond my grasp of comprehension.'

'Your mother?'

I nod. 'She was an unusual woman.'

'Don't you miss her– even a little?'

'I wish I could remember her kindness.'

'I'm sorry.'

'It's not your fault.' Silence stretches between us like a taught tightrope. 'Were you close to your mother?'

She brightens pleased I want to know about her past. 'My parents were very poor. They were humble farmers and they both worked hard to support me. My father died when I was in New York but my mother still encouraged me to come to Europe.'

'Does she – is she…'

'Still alive? She's almost ninety. She moved to Florida ten years ago and developed a new lease of life,' she laughs.

'Do you visit her?'

'Not for a year or so but I will soon. Once I'm well enough to travel long haul. Did you know your neighbour well?' she asks, changing the subject.

'I think so. She had terrible arthritis and didn't go out much. She liked company and she took a great interest in art.'

Why do I imagine Mrs Green would be like Josephine's mother?

I shake my head to rid myself of the confusing images and wish that Javier would walk through the door.

'And she liked opera music,' she adds.

'Didn't I read somewhere that you once saw Vermeer's *The Concert* in an apartment somewhere?'

She closes a book decisively and walks toward the breakfast bar where I am standing. 'Yes, in Munich. Why?' She picks up the chilled glass of wine.

'Obviously not the original,' I probe.

'It was an excellent copy. The man I was visiting – a German called Dieter Guzman – told me it was a forgery but I would never have known. This is a charming apartment and so close to the river…may I have a look around? What a lovely little patio.'

It wasn't the original.

'What about the story in the newspapers about the Romanian who–'

'Written by Karl Blakey? I wouldn't believe a word.'

She wanders around the apartment trailing a finger across the furniture

'Checking for dust?' I ask. 'I'm untidy. I'm not house proud.'

She smiles and takes a step toward the corridor – toward my bedroom. 'Can I look down here?' She walks with confidence and her heels click on the wooden floor. She opens the door to Javier's room. It is tidy and she stands in the doorway as if memorising every detail.

My room by comparison is untidy. Drawers lay open, clothes have been tossed on the floor and the duvet lies in a heap on the double bed. I am conscious of the Vermeer hiding in my wardrobe.

She utters a small cry. 'My goodness – he paints at home too.'

'These are not Javier's – they're mine.'

Her eyes travel quickly over old prints and frames that I brought at the markets. The easel is covered with a discarded sheet.

'But you said that you don't paint. Is this a water colour?' She moves the sheet to one side and regards the painting.

The front door bell buzzes. We both stare at each other. I don't want to leave her alone with my painting.

'There's someone at the door,' she says unnecessarily when it rings for the second time.

'That will be Javier. He's forgotten his key again.'

I wait for her to leave the room but she seems intent on staying so I move away and when I open the front door Annie is standing on the step and the white van is gone.

'I wanted to speak to you – just in case I don't get chance to at the funeral.'

'When is it?'

'Not sure yet – maybe a week – ten days.'

'What are you doing with Mrs Green's furniture?' I ask.

'Roy is selling some things. He's taking them to an auction. We're moving back to Newcastle.' She stands just inside the door and faces me. 'But the thing is – I found out Roy wasn't in Poland or Slovenia when Gran died. He was here in London. I found his flight ticket in his pocket. I think he killed her, Mikky.'

'What?'

'I think he came to the house that morning and killed her.'

'But we found her…'

'I know but think about it. You went to the corner

shop, didn't you? Remember? To buy doughnuts and you thought you saw his car.'

'I did but–'

'He must have come back and killed her.'

'But how? Why?'

'He suffocated her – with a cushion – don't you understand. He owes so much money. He's a gambler, Mikky. He wanted her money all along. He only moved in because he was going to inherit everything. He never loved her. He hated her. He's even hidden the Vermeer that's supposed to go to a man in Bruges.'

Hidden the Vermeer? He hasn't noticed I have swapped it.

'There's a terrible draught with the door open.' Josephine's voice cuts across the lounge and we both turn around.

'I must go and collect Max,' Annie whispers, ignoring Josephine. She has one foot outside the door as she adds. 'I'm worried, Mikky. I'm really frightened of him.'

It is only after she is running down the path toward the nursery and I am closing the door behind her that I realise Annie has a bruise around her swollen left eye that she has tried to conceal with thick makeup.

***

'You left me with her all afternoon,' I complain to Javier after Josephine leaves in a black cab. It's after seven o'clock and I'm tired. I put my feet on the coffee table and yawn. 'You have no idea how difficult she is. All she wants to do is talk about you. She even wanted to see where you slept. She made some pretence of wanting to look around. That woman is seriously creepy.'

'And you are so intolerant,' he replies. He smiles at me, which only increases my irritation. He sits beside me and crosses his legs nursing a glass of Pinot Grigio.

'Why did you insist that I go to that bloody opera?'

'You need educating.'

'I don't want to go.'

'You'll love it,' he replies. 'Glorietta Bareldo will be amazing and besides Andreas is also coming so we will all be together – one big happy family.'

'Yippee dooh dah – I should have gone to South America with Oscar – I could have been his secretary.'

He laughs.

'How do those two women become best friends after sleeping with the same man, anyway?' I ask.

'They've a lot in common.'

'You're impossible, Javier and this is a nightmare. Can you hurry up and paint her bloody portrait and we can go back to normal?' But as I say this I realise nothing will be normal again. There is no going back. Mrs Green is dead. The painting is in my room and everything has changed.

'Annie was hysterical when I saw her and she had a bruise on her face. She seems to think that Roy killed his mother to get his inheritance.'

Javier looks at me with interest. 'Really? What about the painting?'

'He's giving it to a man in Bruges. Mrs Green left it in her Will.' And to change the subject I tell him what Annie told me. 'Roy was in England, that's how he came home so quickly yesterday. She found his flight ticket. She thinks he came to the house while she was painting and he suffocated his mother with a cushion.'

'And you think you saw his car?'

'I did but I also thought I saw you. I went running down the tow path thinking it was you.'

Javier looks at me. 'It's beginning to make sense then.'

'What is?'

He leans forward and pours wine into our glasses. I am beginning to feel light-headed but I drink it anyway.

'You will never guess who I spoke to?'

'Who?'

'Karl Blakey.'

'What? Are you nuts?' I sit up straighter.

'I had to.'

'Why? Josephine has an injunction against him to stay away from her and if she finds out that you have spoken to him she will be furious and will probably even cancel the commission.'

'Karl won't say anything. He's promised me. Besides I'll be finished Josephine's portrait in a few months then I can do what I like and speak to who I want.'

'And you believe him? You trust Karl Blakey?'

'He's a really nice guy. He's intelligent, articulate and interesting. He's a professional. He's an investigative journalist and I like him.'

I stare at Javier. 'You spent the afternoon with him, didn't you? That's why you were late back. Did you have lunch with him?'

'Mikky, I–'

'Tell me the truth, Javier. Is that where you were? With him?'

'He's different. He's special. He understands, Mikky. It's like…it's as if he knows me–'

'He's gutter-press Javier. He digs for dirt then writes trash to ruin people.'

'I thought he was awful but he's really nice. We have a lot in common and he's interesting. It's his job to investigate.'

'I can't believe you've met him again.'

'He wants to raise my profile – he can introduce me to–'

'How can you be so naive?'

'He's working with Alexandru Negrescu and if *he* trusts him, then–'

'He's Romanian Mafia, Javier. He's probably paying Karl big money to dig around for information. How can you be such an idiot? What have you told him? Poor Josephine, I thought she was your idol.'

'She is. The Romanian is only interested in the painting. He told me they want to find the Vermeer that was hanging in the apartment in Munich–'

'How can you be so stupid, Javier? They want it to sell for drugs or to finance prostitution. Besides the painting in Munich is a different one to Mrs Green's. She has had this one for two years. If there are two paintings, and the one next door isn't the original Vermeer then the one in Munich must be. You're looking in the wrong place if you keep thinking Mrs Green has it. You mustn't get involved, Javier. They're all crooks.'

'They want to know about the painting Josephine saw in Munich. They think it has turned up in Eastern

Europe but Christie's don't seem to think it could be the original.'

'Then they are both fakes, Javier. It's simple. The original is lost – gone to Eastern Europe or China or further afield – forever. It's not hanging next door.'

'I'm just curious. I never saw it. It seems a coincidence that Mrs Green has the same painting – even Karl said so.'

'Oh no, Javier! Don't tell me that you told Karl Blakey about Mrs Green's painting?'

His olive cheeks flush and he looks down into his glass. 'It wasn't a secret – was it?'

'You have told him, haven't you?' I stand and walk to the kitchen and flick the switch for the kettle.

'We were just talking,' he says. 'It was conversation about art, nothing else. Karl cares–'

'Cares about what? Himself?'

'He knows about art. He's knowledgeable about these things. Besides he knew about the other copy. He told me that Roy is trying to sell his mother's painting.'

'He knows Roy is our neighbour?'

'Well…'

'You told him that too?'

'He knows that Roy is trying to sell a painting – he heard about it–'

'Mrs Green only died yesterday,' I say. 'How can he be trying to sell it?'

'Annie lied to you about him sending it to Bruges or he lied to Annie.' Javier stares at me and I glare back at him.

'But this must have all happened this morning,' I say.

'It did – I was with Karl when the dealer phoned

to tell him about Roy and the painting. It seemed an amazing coincidence. But Karl knows everyone.'

'How could you speak to Karl about all this? Where is your loyalty to Josephine? I thought you wanted to be recognised for you own art work and now Karl is dragging you into this murky world of stolen paintings and trying to cause trouble.'

I reach for a coffee mug and slam it onto the counter and heap in a spoonful of coffee. It was going to be a long night. The net is closing in.

Javier stands up and leans across the breakfast bar. 'I know you're angry, Mikky. But Mrs Green isn't here now and Roy shouldn't have that painting. We need to get it from him and get it valued. Now, we're both tired. I'm going to bed and I'll talk to you some other time when you are not so emotional—'

'Emotional? Me? Listen to me, Javier – I went to Dresden because you begged me to go with you. I have supported you and your career. I have avoided Karl Blakey twice to be loyal to you and to make sure your career isn't damaged. I have even spent hours with Josephine Lavelle – all for you. And now you turn around and tell me you have not only spoken to Karl Blakey but that you actually like him. I'm furious with you, Javier. Go to bed! And you can go to the opera on your own next week because I'm not going with you. I've had enough. She is your muse not mine.'

I place the milk in the fridge and slam the door.

Javier doesn't say goodnight. He leaves the room silently leaving me to switch off the lights and put the fireguard across the dying embers. Twenty minutes later as I walk down the hallway I hear Javier murmuring into his mobile. I close my bedroom door but instead of going to sleep I illuminate the room professionally. I must finish my work and when it is dry I will be the first person in the post office queue.

Chapter Seven

'Have no fear of perfection, you'll never reach it.'
Salvador Dali

During the next week I hardly see Javier. He is busy with Josephine and I am working on Sandra Jupiter's exhibition. It is only when Annie slips a note through the letterbox with the funeral details that Javier insists he will come with me.

Inside the church of St Nicholas there's a tall archway leading to the west tower and a stone altar below the east window. My body is shaking inside my skin, rattling like a skeleton in an empty cupboard, and our footsteps echo as we walk down the aisle.

'There are only a dozen people here,' I whisper to Javier as we slide into our pew. 'There's no recognition of her life, her loves, her achievements or her personality just that brown box.' I shiver and nod toward the altar.

'Most of her contemporaries and friends are probably dead,' he whispers.

I stare ahead. 'It looks too small for her. It's like a child's box.'

Roy and Annie sit slightly apart in the front pew. Behind them is a chubby man in a dark suit and with him an older man with grey hair who regularly checks the Rolex on his wrist.

'Lawyers,' Javier murmurs.

Behind them Aaron and his wife sit with their heads bowed. Only their son Salman, turns and he smiles at us and I wonder who is looking after their corner shop this morning.

On the other side of the aisle five old people are spread out among the pews. They appear to be lost in memories or was it grief? Did they know her? One old man coughs and blows his nose. He looks gaunt and ill – one more cough and it could be his last.

I sit and stare at the stained glass and think of Jesus dying on the Cross – for all our sins – and I am filled with a sense of melancholy and déjà vu.

Mrs Green had been like my own grandma. I miss her sparkly blue eyes and her inquisitive train of thought. I wish I had done more to protect her. I should never have left her with Roy and Annie. I should have looked out for her.

Had Roy really killed his own mother?

Javier squeezes my finger. He doesn't let go and I am comforted by the reassuring warm grip of his hand.

Was he walking along the riverbank that morning?

I wish I could stop shaking. I am remembering another funeral seventeen years ago in another church, another country, at another time. Then I had kept my eyes firmly on a life-sized figure of Christ carved onto a wooden cross behind the modern altar. It hung against natural stone and was illuminated from dormer windows in the roof. I had concentrated and I had prayed. Never believing for one minute that Mama was in the small coffin only two feet away – she was too tall to fit inside. Not even the strong grip of Papa's trembling hand could make me look up from the floor but when I did, all I saw were his swollen eyes and tears cascading silently down his stubble cheeks.

Roy stands up. He is slim and handsome in his dark suit and his hair and beard are neatly trimmed. He was so different to the intoxicated and angry man that had forced his way into my apartment.

The balding and bespectacled vicar moves aside as Roy takes his place at the lectern. He coughs and stares around at the small audience but without focusing on us.

'Adeline Green was a kind and loving mother and a thoughtful and fun-loving grandmother.'

Adeline? How pretty! Why had I never known her name?

'Ecclesiastes 3, verses 1 to 4.' He clears his throat and reads from the scriptures. His voice is melodious and strong. 'For everything there is a season and a time for every matter under the heaven.'

I will not look at her coffin instead I think of her sparkling eyes and her delight when she saw me. I think of her eagerness to chat, her persistent optimism and how she pressed her door key into my hand – 'just in case,' she had said.

'A time to weep and a time to laugh. A time to mourn and a time to rejoice.'

I hear the tinkle of her laughter and remember the way her eyes crinkled when she ate biscuits always pushing crumbs into the corner of her mouth and dropping most of them in her lap. She had been happy to be reunited with Roy. She had company. She was willing to change. She had stored her things in the attic and they had taken over her home.

'A time to forgive and a time to be forgiven.'

Someone behind me coughs, hairs prickle on my neck and I turn my head.

On the other side of the aisle Karl Blakey sits two rows behind us. His expression is downcast as if he knew the dead woman.

Who told him when the funeral would be?

I glance at Javier but he remains focused on Roy.

When Karl sees me staring at him he winks and I want to drag him by the collar away from Mrs Green and away from us all. I want to reach out and thump him.

'A time to hurt and a time to heal,' Roy reads.

Javier notices Karl and I see a conspiratorial smile pass between them and so I pull my hand from his grip. I will have to be more careful with my emotions. I must not under estimate the headiness of fame or the desire for opportunity that he will pursue at the expense of others. I am on my own as I have always been.

***

The following night we attend a pre drinks reception at the Royal Opera House in Covent Garden. Glorietta and Josephine are regal divas casting a warm glow over handsome couples, men in dinner suits with manicured fingers and women with designer dresses and matching handbags who fill the room with tinkles of laughter. They are people whose names I barely hear and have already forgotten when greeted with air kisses and fake smiles. It makes me think of Josephine. I'm like her acting a part and tonight is my debut performance at the opera as I smile and air kiss in return.

Andreas is broad shouldered and handsome in a white dinner jacket so I smile and flirt with him taking refuge in the company one of the few people I know.

'London life suits you Andreas,' I say. 'You look very happy and debonair.'

He nods curtly. 'I wouldn't recognise you, Mikky.'

'What? In this old thing?' I laugh and tug on my expensive black dress but the joke is lost on him.

'Nice aftershave, *Hugo Boss?*' I ask, frightened he may wander off.

'*Bulgari.*'

'It suits you.'

He glances over his shoulder and moves closer to whisper in my ear. 'How are things with Josephine? Are you getting on any better?' His voice is warm and deep and I imagine him singing Meat Loaf, *Bat Out of Hell*.

I hold out my hand and undulate my palm. 'So-so. I think she needs educating. I might take her to a rock concert.'

'It would mean a lot to her.'

We both smile.

Josephine's hair is cut in a fashionable bob and makeup hides the pain and grief normally etched around her eyes. She wears a pearl grey dress and carries a red shawl across her shoulder. Diamond earrings match a gold musical clef brooch on her chest and she weaves her way effortlessly through the small groups until it is time for us to be seated.

As she steps into the box she is greeted to a standing ovation. She stands in the spotlight, raises her hand and smiles graciously. Tonight, momentarily, she is a star again.

Beside me Bruno, Glorietta's Italian boyfriend, seems to find amusement in everything around him including admiring glances from women of all ages. His arrogance is refined and filled with confident humour. When he sees the tattoo on my forearm he says. 'Is that you screaming at the opera?

'Yes – to get out.'

He laughs and when he turns away I poke my tongue playfully out at Javier. I am still angry with him but he has promised not speak to Karl Blakey again until after he has finished Josephine's portrait.

Andreas guides me to the front of the box to sit beside Josephine. Her eyes shine when she sees me. 'That was very special,' she says.

'They clearly remember and adore you,' I reply.

'Indeed.' She gazes around the theatre lost in thought absorbing details of the scene below us.

I sit back and Bruno refills our glasses with a seemingly endless supply of champagne. I relish the fresh fruitiness on my tongue and wish I could have brought my camera. I could snap images of the audience looking at the stage, so many varied expressions, so many faces and so many poses.

Norma – I hold a glossy programme in my hand.

A sudden butterfly quiver wells up inside my stomach. It takes me by surprise and I breathe in quickly. Surreptitiously, I cast a quick glance at Josephine. Is this what she feels – this sense of nervous anticipation?

I cannot take my eyes from her face. She is caught up in rapture, lost somewhere in the past and I see a tremor of excitement ripple through her slight frame. She pulls her shawl closer to her throat, squares her shoulders and blinks away a tear from the corner of her eye. She must have memories, flashbacks and images of her past life and they have returned to haunt her this evening. The smell of grease paint and the lights on the stage must be like old friends but she will never perform with them again. She grips the rail closing her eyes inhaling deeply. I want to reach out and touch her hand but then she turns and our eyes meet and I am drawn in to the intensity of her black irises and her hypnotic gaze, broken only when the orchestra appear and begin tuning their instruments. Only then the spell is broken and she blinks and turns away. Behind us Andreas, Bruno and Javier share a joke.

A surge of expectancy tingles through my body, my chest tightens and I straighten my back listening to strings, wind instruments and drums fine–tuning and getting comfortable.

The audience's faces are eager with anticipation, flashes of glossy lipstick, cufflinks and expensive jewellery. Hushed tones, gentle coughs and the tinkle of laughter carry upwards toward our box and I wish I could capture it all on camera.

Karl Blakey is sitting in the front row with the Romania and his two daughters and as the lights dim he stares up at me. Javier squeezes my shoulder but Josephine's gaze remains firmly fixed on the stage so I breathe deeply and settle back into my seat just as the opening Act begins.

Tonight belongs to Glorietta Bareldo the opera star who replaced Josephine Lavelle as one of the greatest sopranos in the world. Bellini's melodies, the drama of the opera and Glorietta's intense performance of *Norma* portrays strong passion and at the end, after the battle and huge sacrifice, I sit transfixed. I cannot take my eyes from her when she sings *Casta diva* and it's as if the whole audience has collectively stopped breathing. The auditorium is alive with her voice. Nothing else matters and I am caught in the sheer beauty and emotion of her tone and timbre. It is magical, beautiful and bewitching.

Josephine rises to her feet applauding with rapturous enthusiasm. The audience join in for a standing ovation and cries of 'bravo,' and 'more' fill the auditorium. The noise is deafening. Glorietta is called again and again for over fifteen curtain calls and when Josephine turns to me her eyes are filled with tears. She grips my hand and for a fleeting moment I am proud to be associated with these strong and talented women and I brush away a tear that slides down my cheek.

Afterwards we make our way to a small Italian restaurant where a table has been reserved for our small party. A little later when Glorietta and Bruno join us, diners stand and applaud as she weaves her way gracefully to our table. She takes Josephine's elbow and lifts her gently to her feet and the crowd cheer with more enthusiasm and excitement as the two divas stand side by side, smiling – best friends. Mobile phones are held high and snapshots and video clips are taken.

'They'll probably appear on the Internet later this evening,' Andreas whispers.

'I had never realised that they were so famous or so popular,' I whisper back.

He beams at me. 'This is truly a special moment.'

Glorietta is filled with adrenaline and energetic rays of magical light seem to radiate from her eyes. She is both charming and gracious as she regales us with amusing and entertaining stories about life back stage, catastrophes and rehearsals that don't go to plan as well as anecdotes of stage and crew.

She involves Josephine in her tales and they reminisce, talking of productions, conductors and venues around the world and Josephine comes alive. It is like she is transported to the opera star she once was; animated, passionate and entertaining and her laughter is happy and warm.

Like me Andreas is happy to take a backseat out of the limelight. We are listeners. Occasionally his eyes linger on me gauging my reaction but I won't meet his gaze, instead I focus on Bruno and Javier and when Glorietta joins their conversation Bruno sighs theatrically and calls across the table.

'This is your life Andreas – your future.' He is helping himself to a slice of Carpaccio. 'This is how you will spend you evenings when you are a famous Tenor – in the company of excited, babbling women.' Bruno's good humour and laughter is contagious.

'Babbling?' Glorietta says turning her lips down at the corner to look sad and serious like a clown. 'I think you mean entertaining, my darling.'

'But it's true, Andreas,' Josephine says, 'you will soon be performing on stage with Glorietta – I am convinced of it.'

He blushes so I wink at him and drain my glass.

Since Javier began painting Josephine he has become more serious and introverted. It happens each time he is with a new model. His concentration is so focused and intense. He remains partly in another world and I am pleased. It means he is concentrating on his career and enjoying his talent. But he fits easily into this group of people, smiling, nodding, saying the right thing and his manners are impeccable. But as the conversation flows amid plates of chicken, steak and pasta and chilled glasses of prosecco he is quiet and watchful.

Opera has opened my eyes to a style of music that I have never appreciated before. It seeped into me from the moment the orchestra began its first note and I was mesmerised by the range and tone of Glorietta's voice. Both on stage and off stage she has elegance, style and deportment that is at once intimidating and inspiring. It is a talent that I can now appreciate, one that comes with hours, days and months and years of hard work and dedication.

Bruno refills my glass but I watch Glorietta and Josephine. How hard it must be to reach the pinnacle of a career through professionalism and dedication that is so publicly endorsed. It is a life of endless endurance and hard work; both physically and mentally and I begin to understand the perseverance and energy that Josephine invested in her profession. I also understand how pressure and stress took its toll – even understanding why she took cocaine. To rise to the top of the opera world and then to lose it all and to be abandoned by the public must have been devastating – it would have been a tragedy.

Crash and burn.

'What are you thinking?' Gloriettta asks leaning across the table and addressing me.

'How different your life is to mine,' I answer.

'And what sort of photography do you do?'

'Mainly exhibition work for galleries and museums.'

'Perhaps you would like to photograph me?' she

says engaging me in conversation and I am surprise and embarrassed that I am the focus of her attention. But before I reply she asks. 'You were brought up in Spain – what a delightful country – do you miss it?'

'Yes.'

'But you will stay in London?'

'Perhaps not.'

'Do you know Italy?'

I shake my head. 'Not as well as I would like to.'

I don't mention Raffa. Now is not the time, nor the place. But he is in my heart and this is the common bond that links the three women at the table.

After coffee and liquors Glorietta and Bruno stand up to leave.

'Another party,' Bruno raises his eyes to the ceiling.

'But not a late night.' She rests her hand on my arm. 'We shall meet again, Mikky. I know we shall. Please come and stay with us in Italy. If your portrait turns out well then I might consider one myself.' Glorietta announces with an air kiss to Javier's cheeks.

'We need a new one for our new home in Gsstad,' Bruno adds shaking Javier's hand. 'The walls look empty without her picture hanging up.'

Then they sweep out of the restaurant leaving a trail of magical mystery dust in their wake and we are all in a hurry to leave before the glamour and afterglow of their presence fades completely.

I wait in the small foyer near the bar for Josephine to return from the ladies toilet. I'm glancing through the programme when Josephine appears smiling but a fan – a man – blocks her path and her face freezes. Her hand reaches to her throat. Her eyes are wide in fear.

'Josephine?' I call.

There is something familiar about him then I hear his voice. 'I know what you're hiding. I know about your secret, Josephine. There's no hiding from me.' Karl Blakey reaches out to her but I'm faster. I shove him away but his shoulder is hard and he stands resolute so I push myself between them and face him.

'Piss off! Leave her alone.'

He is stronger than I expect and he slaps my hand away and says to her. 'I know your secret, Josephine. You can't keep it to yourself for much longer– Arrhh.'

I grab him by the balls and push him back against the wall squeezing hard. He staggers and attempts to grab my hand but I karate chop hard with my free hand across his throat. 'Stay away from her you arsehole,' I hiss.

He chokes and doubles over clutching his crotch. I grab his hair and pull his head back, ignoring his moaning. 'Keep away from Ms Lavelle – or I'll call the police.' I spit then I smack his face with my elbow and watch him slump back against the wall and slide to the floor with blood streaming from his nose.

A waiter appears and sees Karl on the floor. 'Are you alright?'

'This fan got too excited,' I say taking Josephine's shaking arm and I guide gently out of the restaurant and into the street where Javier and Andreas are waiting beside the taxi.

They register the look on Josephine's white face.

'What happened?' Javier says.

I ignore him and settle Josephine into the back seat. 'Do you want me to come with you?'

She shakes her head. 'No – thank you.'

I stand aside to let Andreas sit beside her then I slam the door and watch it pull away into the busy street.

When the rear lights disappear around the corner I turn on Javier and push my finger into his shoulder. 'You'd better sort out Karl Blakey. He nearly gave her a heart attack in there – the man is a nutcase – he wants to cause trouble.' I don't wait for him to answer instead I turn and walk down the street without waiting for him to follow me.

I should go now. I should leave. The painting is mine. The funeral is over but I have the exhibition to finish then I can go. I must make things look normal and natural, perhaps even wait until Josephine has gone. But I will go soon. I will tell Javier that I need a change of scene and that England is too cold for me. I will say I am going on holiday then I will not come back and my new life will begin.

***

Glorietta Bareldo and Bruno are unable to attend the opening of Sandra Jupiter's Baroque Exhibition in the Kensington Museum but to my surprise and dismay Josephine Lavelle accepts with delight.

The exhibition is busier than I expected and Sandra Jupiter moves elegantly between groups; networking, socialising and smiling. When she meets Josephine she is in awe, gushing praise on her performance as *Carmen* that she saw years ago in the Royal Opera House. When they realised it was ten years ago they laugh self-consciously.

'It seems like yesterday,' Sandra says.

'Indeed.' Josephine returns her smile but it doesn't reach her eyes.

How many times does she have to go through this performance, I wonder? So I take Josephine's elbow and making excuses I lead her carefully away.

'Are you protecting me again?' she asks.

'Do you need protection?'

She doesn't answer but she leans against me and we walk arm in arm companionably around the gallery. She doesn't mention the incident with Karl Blakey two nights previously and we finally arrive in front of the Caravaggio.

'*The Cardsharps* – it's from a private collection and it is on loan for this exhibition,' I explain.

It measures thirty-seven by fifty-two inches and it shows a brutal low life scam – a sinister looking man, the boy who is duped and the cardsharp with an extra set of cards in his back pocket.

'The dagger makes it seem that violence isn't far away,' she replies.

I'm conscious of people in the gallery watching us as we discuss the painting and I grow in stature – being with Josephine makes me walk taller. She undoubtedly has an aura – a presence – a certain head turning effect on those around her.

'He's your favourite artist.' She remembers.

'And Raffa's,' I add.

'Indeed.'

'Do you have any of his paintings?'

'One or two, Glorietta kept most of them and his wife – of course. It turns out he never divorced her. He didn't want to upset his two children.'

'He was a bit of a playboy, wasn't he?'

'That was his attraction.'

We both smile.

'When are you returning home – to Dresden?' I ask, linking my arm though hers to continue our walk through the gallery.

'Dresden is not my home. I was staying there temporarily to mentor Andreas but it is time for him to move on. I have given him confidence and I have trained him as much as I can. Now he needs a teacher better than me and I have someone in mind for him – someone in New York.'

'That will be a big step.'

'Yes, but a necessary one, he must grow and develop. He is outgrowing me and this is his time to shine.'

'So where will you go? Where is home?'

She sighs. 'I don't know. I like it here.'

'London?'

'Don't sound so surprised.'

'I'm not – it's just that…'

'Well, now I am making new friends, it may make sense for me to stay here.' She squeezes my arm. 'And I've caught up with old friends and they have made me welcome. I have Javier – and you, if you will both let me into your life…'

Thankfully Javier, Andreas, the artist – Marcus Danning and Phyllis Laverty from the art gallery in South Moulton Street make a beeline for us and I make the introductions.

Marcus is bald. His head and neck are perspiring. His tight yellow jacket is fastened in the middle by a large gold button and a purple bowtie at his neck reminds me of a hangman's noose.

'I'm delighted to meet one of the greatest sopranos of our time,' he guffaws. 'You look beautiful, Ms Lavelle – all things considered.'

'I'm still alive,' Josephine remarks, shaking hands with him.

'I work with the Laverty Art Gallery. Phyllis is kind enough to employ me on occasions,' I explain to Josephine.

'You're the best,' Phyllis says. 'Although sometimes a little distracted by the beauty of the art but I always call on you first, in fact there's a job I need you to do, so call me soon.'

'I won't be able to take on any more work for a while.'

'Oh?'

'I'm going away…'

'Back to Spain?' ask Phyllis.

'Yes.'

And I don't know who is more surprised Josephine or Javier.

***

A few nights later Javier tells me Josephine has booked her flight. She has finished her sitting with him, she has seen Glorietta in *Norma* and there is no further reason for her to stay in London. It is late and we are at home drinking coffee and I am watching the dying embers in the hearth.

'I can't believe Annie painted over my mural. I wanted Josephine to see it.' It's the first time we have been alone for a week and I assume he has been sleeping at the studio working on the portrait. He looks tired and there are dark circles under his eyes.

'She did that the morning Mrs Green died. You'll have to do another one,' I suggest. 'When Oscar gets back – perhaps a London scene this time?'

'I want to invite her for dinner before she goes.'

'Can't we just go out?'

'She told me what happened in the restaurant with Karl. She seems genuinely upset. She has been talking about him all week. It's like she is obsessed. He has unsettled her and except for the Baroque Exhibition she hasn't been out at all.'

'Karl terrified her that night. He accused her of having a secret.'

He rests his head back against the sofa and closes his eyes.

'Do you know what it could be?' I ask.

'Karl said that Josephine saw several paintings in an apartment in Munich last August but they found the guy dead – who lived there – a few days later. And when the police got there, the paintings were gone. Karl seems to think she took them.'

'Josephine – an art thief? That's crazy,' I laugh.

Javier shrugs and looks at me. 'He thinks that she only handed over the Golden Icon because Raffaelle brought it to her back stage before her final performance. She had hidden it.'

'She wanted to give it back to the Italian people. Isn't that what you said?'

'Yes but Karl said that she wanted to keep it, but because she was shot and Raffaelle was killed, it's like the authorities have agreed to cover it up. Karl wanted to tell the truth but no one would print it.'

'So they made her out to be a hero when she was

really a thief? I don't believe it. She's not the type.'

'He's convinced. He's certain that she knows where the painting went to–'

'What sort of hold has Karl Blakey got over you, Javier? Why do you believe everything that scumbag says when Josephine quite clearly tells you another story.'

Javier looks away and will not meet my eye.

'Don't let fame go to your head,' I caution.

'It isn't.'

'He's not worth it.'

'I know.'

'You promised not to see him – and besides Josephine is your friend.'

'I do like her.'

'All right, invite her for dinner. You're making me feel sorry for her. She can't rely on anyone. Not even you, Javier. She told me over lunch that all the men in her life – all the men that she has ever met – have let her down and it would appear that you are no different, Javier. You should be ashamed of yourself.'

***

A few nights later Josephine arrives alone and in a taxi. She is dressed in navy slacks and a pink shirt. Her eyes are ringed with dark circles but she looks appreciatively around the room and the dining table with its red cloth, silver napkins and burning candles. The wine glasses have been polished and fluted champagne glasses are chilled. A dish of homemade guacamole and tacos are on the coffee table beside the fire and a warm glow fills the room.

'How delightful.' There is real warmth in her eyes and there is a hint of what she may have looked like as a young girl before the stresses of life ravaged her and the drudgery of fate subjected her to its hidden dark side.

'I hope Javier hasn't been tiring you out? He can be quite ruthless when it comes to his models,' I say.

'He has given me regular breaks. He has been very considerate but I can't pretend that I would like to sit for any longer.'

We drink prosecco and Sade's *Sweetest Taboo* melodically fills the room. Javier's choice – not mine.

He refills our glasses and wanders over to the kitchen leaving us to talk, encouraging us to bond and to make friends. It's the last effort I will have to make. This is the last time I will see her.

'A girl from our class at Uni, Carmen Muñoz, vowed never to sit for him again.'

'She was twitchy and nervous,' he responds in defence. 'She was a great artist but lousy model.'

'Three days in the same position, standing – Carmen wanted to sit down– and you didn't give here any breaks,' I tease.

'She was young and she moaned a lot,' he grins.

'And have you never modelled for Javier?' Josephine asks.

'You must be joking. He tells me that my nose is too long and my mouth is far too wide.'

'And you can't sit still either,' he adds.

'That's true. I do like to be active. Besides I'm not model material.'

Josephine stares at my baggy black *Nirvana* T–shirt, tight jeans and unruly hair and I can tell by her smile that it is something they both agree on.

The room is filled with spices and warmth; Thai green chicken curry, jasmine rice and Nan bread and I sit watching the flickering flames suppressing a yawn, determined to be polite.

Javier has betrayed her. He spoke to Karl Blakey. She deserves more. She deserves better. Just like Carmen did all those years ago.

'I hope you will come to Lake Como for the unveiling of my portrait in the summer,' Josephine says.

There is silence and when I look up I realise she is speaking to me.

'Delighted,' I reply. I have no intention of going to Italy. My plans are already made. I will be spending the summer in Spain and after that South America and travelling the world. Photography is my passion and one that takes time and money both of which I will have in abundance.

'I had the impression you were an opera convert when you saw Glorietta in her role of *Norma*. Perhaps I can invite you to the opera in Verona?'

'Don't get too carried away, Josephine. I was impressed with her but I'm not making a habit of it.' I smile to cover the harshness of my tone.

'She's a rock chick, Josephine and if you ever met her father you would understand why,' Javier calls out from the kitchen.

'Does he sing?' Josephine asks.

Javier walks round and refills our glasses. 'Her father's a hippy – the man's a biker. He's covered in tattoos and blasts heavy metal or rock music all day. He's got eight speakers running through his garage and he struts around playing air guitar. He's nuts.'

'He's not just nuts. Papa's an enigma.' I am savouring the tangy bubbles on my tongue.

'He has no morals or scruples, and he would sell his own mother for a joint – and I'm not talking about a Sunday roast,' Javier adds.

Josephine looks concerned and I am irked that Javier is speaking badly about Papa when he hardly mentions his own dysfunctional family.

'How did you manage as a child?' Josephine asks.

'It was the only thing I knew. I saw other kids at school and their parents were just different to mine. Some kids envied my life. It was unconventional but they saw it as exciting.'

'What about the rest of your family? Where are they? Didn't you have aunts, uncles or grandparents?'

'Papa was from a remote village in Asturias in the north of Spain and my mother's family lived on the west coast of Ireland.'

'Did she ever go back to Ireland?'

'Not that I remember.'

Javier calls us to the dinner table and Josephine sits between us.

'I was married once – to an Irish man,' she says unfolding her napkin and tucking it onto her lap. 'But we weren't together for long. He wanted me to stay at home and be a housewife–'

'I bet you never dreamed you would become such a big star,' Javier interrupts, taking a mouthful of curry.

'Never in my wildest dreams but it was hard work and I made many sacrifices…'

'Did you sing as a child?' I ask.

'My mother hated me singing. She had no

appreciation of music. In fact, I think she was quite deaf. She thought I was shrieking but she sent me to classes anyway. I left home at an early age to pursue my dream. I stayed with an Aunt in New York and went to various voice coaches and then I was offered a place with a group to tour Europe. I was only young, barely twenty…' She wipes her mouth with a napkin and continues. 'We went on tour to Ireland and I met a young man. I thought he was so charming. He had brought his parents to the opera to celebrate their wedding anniversary. I had only just left home… I was homesick and he was funny and handsome and he made me laugh.'

'What happened?' I lean across the table.

She pauses distracted by the tattoo of the Virgin on my finger.

'He pursued me. He wouldn't take no for an answer and when the tour ended, he insisted I returned to Ireland to stay with him. It was all heady romantic stuff. The tour had gone well and I was making a name for myself and we were married within three months.'

'Wow,' I say.

'I never knew you were married,' Javier says.

'I was Seán's wife for a few months but then I realised he wanted a trophy on his arm. He was a budding businessman and Ireland was changing. It was back in the eighties just before the Celtic Tiger and the boom in the economy. He started a construction business and he wanted me on his arm to make him look good but he didn't want me singing professionally–' She pauses, twisting the napkin around her index finger.

'How could he deny the world your voice?' Javier

butts in diplomatically.

She looks up. 'Ah, but I didn't sing at my peak then, that came afterward and with lots of practice. It was Seán's father, Michael who insisted that I sing. He encouraged me and paid for my tutoring. He saw my potential. He was my saviour.'

'That must have made his son happy,' quips Javier.

Josephine regards him silently before replying. 'His wife had just died – my mother-in-law – and Michael was very lonely. He was a Doctor and after she died he lost interest in just about everything. At first I was flattered that he took an interest in my singing and my career. But he wanted me to succeed. He believed in me.'

'That must have put a strain on your marriage?' I say.

'It wasn't an easy time and I paid a very heavy price. I was invited to an audition in London. My career was taking off then...I was... ill for a while–'

'And then you became famous,' Javier laughs.

'Who needs family? That's what I say,' I add.

'I think family is important,' she replies. 'Did your family encourage your passion for art?'

I think she is asking Javier but she is looking at me.

'Never–'

Javier interrupts me. 'My father remarried. They didn't think they would have more children then suddenly my twin brothers came along when I was nine and all the attention went on them. So I sat and painted...'

'Are you a close family?'

'My brothers are spoilt. I love them but we're not alike.'

'They don't even look similar,' I interject. 'They are fair not dark like Javier.'

'Are they artistic?'

'Not at all, one is studying chemistry and the other physics,' he replies.

'Do you think painting is an outpouring of your soul?' she asks.

'It's deeper than that, Josephine. It's my solace. My life. It is the only thing that is true to me.' Javier wipes his plate with the last of the Nan.

'Opera is art. I had the same passion for my art as you have for yours,' she says. 'I was the same with my music. It fulfilled me emotionally and took me where I could not be reached. I escaped via my music. I would lose the demons so I understand you.'

'What sacrifices did you make?' He is probing.

How can he be so two-faced? Is he encouraging her to open up so that he can find out her secret? Would he tell Karl Blakey?

The silence is deafening until eventually she says, 'I sacrificed the most important thing in my life.'

The air between them is palpable. I don't want her confiding in Javier. Let her keep her secret and return to Dresden in peace and I will go to my new life in Spain. Let us all go our separate ways without any confessions or emotions. Karl Blakey will have to look for another font as the source for his vital information and I am angry with Javier.

'What is it Josephine?' he asks softly.

I drop my fork loudly on the plate. 'More wine?' I ask.

'There is something…the most important thing I gave up…'

Javier leans forward, his eyes alert and an encouraging smile on his lips.

I hold up the palm of my hand. 'Come on, you wouldn't sacrifice a thing, Josephine,' I say.

She blinks and tilts her head. 'What do you mean? I–'

'You're a selfish prima donna. You clambered over everyone and everything to seek fame and money and glory – and you got it. I read your stories on the Internet. So don't start bellyaching now about all the sacrifices you made because it all sounds very hollow from where I'm sitting.'

Javier clenches his fist around his wine glass and frowns at me.

Josephine shakes her head, her eyes are filled with hurt and confusion but I stand up from the table regardless of their emotions. I don't want to know her secret and I certainly don't want her to tell Javier.

'Where are you going?' she asks.

'It's late and I'm going to bed. You are welcome to stay the night if you like. You can sleep with Javier for all I care. But if you want to climb into bed with me then think again. You're not my type and beside you are way too old for me.'

'Mikky!' Javier jumps to his feet.

'I've learned a lot Josephine and one thing I do know is that no one wants or does anything for nothing. People don't just come knocking on your door and ask you to paint their portrait. I think you're a bit weird and that's fine. Javier is good with weird but personally I can't be bothered–'

'Weird? Stop it! Please don't think that! There's something else. There's something far more important than all this. You're right! This opportunity has been…is …' She reaches out and grips my hand. 'Please,' she whispers, 'please listen to me. I need to tell you both something very important. Something I have never told anyone–'

The doorbell rings, shattering the tension between us. It is late and I glance at Javier. Then someone thumps on the front door.

'Who is it? It's almost midnight!' she asks.

'I don't know,' I reply.

Javier moves quickly but he barely has time to open the front door before it is pushed from his grasp. Roy propels his way inside and grabbing Javier's collar he shoves him up against the wall. His fist is raised in Javier's face.

Behind me Josephine gasps.

I grab the neck of the empty prosecco bottle and rush to the door. 'Get off him! Get off him now, unless you want this bottle in your face.'

'I want my painting,' he shouts.

His arm is across Javier's throat.

'Get out – now!' I shout.

'Where's my painting?' he hisses at Javier.

'He doesn't have your painting,' I shout.

'He stole it.' He pushes on arm against Javier's windpipe. 'He's swapped it with some crap that isn't mine. Where is it? I'm going to kill you, unless you tell me…'

'You have two seconds to let him go.' I move forward threateningly, holding the bottle inches from his face. 'I'll kill you first,' I say through clenched teeth.

Behind me Josephine says, 'I have taken your picture on my mobile and I'm calling the police. They can see who you are and what you are doing. I will video it all.'

I follow Roy's gaze. She holds the phone to her ear and begins speaking calmly. 'Police, please – I want to report an intruder. Now, yes, he's armed. I have his photograph…'

When I turn back Roy has gone and Javier is bent over leaning against the wall and choking with relief.

***

In the daily newspaper the following day there is a double page spread written by Karl Blakey with the heading, *Vermeer's Secret – No Longer*. After Roy's visit last night and now this I am frightened that if I leave the country – the finger could be pointed at me. I must be patient. There is no evidence and no proof. I phone the newspaper to get Karl's mobile number.

'This is a pleasant surprise,' he says, by way of greeting two minutes later.

'Cut the crap. I want to speak to you.'

'It's about time.'

'Meet me in Chiswick Park at the coffee shop in an hour and don't be late.'

When I see him the rain-splattered glass is between us. He sits with his shoulders hunched and his hands clasped around a mug of tea. I brush the rain from my jacket and scowl at the women with two prams and a screaming toddler.

He stands up when he sees me. 'Would you like a

coffee, tea – breakfast?'

'Just an espresso,' I reply.

He returns with my coffee and slides into the seat opposite me. 'I'm pleased you want to talk to me about Josephine? She's a thief.'

'She's not a thief but you are a liar.'

'Why do you think that?'

'How else do you explain that article you wrote. I want to know how you got the information. How could you write these lies?'

'It's what I do for a living…' He gazes out of the window. His features are small, and his pointed nose and pink eyes are like a wary rodent's. 'Besides, it's all true.'

I pull the newspaper from my bag and place it on the table between us. 'How do you know Roy Green?' I ask.

'Roy's first wife – Ella Steinberg – was German and five years after they married she committed suicide.' He surveys the café then levels his gaze at me and waits.

'You say in here that Mrs Green was an art collector who sold her expansive art collection to pay her sons gambling debts. You then go on to describe Roy's sleazy past, his gambling addiction and his relationships with numerous prostitutes. I would expect nothing less of you – and true to form – you don't hold back. You also state that he owns the original; Vermeer's *The Concert.*'

'He does.'

'Impossible.'

He shrugs. 'His mother's dead. Roy is the inheritor and he's trying to sell it. He's made no secret of it.'

'It's a fake.'

'I don't think so,' he says.

I stare at him. 'It was a stolen painting. The whole world knows it was taken from the Isabella Garner Museum in Boston. They would pay a considerable sum to have it returned…'

'Roy isn't interested in returning it to the museum. He wants to sell it to a collector. That's how I know about it.'

'If it was the original, it would be impossible to sell legally.'

'His intention is to sell it on the black-market to an Eastern European.'

'He would have to settle for a small percentage of its value, probably less than the museum would pay to have it returned.'

'The Eastern Europeans will pay more on the black market than anyone, even more than the Isabella Stewart Museum – just to own it and to have it in their country.'

'But getting back to your article.' I stab the paper with my finger. 'You're suggesting here that Roy has sold it to Alexandru Negrescu's business rival, a man called Petre Ardeleanu. It says here he's a wealthy Romanian and a philanthropist with interests in gas, petroleum and coal,' I read aloud.

'Roy agreed to the sale but the original painting has gone missing.'

'Missing? You didn't say that in the article.'

'I only found out last night. Roy was dealing with them both – a dangerous game – playing one off against the other. Now he can't produce the original painting and Petre is accusing Alexandru of doing a deal behind his back. Each of them believe that the other has bought it and that Roy has led them on a goose chase and they are not happy.'

'What will they do?'

'Something not very nice to him – but why are you so interested?'

'Because Mrs Green was my friend.'

'And?'

'Nothing! I liked her. She told me she had left the painting to a friend of hers in Bruges.'

He frowns. I don't know if this is news to him but I am hoping it will push him in another direction. Karl sips his coffee. 'It's life and death – not just money – Roy needs to get the original painting back urgently. I wouldn't want to be in his shoes.'

'How is this article going to help him?'

'It won't. It's not meant to'

'You are despicable.'

'That's my job, Mikky. I find out the truth.'

'You have no regard for anyone. You are a seedy, low-life–'

'I've been called worse.'

'And now you have made Javier, your friend – and that does worry me.'

'We have become very close,' he smiles smugly. 'Javier enjoys fame. He likes to be recognised and invited to nice places. He also has expensive tastes.'

'Stay away from him.'

'He is easy to buy. He likes a good time and he has no loyalty–'

I throw my untouched, lukewarm coffee into his face and walk out accompanied by the screams and tantrums of the toddler and its shushing mother.

***

The next morning I am photographing landscapes for a new exhibition for an art gallery in New Bond Street and I am lost in thought. If only things were simple. Why didn't Roy give the painting to the art dealer in Bruges as Mrs Green wanted him to do?

My mobile phone rings and I answer it distractedly.

Annie's voice is tense and she whispers. 'Roy is going ballistic. The painting's been stolen. He said someone has swapped it. He was going to sell it and the men who were going to buy it are very angry with him–'

There is no point in me lying. 'He came around to my flat on Saturday night and threatened, Javier. He accused him of stealing it and replacing it with a fake.'

'Oh my God. Did Javier steal it?'

'Of course not.'

'Roy is so angry.'

'I thought Mrs Green left the painting to a friend of hers in Belgium?'

'She did. But that Will was two years ago. She was changing it when she died. She wanted Roy to keep the painting. It was a good fake and I think he was trying to pass it off as the real thing. But now it's not the same painting that Mrs Green had in her bedroom.'

'Really?'

'Her friend in Bruges is furious. He's an art dealer. He wants to take Roy to court – he's threatening all sorts of things. He's the one who said it wasn't the same painting. That's how Roy found out someone had switched the paintings.'

'But it must be the same painting,' I protest.

'It's not. Don't you understand, Mikky? This means someone thought that the painting Mrs Green had hanging in her bedroom was the original. They stole it and replaced it with another one. That's why Roy suspects Javier.'

'But Javier wouldn't do that.'

'Who could have done it then?'

'It could be anyone in the art world. Was there anyone else who knew about the painting?' I need to deflect her attention from Javier.

'She didn't know many people but Roy is determined to find out – the art dealer is furious. It was a secret—'

'Why was Roy in London when Mrs Green died? You thought he was abroad?'

'I don't know. I'm sure he killed Gran but I have no evidence.'

'There was no sign of a struggle. We saw her remember?'

'He suffocated her with a cushion. I found it on the floor.'

'That would have come out in the autopsy,' I reply.

'Maybe they got it wrong? I had no idea she was really rich. I'm going to confront him. I know he did it. He killed her. I'm going to record our conversation and then present the evidence to the police.'

'That will be dangerous, Annie. He's violent—'

'We're moving. The removal men are here. They're packing everything. He's pushing me to my limit. He's crazy, Josephine. He's like a mad man. I can't live like this. I can't live with him. I–' She can barely catch her breath. Her words are lost in tears and choked emotion.

I push the phone against my ear. 'Annie? I can't hear you…'

My mobile goes static.

'I can't go on...Kill me – if Roy…I–'

'Annie?' I shout.

The telephone goes dead in my hand.

Chapter Eight

'I never paint dreams or nightmares. I paint my own reality.'
Frida Kahlo

That evening I work late with Sarah Wozniak an art gallery owner on the King's Road. It's the last project that I have booked and my last commitment before I pretend I am taking a holiday – never to return.

It's dark and almost eight o'clock when I am walking home from Kew station. Mrs Green's death, Josephine Lavelle's intrusion, Karl Blakey's maliciousness and finally Annie's frantic phone call yesterday have all left me exhausted. The thought of a glass of red wine in the bath and dinner cooked by Javier spurs me on. He texted me earlier promising my favourite seafood paella and as I skipped lunch, my stomach rumbles. I can already taste the succulent squid, the saffron rice and juicy mussels.

Outside my flat a black cab is waiting with the engine running and I wonder if Oscar is back from South America. Mrs Green's house looks dark and naked as if the curtains have been taken down and as I fumble for my key the cab door opens.

'Mikky?' Josephine dismisses the taxi driver with a wave and Andreas follows her up to the front door wheeling two small suitcases.

'Josephine?' My mouth hangs open.

'May we come in?'

'I thought you'd left – gone back to Dresden.'

'I was on my way to the airport but I couldn't

leave without seeing you again. I want to speak to you. It's important.'

I stare at her, lost for words wondering what could be so urgent.

'May we come in?'

'I'm sorry about Saturday night but it's all right. There's no problem. Javier and I can look after ourselves.'

'Please,' she says and I see determination in her eyes.

Over her shoulder Andreas stands like an armed guard, his face impassive, so I sigh and open the front door.

'You'd better come in.'

The kitchen light is on but there is no smell of dinner and certainly no paella.

'Javier?' I call out.

'I need to speak to you both,' she says. 'Is he here? I rang the bell a few times…'

I dump my bag on the floor and flick on the lamps. 'He texted me over an hour ago to say he was home. That's strange…'

'Did you see the newspaper article that Karl Blakey wrote? I'm worried about your neighbour thinking you stole that painting. Did you say it was a Vermeer, Mikky?'

'Yes but it's a fake. We told you on Saturday. Javier hasn't taken it.'

'And you? Did you steal it?'

'Me? Why? Why would–'

'I need to know – it's important. I must stop history repeating itself.'

'What history?'

Andreas hovers by the front door with their bags at his feet. He seems embarrassed and unsure what to do.

'Tell me the truth,' she insists.

'This is ridiculous,' I reply.

Perhaps she's ill and the strain of the last few months is too much for her. She looks feverish and nervous but I leave her pacing the room and head down the hallway calling: 'Javier?'

His bedroom is empty. The bathroom is empty.

'Javier?'

He's not in the flat. I return to the living room wondering how to get rid of this infuriating woman but she is standing beside the breakfast bar holding a scrawled note in Javier's handwriting.

I'm next door with Annie.

I check my watch. 'I didn't see any lights on, did you? She said, the removal men were here...' I mumble.

Josephine shakes her head. She is pale and her eyes are bloodshot as if she hasn't slept. She leans against the breakfast bar as if she needs support and I wonder if she is well.

'I don't want you to miss your flight,' I say to them.

'I'll get another one. This is important. Where's Javier? I must see him.'

'Wait here. I'll go and check next door.'

'Is there something wrong?' she asks.

'I'm not sure,' I answer but my heart is hammering and my mouth has dried up. 'I won't be long. Make a coffee or pour a drink.'

The street is bathed in yellow light but Mrs

Green's house is in darkness and looks empty. The windows are black and bare. Then I think I see a flicker of a shadow or is it a torch upstairs in the front bedroom?

In seconds I am over the wall and at the front door. I pause wondering if I should ring the bell but I'm surprised to find the door ajar so I push it open.

Inside, the hallway is silent and in darkness, I take a step forward and cross the thresh-hold. There's a chill in the empty house and I shiver. Walking home I was weary but now my body is wired; taught and tense and I grasp my mobile reassuringly.

The sound of scraping comes from upstairs like something being dragged over floorboards so I take a step forward to listen. The lounge is empty. Mrs Green's belongings are packed and gone. The leather sofa and the family photographs are all gone. The grandfather clock no long ticks whirls or chimes in the hall and even the heavy damask curtains have been removed.

A thud from upstairs startles me. My heart rate increases and I tremble as I did when I was left alone in the caravan as a child so I breathe slowly. I know fear.

As a precaution I tilt my mobile to the streetlight from the window and dial the emergency services number. Now I only have to press the green button and I will be connected immediately. I'm not going to take unnecessary risks. I pause at the foot of the stairs and concentrate on my breathing hoping it will calm the irregular beating of my thumping heart.

The house is silent as if the soul has gone, leaving bare walls and hollow floorboards.

I'm about to call out but murmuring voices caution me then a man groans.

Roy? Javier? Where is Annie?

I tiptoe upstairs and peer around the banister and I am reminded of the night I crept in and stole the Vermeer but this time, in the large bedroom at the back of the house, footsteps echo on the wooden boards as someone paces backwards and forwards. A dim light casts strange disproportionate shadows on the wall like an illusionists trick so I take another cautionary step forward. Inside the bedroom Annie is leaning against the wall. I open my mouth to call out but then she turns away and her hair is tangled and matted. Her shirt buttons are torn and blood drips down her cheek. Clutching my phone I inch forward my hand resting reassuringly on the wooden banister.

Roy's shaking voice crackles through the darkness. 'Annie, I swear you'll never get away with this.'

I step forward, the floorboard creaks and Annie spins around her green eyes blazing like headlights.

'Mikky? Thank God you're here! I was going to call you.'

I move warily into the room.

Roy's head hangs on his chest. His hands are bound behind his back and his ankles tied to the legs of an upright chair. There is a large wound on the side of his temple and blood drips down the front of his denim shirt.

'What's happened?'

'Don't!' Annie shouts and as she holds out a poker that I recognise from the hearth downstairs, Mrs Green's large diamond ring glistens on her blood stained fingers.

'Why is Roy tied up?'

'He attacked me.'

'You can put that down now, Annie. I'll call the police.' I hold up my phone to show her what I'm about to do.

She wipes perspiration from her forehead onto the back of her sleeve and glances from me to Roy. Her breathing is laboured and her voice shakes. 'I haven't got his confession yet.' She backs away from me and circles Roy like a predatory barn owl studying its prey before the kill. She flexes her fingers around the handle of the poker.

'Annie, stop. You can't do this.'

Roy spits blood from his mouth. 'Stupid bitch! Why would I kill my own mother?'

'For the painting.' Annie circles him.

'It's not real. It's a fake.' He speaks slowly shaking his head as if words are an effort.

'But, you didn't know that, did you?' Annie moves closer to him. 'You thought it was the original. You wanted her money.'

'I'm going to call the police, Annie. This is wrong.' I raise my mobile but quicker than a bolt of lightning the poker cracks down on my wrist. The bone splits and I scream. The pain is unexpected and I slump to my knees gasping and holding my hand while my mobile crashes to the floor.

'You stupid woman.' She leans over me and shouts in my ear. 'Stupid, stupid, woman! Why did you make me do that?'

'She's nuts.' Roy shakes his head.

I'm dizzy and my throbbing wrist makes me want

to vomit.

Roy shouts, 'Don't Annie!'

She turns away and spying my mobile she stamps on it and kicks it in across the room. I reach out but she boots me in the shoulder, knocking me off balance and sending me flying backwards against the wall. Pain is reverberating through my body and as I shuffle to sit up I am holding my wrist and weighing up my options.

'Where's Javier?' I demand.

'She's killed him,' Roy replies. 'You see what she's like. She charmed you but this is the real Annie.'

'Shut up – let me think.' She whacks his arm with the poker and he screams.

'No!' I shout.

'I tried to warn you.' Roy coughs. His face is twisted in pain. 'I didn't want her in your house – painting for you.'

Annie steps forward and with the tip of the poker she slowly lifts his chin, tilting his face to one side. One of his eyes is completely swollen and closed. 'You're not so brave now are you, Roy Green? You thought that by taking Max away from me, you would control me.'

'I took Max away from you because you scare him.'

'Liar!'

'You frightened my mother too! With your stupid stories of murder and death.'

'She was a slow old woman.'

'She was my mother.'

Annie cracks the poker on the back of his chair and I jump.

'I've only just started on you,' she hisses in his

ear. 'You haven't even begun to suffer yet.'

'You can have it all. You can have everything.'

'You're a liar.'

'So what are you going to do, murder me? Is that the plan?' Roy's breathing is harsh and when he coughs a spasm of pain flickers across his face. 'You were going to kill me and make it look like self-defence, but now what? You can't kill us all.'

'Where's Javier?' I shout.

In the scant light I see a flash of cold steel as Annie pulls a knife from the waistband of her trousers. Her eyes are cold and calculating as she raises the blade at Roy.

A sense of calmness and determination descend on me and as she plunges the weapon I move quickly unfolding my legs and lunge myself at her. Roy senses my attack and with the bound chair strapped to him we both hurl ourselves at Annie and in one quick, deft movement we all collide in the air. It's like slow motion as my cheek crushes Roy's shoulder, my hip bounces against something hard and I spin away falling backwards. Annie's flailing arm catches my chin and the knife spins from her grasp. There's a crack and a thud as Roy and the chair collapse in a heap and the poker smacks on the wooden floor. Someone moans then it's quiet. My feet are trapped under the weight of their bodies, something sticky trickles down my leg, my wrist throbs and my chest heaves.

'Mikky?' A man shouts from downstairs. 'Javier? Oh, my goodness, Mikky?' Andreas appears in the doorway.

Andreas is surprisingly strong and he works quickly, dragging Roy and the chair off my legs. He unties his hands and lays him gently on the floor then he lifts Annie's hips and I slide my numb foot away and kneel beside her motionless body.

Andreas feels her pulse and shakes his head, his eyes are wide in disbelief.

Roy is groaning and blood covers the floor.

Outside sirens whine in the street and voices call out.

'Upstairs!' Andreas shouts back. Then he turns to me and says more quietly. 'It looks like she hit her head. She's not moving.'

I stand up holding my throbbing wrist and I lean on his shoulder, wiping blood from my face onto my arm. 'I must find Javier.' I push past him and stumble out onto the landing, throwing open doors, calling his name until I reach the front bedroom where the Vermeer was hanging. Now the room is empty; the bed, curtains and carpet are all gone but Javier is lying curled up on the floor with his back to me.

I slide down onto the floor and turn his body toward me. The room swims. My head is fuzzy with white noise and my vision goes dark as I lose consciousness.

When I open my eyes a colourful eagle with a large beak flutters before me, I am flying through the air but gentle and firm hands touch my throbbing wrist and through my hazy vision I recognise a familiar face.

'I know you – this has happened before,' I mumble, struggling to recall the details.

'You're right,' she says cheerfully. 'I hope this isn't becoming a habit. You called us a few months ago. You saved an old lady who live here...'

***

Javier is alive. When I hobble into the street they are loading him into the ambulance. I push past Josephine and Andreas and throw myself at him just before the door closes.

'You look worse than me,' he says.

I hold up my left wrist for him to look at. 'The bitch hit me with a poker.'

'She smashed my leg and cracked a few ribs.'

'At least she left your handsome face alone.'

The ambulance girl with the tattoo has a syringe in her hand. 'Painkiller,' she says.

I ignore her and Javier says. 'I'll be out of action for a while but at least my hands aren't damaged. I'll still be able to paint.' He holds up his scraped and bleeding knuckles.

'What happened?'

'I'd just arrived home and Annie phoned. She told me Roy was threatening her so I went round but Roy jumped me.'

'Roy?'

'He still thinks I have the Vermeer–'

'So, how did–?'

'She smacked him on the head. I think she knocked him unconscious. It's all a little fuzzy but Roy's first wife killed herself and he turned to gambling. Annie was a croupier. Is she alright?'

'I don't think so,' I say.

'Where are they? Where's Roy?'

'In another ambulance.'

'And the painting? Where do you think it is, Mikky? What do you think happened to it?'

I look away distracted by the girl with the eagle on her hand who is pushing the needle into his arm.

'Did you take it?' he asks.

'Get some rest.' I kiss him on the cheek and jump out just before she slams the ambulance door behind me.

***

After making a police statement and explaining my version of events I return home with Josephine and Andreas. It's past midnight and my body is filled with dull pain and I stretch my neck and my shoulders to ease my throbbing head. My wrist is swollen and bandaged but I manage to pull a vodka bottle from the cupboard without any problem and I wave it at them.

'Want some?'

'I'd prefer brandy,' replies Josephine.

'Me too,' says Andreas.

I pour them generous measures of Courvoisier and sliding Josephine a large glass across the kitchen counter, I say.

'You might as well stay the night. It's too late to go anywhere. Andreas can have Javier's room and you can have mine.'

Andreas sips his drink. His shirt is bloody. 'May I have a shower?' he asks.

'Of course.'

We leave Josephine in the lounge and I find him fresh towels and together we make Javier's bed with clean sheets. 'I appreciate your help tonight – thank you.'

'I've never seen a dead body before,' he says.

'Have you?'

'Only my mother's.'

'I'm sorry.'

'It was a long time ago.'

'No, I mean about what happened tonight. I should have gone with you.'

'You weren't to know. Javier will be alright – that's the main thing.'

'You were fortunate.' His voice and manner are both grave.

'Well, maybe my luck is finally changing,' I smile, kiss him on the cheek and leave him to shower and sleep.

The central heating has gone off and the room feels chilly so I pull a sweater over my head and Josephine sits shivering in her coat while we wait for the room to heat up.

'The brandy will warm you,' I say. 'Go to bed and get some rest.'

The nervous energy that she had earlier in the evening when she arrived has been spent. Her eyes are bright but the dark circles under them only emphasis her grey pallor. She yawns then sips her brandy and lays her head back and closes her eyes.

'Thank goodness Javier is all right. I don't know what I would have done if anything had happened to him or–'

'His hands aren't damaged. That was his main concern.'

'How awful everything is,' she says.

'It was a trap.'

'Did Roy kill his mother for the painting?'

'I'm beginning to think both of them are capable

of it. I had no idea Annie was so aggressive. Mrs Green was such a dear old lady. I really miss her. She deserved better…'

'Will he be prosecuted?' Josephine breaks into my reverie.

'The police have gone with him to the hospital.'

My eyes begin to close and I yawn. 'Poor Max will be devastated without his mother. He loved her so much. He'll be another child growing up without his mother's love,' I mumble.

I am thinking of another child in another country, in my other life. It will be a hard life for him. I remember the effect it had on me. Even though we didn't get on my world turned upside down when Mama died. The smell of damp and paraffin oil in the caravan still haunts me and I remember the times I slept outside on a worn mattress under the stars looking up at the night sky listening to crickets clicking their legs in unison. They were my childhood lullaby and I am suddenly a child again overwhelmed with loneliness and I swallow the lump growing at the back of my throat knowing it's the aftermath of shock and it will pass.

I squeeze my eyes shut and concentrate on breathing deeply. I'm lying hidden on an empty pew at the back of a church, my cheek resting on my hands like a pillow. The lingering smell of incense envelopes me, and the haunting tune of *Pan Angelicas* comes into my dream and I believe I can sing. My voice echoes in the confines of the closed, dark church and I am a lone choirboy with a falsetto voice.

A hand soothes my forehead pushing wispy strands of hair from my face and a gentle voice whispers comforting words of love: soft words of apology, guilt and doubt. The Virgin Mary looks down on me. She couldn't protect me, any more than she could protect her son from his destiny but she knows he is The Chosen One just as she was chosen as the Holy Vessel to bring him into this cruel world. A mother's love, a mother's sacrifice and my pain, neglect and sorrow, are all stroked away by soft caressing hands and my soul is released – transposed into softness and joy and I sleep; finally released from the demons that continually haunt me.

*****

When I wake it is still dark and I'm lying on the sofa. My back aches and my wrist throbs. I stretch the length of my body from my toes and my arms. To my surprise Josephine has not gone to bed but has stayed awake. She is watching over me and watching me as I stir.

'Good morning,' she whispers.

'Hello.' I check my watch. It's 5am. I have slept for three hours. I let her make me coffee while I rub sleep from my eyes. The fresh smell wakens me and as I sit up I know my decision is made. I will leave today. It's time for me to get on with my life. The events of the past twenty-four hours will be my excuse and my reason for leaving.

Josephine brings us coffee and sits beside me.

'Andreas will sleep until noon if I let him,' she says.

'There's no hurry,' I reply. I will not let their plans affect me.

'There is something you should know. I should

have told you before but–'

My mug is half way to my mouth. I hold my breath. It's as if I have always known there is something else and I sigh. 'Is this about Javier?'

She leans forward and clasps her fingers. 'It has been a secret I have kept for over thirty years. No one knows. I have been so frightened.'

'What is it?'

'I wanted to speak to you and Javier together. But now, I want to explain–'

I do not want a confession. Not here, not now. There has been too much emotion. I want to escape. I want Javier to be here. She is his friend – not mine. They are the ones with a special bond. And it dawns on me this must be it. This is the secret that Karl Blakey talked about – the secret he is convinced that she's hiding – and now she wants to tell me. But I don't want the burden of her problems. I want to escape and to be alone.

'Is this what Karl Blakey wants to know?'

'So far, I have managed to keep it from everyone.'

'Is it about the painting in Munich?'

'Sadly, it's not that simple,' she pauses. Her eyes meet mine and I am drawn into the depths of her dark irises and I fear I may drown there when she says softly.

'I have a child.' Her face is ashen and her eyes are filled with pain. The strain of her secret like a tree in a storm has caused her to bend, her shoulders are hunched and she looks broken but she continues speaking.

'I'm not the maternal type. Or rather, I wasn't. I was a professional singer but I have changed and I'm different now and I hope – I hope – my child will forgive me – and will be my friend.'

'J… Javier is my friend too,' I stutter. Why do I think this has something to do with him?

'I hope you will be…' She reaches out and I hold her fingers searching for words of reassurance – *nothing can be this painful, can it?*

'You need to confide in someone like Glorietta,' I suggest gently and I want to add someone your own age but I don't. She looks too broken for me to reject her. 'Someone who can help you–'

'I'm hoping my child will forgive me.'

It dawns on me then. All these months and all the interest she has shown in Javier. It makes complete sense. The way she has looked at him and behaved toward him and the opportunity she gave him to paint her portrait. I piece together what I know of Javier's past. His father was married before – did they have children – was Javier illegitimate? Could Josephine?

'I'm your mother,' she says.

'That's kind of you to say so but–'

'It's the truth, Mikky. You were adopted when you were a few hours old. 'I'm your birth mother. It's why I came looking for you.'

***

I don't know what to say. The events of the past twelve hours have been traumatic and perhaps she is unwell – unstable. Perhaps she has been affected by her past – by her accident last year and Raffa's death.

'I had to find you. I had to know that you were all right,' she says, gripping my fingers as her words gush out as if the safety valve of her soul has been opened. 'I needed to know that you were safe and happy. I wanted to make sure–'

'But – Javier?'

'I want you to know that I did it – that I gave you away – for the right reasons. It was the only thing I could do. I had no choice. It was the only way I could save you – the only way I could save my daughter. '

'Me?'

'I'm so sorry, Mikky. I wanted to know that you had a good and happy upbringing and that they were kind to you. But when I met you, I didn't know if you knew – if they had told you or if you had found out the truth.'

I shake my head. 'This is impossible.'

'I was frightened when you came to Dresden and I saw you. I couldn't take my eyes off you. You had grown into such a beautiful woman. An adult. You were my baby.'

'Josephine, I–'

'I know this is must be a huge shock to you. I understand. I spent my whole life believing that I had given birth to a son that I called Michael. Your father told me you were a boy. He led me to believe that… he convinced me–'

'A boy?'

'Yes.'

'This is not true.' I move my hands away from her but there is something in her urgency that makes me pause. I cannot take my gaze from the anguish in her eyes.

'It is true, Mikky. Please, wait! I have papers – proof. I'll show you.'

I watch while she pulls a reinforced envelope from her suitcase and extracts a sheet of lined paper torn from a schoolbook. When she passes it to me her hands are shaking and I recognise my Mama's neat handwriting. It's dated 7th September 1984 – one month after I was born.

Dear Nurse Angela Morris,

I am glad to be able to tell you that I have registered Michaella McGreevy as my baby with my husband Franscisco Dos Santos as her father. She will have a far better life with us than with her mother. The opera, music and theatre are no place for a small child.

I told cousin Michael that we are going to live in Madrid and he is pleased, although I am not sure when that will be. We can discuss further details when we meet next week in London.

Yours sincerely,

Alisha McGreevy.

P.s. We have decided to call her Mikky.

'My Mama never used her Irish name,' I say. 'I had forgotten it was McGreevy.'

From the same battered envelope Josephine pulls out a postcard. I gaze silently at the old picture on the front and eventually I meet her gaze.

'Los Cibeles – Madrid – we lived near here for a few years,' I say.

'And I sang in the Teatro Real in Madrid for a whole season. I never knew that you lived so close,' she replies.

I read the smudged ink–stained words on the postcard dated two years after the letter.

Querida Nurse Angela Morris,

We have settled in Madrid. It is warmer here and my husband has found work in a hotel. Although his parents are in Asturias we are near his brother.

Mikky is happy and learning Spanish very quickly. She has settled in to her new life here.

Thank you for all your help in making us a happy family.

Un abrazo,

Señora Alisha Dos Santos.

'Alisha Dos Santos – my Mama,' I say.

Josephine nods and passes me a copy of my birth certificate.

'I'm your daughter?'

'Yes.'

'How?'

'They registered you as their natural daughter.'

'It must have been... illegal.'

'It was.'

'Where is this nurse now?'

'She lives in Islington.' She passes me a manila coloured folder.

'I hired a private investigator to find you. I should have done this through an agency, Mikky. I understand you are in shock. There are professional agencies that can help, they offer counselling and will give us – you – support. We should talk about this and maybe we can go and see someone professionally to help us work things through.'

'It's a little late now, isn't it?'

She casts her eyes downwards and her shoulders

droop as if she is defeated. She sighs before speaking. 'I couldn't wait any longer. It was killing me to be in your company and for you not to know. It's been torture…'

'But why now? Why come looking for me now, after all these years?'

'I had to make sure you were all right. I had to make sure that you had a good life and that you were happy. I had to know I made the right decision.'

I look at her lips, her eyes and her nose. Are we alike? There are dark circles under her tired eyes and I doubt she has slept at all. Even her voice is weary.

'But they didn't look after you. I'm so sorry, Mikky. Can you forgive me?'

'It's not about forgiveness. It's about understanding. Why? Why did you do it?'

'Your father – Michael arranged it all. He was a doctor – an anaesthetist.'

My mind is whirling after the events of the past twelve hours and now this. I cannot make sense of anything. My head throbs, my wrist hurts and my shoulders ache. I rub my sore eyes.

'I wanted – we both wanted – to protect you.'

'Protect me?' My laugh is ironic. 'So you had me adopted?'

'I was married then but your father – Michael was my husband's father.'

'What?'

'Your father was my father-in-law. The shame would have ruined your father's family and my husband Seán. They were Irish and the scandal would have killed them all if the truth had come out.'

'You slept with your father-in-law?'

'Yes.'

'And he was my father?'

'Michael was the only man I ever loved. The only man who ever understood me but we couldn't be together.'

'And he told you, I was ...a boy?'

'I hired a private investigator to find you–'

'When?'

'Last year after my... after my – accident. I looked for you myself on the Internet but there was no birth record of you. I couldn't believe it. I didn't understand why you were not registered as my son. He had told me that my son Michael was happy with a family in America–'

'But my name is Michaella.'

'That's why I couldn't find you. The investigator looked for information in the clinic where you were born and he managed to trace the nurse who had been with me – who helped deliver you.'

'But why only last year? Why did you not look for me before?'

'Your father – Michael – died last year and Seán, my ex-husband, blackmailed me into singing at his funeral in Dublin. He had found a letter in Michael's possessions referring to our affair and because his business was in decline he thought that if I sang at his father's funeral it would create prestige for him. But I was terrified that he had found out about my secret child. I was just reviving my career and about to audition for the role of Tosca. But when I arrived in Ireland he told me that Michael had found art treasures during the war and he threatened to tell everyone about my affair with his father unless I went to Munich to get the Golden Icon. And I thought that would lead to them finding you–'

'He found art work during the war?'

'That's why I went to Munich and I saw the paintings in that apartment. But then Seán was killed and I wanted to make amends for Michael's past and return the Golden Icon. It didn't belong to him.'

'But…I can't take all this in, Josephine – I'm sorry.' I shake my head. 'All these people and the story I read about on the Internet were – are my family?'

'Yes.'

'But you didn't want me.'

'I wanted to protect you from the scandal. Life thirty years ago is vastly different to how it is today. And if I'm truthful, I was ambitious and so was your father. He wanted me to succeed. He wanted me to be famous and he encouraged me. He recognised my talent and would have sacrificed anything. He was more like a father to me… I was young and impressionable… I was in a foreign country with a modicum of talent and it went to my head. I'm so sorry, Mikky. I never wanted to–'

'How can you not know the sex of your own child?'

'I was very ill after the caesarean. There had been complications and I lost a lot of blood. I was sedated. I wasn't well. But they are all excuses…'

'Did you hold me?'

'He wouldn't let me. When I saw you, you were wrapped in a baby blanket. This is all I have.' She takes an old and crumpled photograph from the envelope and hands it to me. I am a baby: tiny, black curly hair, eyes closed, vulnerable. I could be a boy or girl. I'm just a baby.

'This is all I had to remind me of you. Michael took it when you were barely a day old.'

'So my life has been a sham – a complete lie,' I say.

'No, Alisha and Paco were – are your parents.'

'But you're my mother.' I stand up and walk to the window. I tilt the shutter. Outside a storm is blowing. Rain and wind hurls a paper bag along the gutter and a car splashes into a puddle and it washes across the pavement and I realise the enormity of her confession and the impact for her and her child if this became public knowledge.

'It's no wonder, Karl Blakey follows you,' I say, 'with a secret like this...'

'He doesn't know. He follows me because of the artwork in Munich but that's an old story. You are my secret. I will not let him find out about you. I want to protect you and look after you.' She looks stricken with guilt and pain.

'And Michael?' I cannot bring myself to call him my father. 'How did you–?'

'He was sixty when we met – I was twenty-two. We were together for six months. After you were adopted we didn't stay in touch. He lived in Dublin. He contacted me after my break down became public four years ago but I wouldn't speak to him. Karl Blakey was destroying me and delving into my past. Cesare, my voice coach, brought me to live in Lake Como but Karl followed me and I was frightened. I didn't want him to find out about you and destroy your life as he did mine.'

'Did you ever think about me?'

'All the time, but Michael had led me to believe…
I thought you were my son – living in America.'

'He lied to you.'

'Yes.'

I pick up the postcard then the letter and the copy
of my birth certificate and read them all again very
slowly. 'Is that why you banned Javier from speaking
to Karl Blakey?'

'I couldn't take the chance–'

'And the portrait? How did that come about? Was
that for real? Did you really want a portrait?'

'When the private investigator told me that I gave
birth to a daughter and you were adopted illegally I was
shocked. Michael had lied to me. I had a daughter and
I was excited but I didn't want to approach you directly
so I thought if I became your friend you might like me
but I had to find a way to get to know you...'

'So you devised a plan for Javier to paint your
portrait?'

'You were difficult to find, you travelled a lot and
then I didn't know how to meet you. Knowing he was
your flatmate, the investigator searched for
information on Javier and he came across an article last
year in the Sunday Times after he painted the portrait
of–'

'Lady Rushworth.'

'Yes.'

'So you invited us both to Dresden?'

'I wanted to meet you. I wasn't well enough to
travel and I wanted to see if you were happy and if I
had made the right decision.'

'You must have been horrified at my bad
behaviour.'

'You were angry and I wanted to help…I felt responsible. I am responsible…'

'It's not your fault I'm antisocial and have bad manners.'

She smiles. 'I don't believe you are. I see a beautiful, talented, kind and loving woman. I'm very proud of you and I hope, one day, you will be able to forgive me.'

I can't give her reassurance or guarantees but I'll listen to what she says. I stretch my arms trying to free the knotted lumps in my shoulders. 'I'll make breakfast and you can tell me all the gory details and don't leave anything out.'

And, for the next three hours, while Andreas is asleep and Javier is in hospital I listen as Josephine tells me how she had an affair with her father-in-law, became pregnant, divorced her husband Seán and became a world famous opera star.

* * *

Spent of emotion and exhausted I insist Josephine sleep in my bed and by ten-thirty I'm in a taxi heading toward Islington. Today is the first day of March and one of those days that stays resolutely dark and dismal as if it will never be light again. Rain drizzles persistently against the window and the wipers move lethargically backwards and forwards: backwards thud, forwards thud, backwards thud.

She could be lying.

Thud. Lying. Thud. Lying. Thud.

The private investigator followed me. He may know everything. She could be after the Vermeer. Had

I known I was being followed I would have taken more care. Had he seen me go in and out of Mrs Green's house? Had he followed me? Did he know I had worked in Bruges? Has she pieced it all together?

I turn the letter and postcard in my hand and although it looks like Mama's writing it would be easy to copy it. It could be forged. I have spent my life imitating, copying and cloning. It isn't hard. Everything can be faked including – so it would seem – my life.

But I will not be fooled easily. Is it a coincidence that she has come into my life when all my plans are in place – at the precise moment I've taken the world's most famous stolen painting and I'm planning on leaving the country?

How can it be a coincidence?

She has planned it.

I had thought her bond had been with Javier. In Dresden she had pulled him into her web of celebrity charm. She had fooled him. She had won him over. But now she says it had been a ruse to get him to paint her portrait so that she could get to know me. She is not to be underestimated. She is manipulative and controlling.

The taxi drops me in the Angel. I pull my collar around my neck. I have always been alone – there has only ever been me. My birth mother didn't want me – her career came first. My birth father lied about me. My adopted mother resented me and my adopted father would have sold me for beer money.

I don't need any of them. I will move on to my new life. I want to prove Josephine Lavelle is a liar.

I don't need a mother.

I only want one thing. It belongs to me and I will protect it. The masterpiece is mine.

***

My step is resolute and determined. I follow the directions in my hand and it takes me twenty minutes to locate the home of Nurse Angela Morris. It's the address that the investigator discovered and Josephine kept it in the folder. The house is at the end of a terrace set back from the others beside a narrow alley. Steep steps with a collection of hibernating clematis, empty baskets dangling from iron hooks and tired hydrangeas that haven't yet been pruned lead to a blue front door.

In the summer I imagine it to be colourful and warm but today it's frosty and full of decay. There is a light glowing in the window so I knock and wait.

An old lady opens the door. Her left side seems distorted and her arm hangs limply. She wears a floral patterned dress and a lopsided grin but she isn't smiling, she stares at me frowning in confusion.

'Angela Morris? My name is Mikky Dos Santos. You may remember me as Michaella McGreevy?'

'Michaella McGreevy,' she slurs although she is not drunk. 'What's taken you so long? You'd better come in.'

I'm trying to detect a trace of familiarity, some recognition or a sign that I may know who she is but she is a stranger to me. She is also older than I thought and I'm disappointed. She must have been over forty when I was born. Will she remember the details?

Illness has been unkind to her. She walks with difficulty holding onto furniture and leaves me alone in the cramped lounge while she disappears into a galley kitchen at the back where I guess the smell of cooked cabbage originates. I gag before taking a tissue from my bag.

The room is squashed and airless with dark and heavy furniture. Tiny paned windows are cut into squares and a table lamp casts a yellow glow across an open book on the arm of the chair – it's a well-known thriller – and on the floor a stack of celebrity magazines are ringed and stained from damp glasses and crusts of dried food.

Angela Morris returns with two crystal glasses filled with ice. The gin is rough on my throat and there's very little tonic.

'It is barely eleven o'clock.' I cough. The stuffed armchair nearest to the window looks the cleanest so I sit down opposite her.

'Drink it. You'll need it. Cheers!' She smacks her crooked lips and when she sits our knees are almost touching.

'I had a stroke,' she says slowly and deliberately. 'So be patient with me. I was pleased when that nice man came, you know, the private investigator – Joe? That's why I gave him the postcard and the letter. I didn't know what else to do after I read about her last August. You know, when she was shot. I thought she would die. I saw it on the news. It was on the television and I thought, I'm the only one who knows the truth.'

'She almost died,' I say.

'I would like to have met her again.'

'Perhaps you might.'

'Does she know you're here?'

'Yes,' I lie.

'I was pleased when he said she wanted to trace you.' Angela Morris speaks in small measured sentences. 'You were a pretty little baby, curly black hair and deep blue eyes. I held you in my arms. You were a quiet little girl. Very contented.' Her distorted mouth changes into a grimace as she attempts a smile and I imagine this woman holding me – thirty years ago.

'And, you knew I was going to be adopted?' I prompt.

'Dr McGreevy told me. He had all the paperwork arranged. He said your mother – Josephine – agreed but I spoke to her and I could see she was poorly. She was in labour for over fifteen hours. I pleaded with her to have a caesarean but she wouldn't. She said it was God's way of punishing her and that it was his revenge but then it was too late. Michael insisted – Doctor McGreevy – insisted. He said she wasn't in a fit state to argue with him. I felt so sorry for her. She was so ill. But he wouldn't let me near her after that. He insisted on looking after her himself.'

'Why did he do that?'

'She was very distressed. There was a time when I thought she wouldn't let you go.'

'She held me?'

'Yes.'

'She doesn't remember. She says it's like a dream. As if it all happened to someone else…'

'Oh, it was her all right. She didn't stop crying. There's no mistake about that. She wasn't happy. She didn't want to let you go. She kept saying she'd changed her mind but Michael was determined. He could be very persuasive.'

'But it was illegal.'

'Doctors often arranged adoptions like that. I don't think they would get away with it now… Everything's changed. It's more regulated'

'My adopted parents registered me as their child. It's their names on my birth certificate. I would never have known.'

'I think it happened a lot – especially in Ireland. It was Michael's idea.'

'That's awful. There could be more children – children like me?'

'Probably.'

'But there's no way for them of ever knowing the truth?'

'Michael didn't always follow the rules. He was unconventional like that.'

'Unconventional isn't what I would call it. Besides, he was the doctor and you were the nurse. Why don't you refer to him as Doctor McGreevy?'

'Josephine wasn't the only woman to have an affair with him. Once she became famous and travelled around Europe he was all on his own. He was lonely. He came to London a few times and we kept in touch. He wanted to make sure that there were no questions asked and I think he wanted to keep me sweet and make sure I didn't tell anyone.'

'So you had an affair with him?' I sip my drink and gaze at this woman, struggling to understand the complexity of their relationship.

'Only for a few months, I was never an attractive woman. I was a nurse from a poor family and I was flattered by his attention. He could be very charming and amusing and he made me laugh. But he only loved her. I don't think he ever got over her leaving. He listened to her music all the time.'

I am thinking of this old woman with my father. A man called Michael.

'I was much younger then,' she says, as if reading my mind. 'And I was older than Josephine. His wife had only died a year or so before. He was very handsome and fit for a man in his early sixties. He flew to England regularly and he often went to where she was singing. He followed her around for many years.'

'I don't think she knows that.'

'She had her career. It's what he wanted. What they both wanted.'

'And you kept their secret. Why?'

'He paid me and I retired early. I never worried about money.'

I sip the gin for reassurance. 'Did you know the couple who adopted me?'

'They worked in a hotel in London and Michael said they were just married. Alisha and Paco – they agreed to take you to Spain.' Her lopsided face tilts to look at me with her good eye. 'Were they good to you?'

I shake my head. 'My mother was very jealous and when my father paid me any attention she became angry and violent.'

'Where are they now?'

'Mama died when I was fourteen. She was drunk and she wrapped a motorbike around a tree. My father spent most of his life playing cards and he would steal money from my piggybank to pay for his cannabis.'

She shakes her head and sips her gin. 'What a waste.'

'Why didn't you contact Josephine?' I ask. 'Why didn't you get in touch with her and tell her that I was a girl. Why did you let her believe I was a boy?'

'Michael only died last year. He would have been furious with me. He would have stopped my income.'

'He still pays you?'

'He did. Until the day he died. He kept his promise.'

'She thought she had given birth to a boy,' I insist. 'How could she think that?'

'Michael insisted that I should never tell the truth to anyone. He said it was to protect you both but he was the one with the secret. It was to protect him too.'

'But you knew?'

'That he was your father? Yes.'

'And you knew Josephine was married to his son?'

'It didn't take me long to find out. Then when Josephine was so ill, she was delirious and she told me it was a secret but then afterwards years later he admitted it.'

'Once I was adopted and gone and out of the way.'

'Yes.'

'He doesn't strike me as being the kindest man in the world,' I say.

'He was–'

'Not to me.'

'He thought you would have a better life. That you would be better cared for–'

'To give me away to strangers – to hippies – to live abroad?'

'They weren't strangers.'

'He knew them?'

'Alisha was his cousin's daughter from the west

coast of Ireland. She had a botched abortion the year before and couldn't have children so Michael forged the papers at the hospital so that she could register you as her baby. She was named as your natural mother that way there would never be any evidence to say that anyone else was your birth mother and Josephine would be safe forever from scandal.'

'Why did they send the letter and postcard to you?'

'I asked her to let me know that they had arrived safely in Spain and that you were all right – you were such a helpless little thing – just a tiny baby and I imagined that like any mother Josephine would, one day, want to find her child. She would want to know the truth and I was right. She went searching for you as soon as Michael died.'

I sit silently absorbing the information about my life. Then she says: 'What happened to your face and your wrist?'

I raise my bandaged hand to the graze on my cheek. 'I slipped on the pavement.'

'And what about that ugly scar on the back of your hand.'

'Alisha did that.' And I tell her then what my adopted mother was really like and the night that she sliced a meat knife through my skin without a flicker of a conscience.

***

The taxi takes me straight to Heathrow. I have a holdall with everything I need and I will disappear forever. My shoulders ache with the burden of past lies and the people around me: Javier in hospital, Josephine in my flat and Nurse Angela Morris begging me to stay in touch.

I don't want any of them.

I only want the Vermeer.

I check my mobile and there is a missed call from Josephine and another from Javier. At the check–in desk I think only of the painting. I will spend my life travelling, taking photographs and picking up interesting commissions and jobs. I have spent years repairing paintings and artefacts and I will easily be able to restore it back to its original condition, once I am alone and safe.

I call Javier as I am boarding. He is in the hospital and Oscar is with him having returned yesterday from his business trip. He tells me Javier is still sleeping and I tell him where I am going but not to tell Josephine.

When I am on the plane I check my voicemail. She has phoned me. 'Where are you, Mikky? I hope you are okay. Call me as soon as you get this message – please.'

She can wait. I lean my head back, close my eyes and I am asleep before the plane is in the sky. When I wake my neck aches, my mouth is dry and my wrist throbs. I drink coffee, eat a sandwich and take two painkillers and when the plane flies over the west of the island I am reminded of the steep cliffs and the scenic villages of Deia and Valdemossa. The plane tilts its wings and a surge of excitement fills me with nostalgia. I think of the numerous tranquil bays, beautiful coves, turquoise sea and memories of barbecues and summer evenings with Javier and Carmen. It's more than eight years since I visited Mallorca. It was the summer after I finished University and our History of Art lecturer Dolores, invited several students here for a holiday. She was retiring from teaching and buying an art gallery in a beautiful village on the north of the island. But I wasn't a stranger here. My parents had brought me the first time when I was twelve. We had lived in Colonia de Sant Pere, a small village on the north east of the island, created by survivors of the bubonic plague who fled the neighbouring village of Arta in 1820.

Along this rocky coastline I had snorkelled and dived pretending to look for hidden treasure from lost Spanish galleons. With its small white sandy beach and little fishing harbour I lived like a street urchin running amongst the boats and along the quay while Mama spent a summer working as a waitress and Papa sold his catch to the small restaurants.

It was an idyllic time and I had been devastated at the end of the season when it was time to move on. Tourists left the island in winter and so, like the masses, we packed our camper van and headed south to the peninsula to find work for the winter.

Now as I disembark with only hand luggage, it is late afternoon and outside the air is fresh and cool. Had it only been this morning when I sat with Josephine and listened to the window screen wipers thudding in the taxi to Islington? The memory pales and fades against the bright sunlight and blue sky, even the air smells more optimistic and my fears lift and my concerns are pushed away. I open the window in the rented cheeky red Fiat 500 and drive toward the north of the island. Once I am past the ring roads of Palma the road stretches ahead of me and I am liberated. Fields of straw and hay stretch between stonewalls, sheep and goats graze peacefully and on the hillside windmills with unmoving sails stand as beacons – a testament to the farmers of the past – now simple decorations in the present.

I am home.

But my mind is occupied like a kaleidoscope of vivid images of past events that I cannot escape. Was Mrs Green murdered? There had been no suggestion of it in the autopsy or doctor's report. Mrs Green had been ill and I knew she couldn't live forever but I miss her. Although she had been a stranger I had respected her. She had been closer to me than a good friend and certainly my own grandmother – who according to Josephine had no knowledge of my existence and lived happily in Florida.

There is no investigation into Mrs Green's death and I consider the reliability of Annie's accusations and Roy's involvement.

Where is Max? Had Roy taken him away from his own mother?

In front of me the lorry brakes and I react instinctively jerking the steering wheel hard right. I skid and steady the car – dangerously close and I'm left shaking. My bandaged wrist hurts and I curse in pain. I must focus. My only consolation is that if I were to die now, no one might ever discover the Vermeer and that makes me laugh aloud and I sing at the top of my voice, *My Hero* tapping the melodic rhythm happily against the dashboard.

The picturesque village of Arta is filled with bars, restaurants and art and craft galleries. The hilltop fortress and chapel of Santuari de Sant Salvador is a steep walk from the town centre but in the main cobbled street tourists are browsing and sitting in outdoor cafes. It's still relatively undeveloped and an attraction for artists, cyclists and ramblers.

I park in a back street and walk around to the front entrance, half way up the old pedestrian cobbled street, opposite a crowded tapas bar and beside an expensive boutique. I peer inside at prestigious gallery; perfect lighting, pine wood floors, whitewashed walls and natural light flooding in through crevices, niches and large skylights from the roof.

The owner is concentrating on bubble wrapping a painting for a Japanese tourist. She doesn't look up so I explore the gallery and admire the artwork on the walls.

The ground floor opens into three smaller separate rooms; a counter with prints and books then an exhibition by local artists and in the third section there are three massive paintings by my fellow student and Javier's ex muse, Carmen Muñoz. I recognise a semi-nude of a plump and voluptuous model that once hung in my bedroom.

There's another painting of the same reclining figure reading a book but the third painting is a large abstract called *Life in a confused form*. Carmen painted something similar when we were at University just after she and Javier separated.

The walls leading up the stone staircase are covered in an assortment of copies: Van Gogh, Rembrandt and Warhol but on the second floor are numerous landscape oil paintings, many with bulbous clouds, windmills, churches and monasteries by a variety of Spanish artists. The most popular paintings of the island are by Blanca Nieves – Snow White – has a whole section dedicated to her work and as I stand there two tourists select three prints and carry them downstairs to the till.

But it is not until I climb to the top floor that I am surprised to see my own canvases prominently displayed alongside two other biblical artists. Each painting fills me with nostalgia and I'm overwhelmed at seeing my work on display; there are eleven paintings in total. One of each disciple's face revealing their traumatic expression taken in a split moment of time, a quick snapshot, revealing their complex reaction to the crucifixion of Christ. The attic windows cast biblical rays of light on the intricacy of their emotions, the anguish in their eyes and their outstretched hands beseeching the Lord as life ebbs from the Saviour on the cross. They are paintings filled with emotion: fear and love, regret, denial, betrayal; a millisecond in time, as fast as a paintbrush; a quick flash of a blade like the knife that disfigured my hand narrowly missing my face.

Each dark painting has only a glimmer of light, a small flicker of hope that divides the canvas: light and dark, good and evil, heaven and earth, chaos and calm.

It's years since I saw them, in my last year at University when Dolores was looking for paintings to open her gallery. I had not thought them worthy enough but she had insisted and now I'm flattered they still hang in here. I don't know how long I spend gazing at them, each canvas the size of a television screen and I wonder why she has kept them for so long.

A couple dressed in hiking boots and walking clothes come upstairs and stand beside me. Seeing me alone they whisper and speak in hushed tones as if in a church. The canvasses do not reflect their happy holiday spirit and they leave quickly after murmurs of disapproval. The paintings are too obscure for them. It was during my dark period when I was obsessed with betrayal, religion and truth. When I was trying to make sense of my life.

'Hola, Mikky?'

The tranquillity of my reverie is broken and I turn at the sound of the familiar and husky voice. 'I hardly recognised you. It's been a long time.'

The tall woman before me is over seventy. Thick black-rimmed glasses frame her serious eyes but she breaks into a grin as she gathers me into her arms.

'You still give a good hug, Dolores,' I say, as we pull apart.

'You see – I still have your paintings, as I promised.'

'You can't sell them, more likely.'

'They're not for sale.' She wears a vibrant yellow and orange patterned silk dress and her fingers and thumbs are adorned with an assortment of large glittery rings but nothing detracts from her charcoal eyes and her steely gaze. 'You're here to stay?'

'If you have a room.'

'There is always room for you. What has taken you so long?'

I shrug.

She scrutinises me as if I am a still-life subject who is to be painted. Her eyes travel over my bandaged wrist, the horrified face of *Scream* on my arm, the old scar on the back of my hand and finally it settles on my finger and the new tattoo of the Madonna.

'You look tired,' she says. 'Is everything alright?'

'How's business?'

'It's quiet now – in the summer it's busier – another month at Easter and I won't have time to chat to you.'

'I can't believe you have kept these.' I nod at my paintings.

'I will never part with them – unless you want them back.'

I shake my head.

'Come.' She links her arm through mine and we walk back downstairs pausing occasionally to look at paintings.

'I take it these are not the originals?' I say dryly, pointing to Dali's *Swans reflecting Elephants.*

'This is the floor of our copies. Anyone who cannot afford thousands or millions of euros for the original but wants a specific painting comes here. We are quite well known.'

'For forgeries?'

'They are copies, Mikky – it's not illegal if that's what you mean. They are genuine fakes and are sold as such, and the artists like to look at it as getting their own back on the art establishment. Many of the so-called art critics cannot tell the difference and the artists enjoy fooling eminent art specialists and gallery owners but these are still copies. You should know that. Didn't I teach you anything or is your head filled with photography now?'

'Are these painted by more than one artist?'

'Of course, I have lots of new artists who paint for me.'

'Students that paint forgeries instead of their own work?'

'In Asia they do both to supplement their meagre income. These modern paintings for example like Warhol are much more vulnerable to fraud than Old Masters and the struggling artist lives in the hope that they will get noticed – so they copy the originals hoping for a lucky break.'

'Things haven't changed.'

'Not as far as the struggling artist is concerned.'

'And the buyer is deceived.'

'It is only a crime if they are sold with intent to deceive the buyer. Pastiches are not forgeries. If you can't afford twenty million euro for an original then why not enjoy a fake?'

I walk along the gallery studying and examining the paintings. 'But these are excellent. It would be easy to pass them off as originals...'

'They wouldn't pass under scrutiny. We have wealthy philanthropists, cosmopolitan art collectors and tourists who cannot tell the difference between an original and a fake – Gaicometti – Van Gogh – Braque – Ben Nicholson – Dubuffet – you name it we can paint it. I have many talented students that can reproduce just about everything.'

'I'm surprised no one tries to buy one and pass it off as an original.'

'Impossible. And you should know that. Did I not teach you anything? To pass off a fake, one has to be very clever and very lucky. Each painting needs to show authenticity through a record of its history of ownership and exhibitions, right down to the alleged current owners.

'It's becoming increasingly difficult to validate bogus provenances. You need to provide rubber stamps, authenticating seals and forged receipts of non-existent sales. Then you need to have a network of unsuspecting salesmen or someone of influence and offer them a percentage to help sell the painting as an original. It is not at all easy and quite honestly, it's not worth the effort and the risk of going to prison if it all goes wrong – because it will. This is a far more honest way of earning a living…' She waves her arm in the air, proud of the copies adorning her walls. 'And I like it.'

'I've never understood how art professionals can be fooled by fakes. It's still a mystery to me,' I say.

'It's because many wish to be misled. They're easily duped into believing they have an original. There are many paintings hanging in famous and prestigious galleries worldwide or paintings cherished by private collectors who refuse to believe they have purchased a forgery. They have been deceived. Their egos over compensate for the extravagant funds they have parted with and they are victims of their own greed. So many prestigious art dealers and auction houses can't even agree on the legitimacy of paintings but I don't feel sorry for any of them.'

'This Rembrandt is an excellent fake. Who painted this?'

'Who do you think?' she replies, tilting her head. 'You want to stay in the studio?'

'Thank you.' I smile and link my arm back through hers but at the foot of the stairs I pause at a familiar painting. 'Carmen Muñoz – is she still painting?'

'A lot has happened,' she says. 'Come on, let's get you settled then we can go across the road for tapas and we can catch up. I will close the gallery. You're lucky the studio is empty. Carmen and Yolanda only left last weekend. She would love to see you again.'

'They were here?'

'Of course – just because you want to live your life as a hermit it doesn't mean that other people do too.'

'Is Yolanda still tattooing?'

'Yes. You have room for another one?'

'Maybe.'

'Then you will have to go to Malaga.'

'It's on my list,' I say.

'I suppose you only came here to collect your parcel.'

'I came to see you,' I lie.

***

I sleep well. I am secure and relaxed. I wake up to a sky so bright and vivid that it makes me feel pleased to be alive. I stretch luxuriously on the mattress on the floor, throw back the light cotton duvet and pad into the shower. Afterwards I dress in black leggings, ankle boots and a *Rage Against The Machine* T-shirt. I pull a brush through my hair and add pink lipstick.

The door of the studio leads into the back street where I parked the car so I walk around the corner and into the cobbled main street where market traders have set up their stalls. Rows of cotton sarongs, trousers and shirts mix with handmade wooden toys, handbags, purses and belts imported from Morocco. Voices rise as a trader refuses to negotiate for spices with a tourist who holds a colourful tub of saffron. The air is filled with herbs, garlic and mustard seeds – all smells from my childhood when I would wander between stalls barely reaching eye level. Another stand, run by an English couple, is decorated with ceramic pots and handmade candles, their sweet scent mingling with roasting chickens turning on a spit. It is bustling and busy but the atmosphere is relaxed and I am filled with energy and my heart is light.

The cobbles are uneven and, shielding my eyes from the bright sunlight, I stumble. I'm suddenly transported to another time and another place – back to Victoria Station when Karl Blakey followed me. Now he is sitting in the tapas bar and this time, instead of hiding, he beckons to me to join him. He stands up and pulls out a chair for me.

His rat's eyes smile. 'What a lovely surprise, will you join me?'

'You're following me.' I don't sit down. 'What do you want?'

'We need to talk.'

'How did you know I was here?'

'Javier told me.' He signals to the waiter for two chilled glasses of cava. He is fluent in Spanish. Antonio remembers me from last night, sitting with Dolores and he winks behind Karl's back as if I am meeting a lover.

'I might have guessed he would tell you.' I sit down, silently cursing Javier.

'You're not answering your phone.'

'That's because I don't want to speak to anyone.'

Karl grips my bandaged wrist. It hurts but I don't flinch. 'He told me everything. He told me how Annie lured him next door and that Roy beat him because he believes Javier stole the painting.'

I pull from his grasp and glare at him. My arm is throbbing.

Antonio returns to our table and uncorks the bottle. It fizzes and he serves us with an unnecessary flourish and a wide smile.

I pick up a ripe green olive and place it between my lips.

'Roy has gone missing,' he says.

'Roy is not my problem.'

'And guess what? The Vermeer is also missing.'

I sip the sparkling wine slowly relishing the cool dry bubbles on my tongue and the slight acidy, sweet flavour on my lips and I realise this is breakfast.

The spring sunshine is warm on my closed eyelids and I lean back and fold my arms knowing Karl is watching me. 'I'm a journalist. My interest is art and paintings and I see the gallery across the road specialises in fakes and forgeries.'

'They're copies.' I don't open my eyes and I force myself to yawn.

'What are you doing in Mallorca?'

'It is none of your business.' I stretch and when I open my eyes Dolores stands in the doorway of the gallery watching us, smoking black tobacco from a long holder. She does not smile and I do not wave at her.

He yawns and covers his mouth with the back of his hand then he raises his glass and drains the last of his cava. 'You know I will find out, Mikky. I'm good at my job. Ask Josephine Lavelle if you don't believe me.'

I lean across the table and gently take his hand and

to my surprise he blushes.

'I'll tell you the truth, Karl. Dolores, the owner of the gallery, was my art teacher. She recommended me to study art in Milan. My teacher was Raffaelle who was Josephine and Glorietta's lover. And I want to know – I have to find out – if he loved me. I couldn't bear the thought that when he died he had loved them more than me. He was my life. I loved him like no other.' I let go of his hand and place it on the table and continue speaking. 'I'm sorry Karl but this is a personal quest for me. I have come here to speak to Dolores about him. Perhaps you will respect my wishes when I say that it is very private and I cannot rest until I know the truth.' My eyes fill with tears. 'Please, Karl. Let me find the truth then I will tell you anything you want to know – if that's what you want. But please give me space. I must heal. I need to know the truth then I can move on and find peace and hopefully one day I will find love again.' I place my hand on my heart.

'You are an accomplished liar,' he laughs.

I lean forward so my face is inches from his. 'So, tell me what you want because if you don't leave me alone and stop following me, you'll regret it. I'm not a soft pussy like Josephine. I'm a tiger and I will maul and scratch you until you can't take any more and it will be far more painful than me squeezing your balls like the last time.'

He pushes back his chair and stands up. 'Javier asked me to find you. Roy has gone missing and so has his painting. Two Romanian businessmen are looking for him and he cannot hide forever. I came to warn you…'

'All of this has nothing to do with me.'

'It's Javier who's worried about you – not me – I couldn't give a toss.'

When I stand and face him he has to look up to meet my gaze.

'Stay away from me, Karl, it's bad enough that you have ingratiated yourself with Javier but I don't like you and I certainly don't want you near me. I know the damage you cause and the lies and crap that you write, so piss off.'

'I hope that when we next meet you will be more grateful.'

'You're not the cavalry, Karl. You're a slimy worm following me on the pretext that you want to help but I want nothing to do with you.'

'Javier didn't take the Vermeer and he didn't replace it with a forgery. There's only one person who could have done that and I won't leave you alone until I find it.' He turns on his heel and I watch him walk away, down the cobbled street until he is engulfed between the market stalls, shoppers and tourists and I am left with the tangy, stale after taste of his visit.

I lean back in my chair and order another glass of cava for breakfast and settle down to brood over my situation. I'm under suspicion and there is no one I trust. I stretch my neck and begin thinking and plotting my next move.

Chapter Nine

'If people knew how hard I worked to get my mastery, it
wouldn't seem so wonderful at all.'
Michelangelo

I spend the next few days thinking of a plan and I start
painting immediately. It will be my safety net – my
security. How could I have been so naïve to think that
I could send the painting here and that no one would
come looking for me?

Oscar, Javier, and Karl – they all want a piece of
me but Josephine is more persistent. She won't take no
for an answer. We have spoken on the telephone twice
and I even promised her a painting hoping she would
leave me alone but after I have been in Arta for a week
she leaves me a voicemail.

*We must talk. Javier's told me where you are and
I'm coming to Mallorca.*

I'm furious with Javier and I won't take his calls
then I wait for her in the tapas bar with my back against
the wall enjoying the sun on my face. She doesn't see
me at first and even though she wears sunglasses she
scans the tables shading her eyes with her hand so I
wave to her.

She walks more upright as she weaves between
the tables. There is an improvement in her posture
since we met in Dresden before Christmas when she
had looked so ill. Now she moves with more freedom,
less rigidity and the pain that was firmly etched across
her face is replaced with a warm and welcoming smile.

'Hello, Mikky.'

I have known for eight days that she is my birth mother but she still looks like an opera star – not a parent.

'You took your time. You said you'd be here at two,' I say in greeting. I don't stand up and I sit with my legs splayed wide and my arms folded.

'I got a little lost trying to find my hotel.' She pulls out a chair and sits elegantly, crossing her legs and placing her elbows on the table. A gold chain hangs around her neck and a matching bracelet on her wrist catches the light. She eludes confidence and seems unfazed at my bad manners. 'You're painting again?' She points at my paint-stained shirt and my favourite blue denim shorts.

I yawn deliberately loudly and don't bother to cover my mouth and I revel in a shiver of satisfaction when she recoils. 'I told you. I need time to think. I want to be alone,' I say.

'I'm worried about you.'

I sigh theatrically.

She is a strong woman and in spite of being ill she is used to getting what she wants. I'm angry that she has manipulated me but worse than that I'm frustrated that I still feel sorry for her. I don't want her to like me and I don't want to form any attachments, certainly not now. Not at this critical stage when my plans are being reworked.

Antonio appears with a chilled glass of beer for me.

'Aguita for the artist,' he jokes. His face is chubby with heavy dark eyebrows. 'Are you going to eat, Mikky?'

'No tengo hambre.'

'Y tu amiga?'

'Tampoco tengo hambre,' Josephine replies. 'But I would like a glass of white wine.'

'You have a good accent,' I say after he's gone. There is so much I don't know about her.

'I'm a trained opera singer. I sing in many languages and Spanish is just one of them.'

'I like Tosca – *Vissa d'arte*. Wasn't that your favourite? You sang it at Michael's funeral.' I cannot bring myself to call a stranger – a man I knew nothing about until last week – my father.

She raises an eyebrow and smiles. 'I'm surprised – you told me you don't like opera.'

'It helps me to paint.'

'To listen to – opera?'

'To all music – it depends on my mood. Normally I like heavy metal… rock. I was brought up on it. Papa loves Iron Maiden – it's his favourite group.' I say deliberately to hurt her as if I am in touch with him and we are the best of friends.

'How is my painting coming along?'

'I didn't agree definitely to paint one for you.'

'I will pay for it.'

'You may not like it.'

'I will.'

I shrug.

'I'm pleased you're painting again,' she smiles. Her mouth is wide like mine but she has told me that I have Michael's eyes.

I wave my empty glass at Antonio to bring me another beer while Josephine tells me how pleased she is with Javier's portrait of her then she says.

'You remember the night in your flat when I came for dinner and Roy came looking for his painting and he threatened Javier?'

Antonio returns with our drinks.

'Yes.'

'I think you took it.'

'Me?'

'Did you?'

I sip my beer. 'Why would I do that? It wasn't even an original.'

'I think you believed it was the original.'

'Think what you like.'

'That's why I want to talk to you. I must stop history repeating itself. I don't want you to be like your father. He was a thief. I want you to be better than that – better than him.'

'A thief? I thought he was a doctor.'

'At the end of the war Michael was a medic in Germany with the Allied forces. I told you that but he found hidden Nazi treasure that had been taken from museums and Jewish people's houses and instead of returning them to the authorities he – along with his three friends – hid them and kept them safe until after the war.'

'So, he found them.' I lean my elbows on the table. She has my attention.

'He stole them.'

'He looked after them.'

'He was a thief.'

'An opportunist,' I argue.

'Do you think he was right to do what he did?'

'Why not?'

'Come on, Mikky! What have you done with it?'

'What?'

'Mrs Green's painting?'

'Why would I have it?'

'A man's life is at risk.'

I focus on a family walking past. 'You're not having an ice cream,' the man says. The toddler whines and lags behind. 'Hurry up, Daisy. Now.'

'I want it, Mikky. I want to return it to Roy.'

I stare at her then I lean back and fold my arms.

'Don't you understand you silly girl, this can get dangerous,' her voice rises.

I look away focusing on a group of tourists but she continues speaking.

'You have no idea the danger you're in, do you? No one is going to let you steal this painting. You will never get away with it. They will follow you and they will kill you. I know what it's like. Look what happened to me, Mikky. I don't want this to happen to you. I want to help you.'

'I can take care of myself. I've had to for all these years. I've managed so far without you.'

She flinches and a thrill of pleasure ripples through me.

'I'm here now, Mikky. I want to–'

'Stay away from me, Josephine! I don't need you.'

'I think you're wrong.'

'Fine.'

'You need a family. You need support and love.'

I lean forward across the table. 'Michael – my real father was Mama's cousin. She never wanted me to go to Ireland or meet any of my Irish relatives – even when she died. I never met any of them. I've managed without a family all my life.'

'I'm here for you now.'

'Mama and I weren't close.' There's a flicker of hope in her eyes. 'She was not an easy woman to live with. She didn't like me. I was a mystery to her. She had no imagination. She had no interest in art or beautiful things. She had affairs with lots of men. She beat me and she treated my father very badly – she was a bully.'

'I'm sorry.'

'You have no idea what it's like to have no one.' I swallow hard.

'Believe me… I do.'

'Even Javier has betrayed me. He's told everyone where I am. Dolores is the closest person to me now.' I nod at the gallery. 'And this is my home.'

***

After my outburst and her calm patience and persistence we speak about art and in the end I relent and take her to the studio where I am staying.

It's an old rustic building with cemented whitewashed floors. The ceiling is rusty pink, the walls are painted in ochre and overhead thick wooden beams have been painted white. Downstairs the living area consists of a kitchenette where I have left plates and dishes to drip-dry amid cooking oils, herbs, jugs and pots of marmalade. In the far corner is a wood burning stove and a basket stacked with chopped logs, pinecones and old newspapers.

An old architect's table is littered with an assortment of shells, pebbles and unusual shaped rocks that I have collected from my walks. Ceramic figures stand beside burnt candle stubs. Empty yogurt pots, a bottle of red wine and empty beer bottles lay haphazardly with discarded CD's and empty cover sleeves.

Sketches and pencil drawings are stuck to the wall and Josephine picks up a photograph of Dolores with her hand held up in protest, squinting into the sunlight, a cigarette dangling from her lips. She looks at one of Carmen and Yolanda beside a beach bonfire, and then one of Javier and Oscar taken last year. She replaces them on the shelf without comment.

An old red sofa is draped with colourful sarongs and an assortment of patterned cushions like those found in a fortune-tellers tent. The open–plan room is divided with a bookcase crammed with art, crime, thrillers and biographies and at the far end is a double mattress covered with a white Egyptian cotton duvet.

'Bathroom is in there.' I indicate a shower room under the stairs painted with aquamarine blue. 'Come up.' I lead the way climbing an open, stone staircase and into a magnificent studio with large patio doors that lead onto a terracotta tiled terrace.

Josephine ignores the paintings and numerous canvases and steps outside where pots are filled with an assortment of cacti and marigolds and the air is filled with the warm aroma of sage and rosemary. She weaves past the old, mismatched wicker chairs and a rickety table where yellow mosquito candles have burnt to their stubs past a faded parasol that hangs lopsidedly and she stands at the low terrace wall and sighs deeply.

'That's the back of Dolores's art gallery.' I point to the building in front of us. In the neighbour's garden below wild blue flowers grow amongst the rubble of the old stone house. A builder calls out from the unfinished building and a three coloured cat stalks along the wall toward the scaffolding.

'That's considered lucky in Germany,' she says.

'And food in Asia.' I reply.

The bell of the old church in the square tolls three. Its square tower rises over the red-slated roof tiles and in the distance the sea glistens like a shimmering illusion.

'At night the tower is illuminated,' I say.

'It reminds me of my terrace in Comaso – in Italy. I had views of the village and the pretty lake below. This is breathtaking,' she says. 'Inspirational.'

A lemon fragrance from the trees wafts up on a light breeze and its familiar aroma comforts me but when Josephine turns there is something in her eyes that I cannot fathom.

'We are quite alike, Mikky. We are quite similar.' She has a half smile on her lips. 'Let me see my painting?'

In the studio she scans the room absorbing the details; canvases all shapes and sizes, some used and some new, paint-stained easels and baskets filled with watercolours, thick and soft brushes and jam jars filled with dirty water and most noticeable of all, tubes of oil paints.

'You don't use acrylics?'

'Sometimes, they dry within an hour whereas oil paints can stay wet for days even weeks depending on the humidity.'

'My goodness, each painting must be five feet square. They're like Caravaggio's,' she says staring at the large unframed canvasses on the wall.

I perch against the bench.

'*The Palm*,' she reads the name aloud before standing back to study my work. 'Your paintings are dark and rich in colour.'

Jesus is lying on the cross as Judas hammers nails into his hands. Much of it consists of shades of brown and grey, which come from Judas' shadow. Light from a lantern above their heads shines onto their faces reflecting the serenity of Jesus' forgiveness that contrasts with Judas' anger and frustration.

'The forty pieces of silver are scattered at Jesus' feet…' She leans forward to scrutinise the painting. 'Is it a woman's hand that holds the lantern? Her face is in shadow. She is hidden. Is it the Madonna? I want to see her face,' she whispers.

I circle the room. 'You'll never see her in one of my paintings.'

Josephine turns her attention to the second painting and I say.

'In the moment that Christ has been pulled from the cross the light has moved and the face that holds the lantern still remains elusive.'

Josephine stands beside me. 'Jesus' chest is smeared with dark red blood. It's the only colour amongst the shades of black and hues of dark brown and grey and his eyes are closed in death.'

I move away but she continues accurately narrating the scene.

'Judas' tears glisten on his cheeks and he cups the falling ones in his hand but they're transformed into glistening silver coins.' She reads its name aloud. '*Forty Pieces of Silver* – money and greed – the love of it – is the root of all evil,' she adds.

'Only for some people.'

'Why don't you paint the Madonna?'

'Her pain would be too raw. Her grief too deep.'

'Because of his death?'

'Because he was her son and she couldn't protect him.'

In that flicker of a moment our eyes meet, so I move to an easel nearer the wall. 'This is your painting, the one you want me to paint for you; *Tones of Truth*.'

'Tones of Truth,' she repeats.

It's my turn to narrate. 'Jesus is in a fishing boat on a wild and choppy Sea of Galilee. Instead of casting a net he has a baton in his hand. It is night and the moon casts an eerie glow illuminating the rapt faces of four men staring at him as if waiting for his word or instruction.'

'My goodness,' Josephine examines them.

'Inside the fishing boat each man holds an instrument: Peter blows into a saxophone, James holds a cello, Mark strums a mandolin and Judas taps a tambourine.'

'It's magnificent. It reminds me of Raffaelle's work. He painted in a similar theme.'

'I need a little more time…to finish it.'

'And why don't you sell more paintings? You should be exhibiting in London or New York or Rome? Why did you give all this up to become a photographer? You silly girl – you have so much talent.'

I snort derisively. 'Tell that to the art critics. They are so up their own arses they know nothing. They're a bunch of self-centred egoists. They're not interested in talent. They think my work won't sell. They say I am too emotionally repressed and that my paintings lack the spark that Caravaggio displays. They say I am a poor imitator of art and that I have no creative skills and that my images are repetitive and dark. The list is endless. I could go on. I won't let it affect me. They know nothing about me.'

'But there must be gallery owners or art dealers who could represent you. A friend of mine has a gallery in New York. I will tell him. I will help–'

'He'll be like all the others. They profess to be experts but they don't even agree with each other. It's a battle of egos and reputation. They have no idea about art or its meaning. They're only interested in money and what sells and how to rip people off. They're an unscrupulous bunch of crooks – and I don't need them.'

'What about Sandra Jupiter or that other lady who owns her own gallery…'

'Phyllis Laverty.'

'Yes, wouldn't she help you?'

'I wouldn't ask them. They only know me as a photographer besides they are no different to any other art dealers. They're just as corrupt.'

'That's a little–'

'It's true!' I interrupt. 'Look at the originals that come to light. They can't decide if they're fakes or forgeries. Besides I don't care any more. I'm a photographer now. I have only painted this for you – as a favour. It's my last painting. '

She ignores me. She doesn't believe me.

'Is this yours too?' She moves over to a second easel facing the window. 'This style is so different.'

'It's a watercolour,' I reply.

'And so much smaller.'

It's approximately three feet by three feet. She leans to examine it closer. 'It's very modern – very different.'

'It's Cubism. Be careful! It's still wet. It's a commission for an Italian and it's what sells in the gallery. Look…' I flick through a stack of paintings propped against the wall pulling them out at random. 'This one is a Frampton, this one a Dali. Here look at this one – hey presto – it's a Picasso.'

'Did you do them all?'

'No! Other artists paint here; students, local artists, Carmen – a friend who once went out with Javier – Dolores gives them a roof over their head and they paint for her. It's what the tourists want. And they sell. When someone likes a painting and can't afford to pay millions for the original they are happy to pay a few hundred euros for a copy to hang on their wall.'

'Is Carmen your girlfriend?'

The bluntness of her question takes me by surprise. 'No.'

'Do you have a boyfriend?'

'I don't want a relationship. I don't trust anyone. They all betray you in the end. It's human nature.'

'Not all men are the same. Michael was the only man I ever trusted–'

'And he lied to you. But it's not just men – it's people. They can't help themselves. My parents were as bad. When I was thirteen I pretended that they weren't my parents. I spent hours on my own and I found refuge in churches, monasteries and chapels.

'It was solitude. It was somewhere to go. It gave

me peace from the never-ending arguments and it gave me security in their continual gypsy wandering. I spent hours studying paintings, sculptures, stained–glass windows and evening after evening I began studying the bible. I even had this tattoo done on my sixteenth birthday. I pretended I was eighteen.'

I turn around and pull up my shirt revealing the tattoo across my back.

'It's the betrayal – in the Garden of Eden. If God couldn't trust Adam and Eve then who could he trust? Man is always out for himself and nothing has changed.' I pull down my shirt. 'After Mama died I went crazy for a while and I thought that I belonged to the Virgin Mary and that she would look after me. I had an affinity with her. I understood her sadness and pain. But no one was there for me. Then for a while I took love from where ever I could find it. I surrounded myself with lovers: men, women, strangers and friends but then I realized…' I glance outside at the blue sky in an attempt to quell my tears. 'None of them ever loved me – it was purely sex.'

'I'm so sorry, Mikky.' She doesn't move but her voice tremors.

'It doesn't matter – I am who I am. This is me and this is now.'

'If I could change things I would, believe me–' She breaks off midsentence. Her hand is warm on my arm and her touch is soft and caring. 'Knowing that I gave you away was the worst thing that ever happened to me. It was more painful than anything I have ever been through. If I could change–'

'You're a very good actress. You must have been excellent on stage.' I pull away from her. 'Your painting will be finished by the end of the week. I can send it to you.'

'I'm happy to stay until then.'

'I need to concentrate,' I say with deliberate malice. 'I don't want you here.'

'Roy promised to sell the Vermeer to a Romanian businessman. You took it from Mrs Green's house and I want to know where it is. You must return it. It's called stealing.'

'You hardly think Mrs Green got it legally.'

'She paid for it.'

'Says who?' I stand defiantly with my hand on my hips so she can see my strength and the muscles in my arms.

'Javier says she bought it from an art dealer.'

'A crook in Holland–'

'A reputable dealer in Bruges.'

'Yeah right,' I laugh. 'Why are you so bothered?'

'Because it doesn't belong to you – it belonged to Mrs Green and it must be returned to her estate or to the authorities or those in charge, and they can do what they want with it.'

'Listen to me, a Vermeer painting supposed to be one of the most sought after and expensive in the world – worth approximately 200 million pounds was stolen over ten years ago from an art gallery in Boston. You hardly think it is going to turn up hanging on the wall in a house in Strand-On-The-Green, where an old lady says she bought it from a reputable dealer in Bruges?'

'You must give it back.'

'She's dead!'

Josephine winces at the coldness in my tone but I continue theorising.

'The estranged son turns up out of the blue with debt problems knowing she has money. He thinks the Vermeer is the real thing but it isn't and these businessmen were stupid enough to believe him and now he's trying to blame someone else.'

'I don't care if it's a fake or not. It doesn't belong to you.'

'I haven't got it. Roy's lying – he has the painting.'

'Javier says, it isn't the same one.'

'It must be.'

'Roy left the painting that you substituted on your doorstep. Javier says it's not the same painting as the one hanging in Mrs Green's house before she died. It's a poor substitute.'

'He never saw the one hanging in her house.'

'He knows by the way it was put back in the frame.'

'So you believe Javier, over me?' I bang my fist on the bench.

She raises her voice. 'In this instance – yes. I know you stole the painting. You think money will save you and give you the security you crave but believe me it won't! I've been there and I know. You can never run from who you are or where you came from–'

'You can say that again,' I shout. A flashback of my empty childhood shocks me: another time, another place and another mother. The image is so vivid of Mama but in an instance her face is gone and I'm standing before a wily and manipulative woman who says she is my birth mother – my own flesh and blood.

We glare at each other. Her chest is heaving as

heavily as my own.

'Where is the painting, Mikky?' she asks quietly.

I pout like a small child. 'Everyone wants the painting for themselves.'

'That maybe true but one thing is certain. It does not belong to you.' She raises an eyebrow.

'It's with a friend. You hardly think I was going to carry a painting in my handbag,' I reply.

'Okay. So return it to Roy and that will be the end of the matter.'

'It doesn't belong to him.'

'Who does it belong to – you?' She laughs. 'You're a thief but you're not stupid. I trust you to do the right thing. It won't bring you luck – it won't buy what you are looking for.'

'It belongs to whoever has it in their possession.'

'Don't speak to me as if I'm stupid! I probably know far more about stolen artwork that you do.' She turns away from me and says in a more reasonable tone. 'Do you not understand? If Roy believes you've stolen the original he will stop at nothing. I know the sort of man he is. He will come after you–'

'He doesn't know I have it.' I begin restacking the paintings on the ground.

'It won't take him long to work it out. Just like I did–'

'I'll be fine.'

'That's what I said when some thugs came looking for something I once had.'

'But you are not me. We're two different people.'

'He will hurt you.'

'I can take care of myself.' I finish restacking the canvasses.

'Return the painting, Mikky. If it's money you want then I will help you. I will promote you. I will hold dinners and fund raising events or whatever it takes. I will make sure that your work is seen and recognised. I have some very good contacts and I will help you get known for your creative talents but not for being a dead art thief. Please, Mikky. Let me help you. Let me be the mother that I was never able to be before. Let me make it up to you.'

I smile slowly. 'I'll tell you what – the Vermeer is a forgery – so go to the dealer in Bruges. Speak to him. Find out the truth and if it's a fake I will keep it but if it is the original then I will return it.'

She seems to weigh up my suggestion. 'Promise?'

There's a noise downstairs, the door opens and a voice calls out. 'Mikky? Where are you? Guess what?' The sound of running flip-flops on the stairs precedes an elfin face and a breathless girl. 'Mikky! Guess – wha– oh? Hello? You're with someone, sorry…'

Maria looks like her grandmother. At only thirteen years old she has the same disconcerting and hypnotic look in her eye as Dolores but she is the shape and size of a young boy. Her hair is cropped short and she rubs her nose nervously looking from me to Josephine and then back to me again. Her eyes are placed wide apart giving her an expression of wariness like a trapped fox.

'What's up, Maria?' I ask. 'Que te pasa? Does Dolores – does Grandma – want me? It's okay. Josephine's cool. You can tell me.'

'There's someone watching the gallery. He's been sitting in the bar all morning and Antonio says he doesn't take his eyes off the door. He takes photographs and makes notes.'

'What does he look like? Is he ugly? Medium height with long blondish hair?'

'Antonio said to tell you, it was the man who was here last week.'

'Karl Blakey.' I glance at Josephine and she pales. 'Do you think he knows – about us – our…?'

She shakes her head and shrugs.

'Go to Bruges, Josephine – go and find out if it's a forgery then you can leave me in peace,' I urge. I want to get her out of the way. It's time for the next phase of my plan – the one where I disappear forever.

Josephine pauses at the top of the stairs then without a word she leaves and I hear the door slam behind her.

I grin at Maria. 'Phew!'

'And what'll I do?' she asks.

'You, my angel, can go to the post office.'

'Post office?'

'Yes. This is a commission for an Italian Count. I need to wrap it up and send it. Give me a hand?'

Her face lights up as if I have given her the best present and the wheels of the next phase of my plan turn into motion.

***

'Mikky? It's Javier.'

'Hi.' I hold the phone against my ear and move around the studio stretching the muscles in my arms and neck.

'You haven't returned my calls.'

'I'm angry with you. You told Josephine where I was and now Karl is hounding me.

'I asked him to warn you. He is not as bad as you think he is.'

'And Josephine?'

'She cares about you. She told me that she's spoken to you. We're worried. Roy thinks I have the painting and he won't take no for an answer. Karl spoke to the Romanian and Roy has three days to get the painting.'

'It's a forgery. And if Roy believes that the one his mother owned is the original then he's delusional.'

'It should be returned to the Museum,' he insists.

'It's not the original.'

'What are you playing at, Mikky? You are the only person who could have swapped the painting.'

'Why would I take–?'

'You wanted to live in this area. You wanted to get close to Mrs Green and I think you made her your friend with the intention of stealing the painting.'

'I suppose you processed this theory of yours with Karl?'

There is silence for a minute then he replies.

'Karl helped me piece it all together and as I can't walk I sent him to warn you.'

'How thoughtful.'

'What's happening to you, Mikky? I don't know who you are.'

'That's a coincidence, Javier – who are you? I always thought our friendship was important but you have betrayed me.'

'You're being ridiculous. These men want the painting.'

'And what is your role in all of this, Javier? What do you want?'

'I want to protect you, Mikky.'

'You've stitched me up. I bet you or Karl have already told Roy where I am.' And I know from his silence that I have spoken the truth.

***

I'm lying in bed with a cool cotton sheet across my naked body but I cannot sleep. I punch my pillow and turn on my side gazing at the patterns and shadows the moonlight creates as it streams in through the open window at the far end of the room.

My mobile tinkles with a text message so I flick on the lamp and squint in the darkness.

You're in danger. Where is the Vermeer? KB.

I type slowly and truthfully.

I have no idea.

Chapter Ten

'I shut my eyes in order to see.'
Paul Gauguin

I lay in bed gazing at the ceiling thinking about the details of my plan. It's not ideal and it's not the best solution but I will be prepared for Roy. I think of what I will tell him – the truth about Josephine will let me off the hook. It's a shock and I want to avoid any publicity but I'll spin a tale of sadness and I will cry and tell him it's the reason I left London. I smile perhaps I have adopted Josephine's acting techniques.

'Adopted, now there's a word,' I say aloud and stretch my hands pushing my palms against the wall above my head.

I was born without a chance but it's up to me to generate my own opportunities. It's up to me to create my own path and my own destiny. There was – and only ever will be – me. I spent hours on my own, a solitary child whose parents never stayed in one place long enough for me to make friends. It made me introverted and I found it difficult to speak to children of my own age. Instead I spoke to priests, nuns and curators, even tourists or worshippers in churches and I saw their faces as they prayed. I listened to their diligent reverie and watched the way their lips moved as they clutched and counted beads reciting their sins, asking forgiveness, begging for a miracle.

I knew the stages of the cross by heart, a million times over. I had seen depictions of them in all shapes and guises; painted, sculptured from wood or cast in reflected light from stained glass.

I understood Christ; his humiliation and betrayal by his twelve closest friends but it had been nothing compared to the betrayal of two mothers. At least Jesus had God on his side.

I was her responsibility and she gave me away. How could she believe – for all these years – that she had given birth to a son? And what sort of man had my father been who could lie about me so easily – a liar, a thief – both?

I swing my feet onto the floor and the cotton sheet slides from my naked body. I shower and brush my teeth.

Who am I?

I go over the details: I have already taken Mrs Green's key and dropped it while I was standing in the middle of Kew Bridge. No breaking and entering, no fingerprints. No proof. Mrs Green is dead. Annie is dead. Roy has skipped bail.

I dry my body and pull on jeans and a loose fitting *Biffy Clyro* T-shirt that I bought at their concert last year and I am whisking eggs when my mobile rings.

'Mikky?'

'Sí,'

'It's me. It's your moth– Josephine. I'm in Bruges. He's admitted it's the original and he'd made a deal with Mrs Green.'

'He's winding you up.'

'Javier suspects you took it and so does Karl. But I *know*, Mikky. I *know* you took it. I'm going to meet a friend of Glorietta's. He's a policeman in Barcelona. He can give you advice–'

'Not interested–'

'He's with the Art Squad. Trust me. I will tell him. You must return it. I will not let you behave like this. You're better than a common art thief. I will not let you behave like your father–'

'What?'

'Like…'

'I heard. Don't be so moralistic. You're the one who slept with your father-in-law.'

'Mikky, I–'

'Listen to me, Josephine. The painting is mine and I never want you to come here again.'

'Please, Mikky–'

'You want the Vermeer for yourself. You've lost everything. You have nothing–'

'I didn't–'

'I don't want to see you and if you start following me I will get you arrested so just leave me alone.' It's an unrealistic threat but I need to keep her away.

I hang up the phone but it rings immediately. I don't recognise the number but I know his voice.

'Mikky?'

'What do you want, Karl?'

'Roy has been here – he's pissed off.' His voice is husky and faint.

'You told him where I was…'

'I've a black eye and I think a few broken ribs–'

'Fuck off, Karl.'

I toss the phone down and breathe deeply. Now the end begins. How can I survive and keep the masterpiece?

***

That evening Dolores smokes continuously. We are sitting on the terrace of her villa on the outskirts of Arta. The sun has long since set and I'm wearing a warm fleece, listening to the clicking of the crickets and enjoying a glass of Armagnac.

I have told her. 'Josephine is my biological mother,' I repeat softly.

Dolores replenishes my glass. She has a cheroot clasped firmly between her lips and she frowns in concentration listening to me.

'At first I wanted her to like me. I wanted her approval. I wanted to be special. Someone she would look up to and respect and be proud to call her daughter but now I don't – I don't care.'

A sea breeze is blowing cool on my cheeks and I push a strand of stray hair behind my ears.

I have also told Dolores about Mrs Green and how Roy believes I have the painting. 'And I am the only one who would know it was a fake, Dolores, but he's going to come after me anyway.'

'We must not take any chances.'

Maria wanders out onto the terrace with a new bottle of brandy. 'Should we tell the Guardia Civil?' she asks.

Dolores takes the bottle from her granddaughter. 'No police – officially – but I will telephone a friend in Palma. He has helped me a few times in the past.'

'No police,' I say.

'You need to be safe. What about your father?'

'If he knew a stolen painting was involved he would sell me to the highest bidder. I won't go to him.' I stand up and stretch my aching shoulder muscles.

'Would you stay with Carmen and Yolanda? You know she's the curator at the Picasso Museum now?' Dolores squints, lifts her glasses and rubs smoke from her eye.

'I haven't decided but when I go away it must be our secret. No one must know.' I lean on the balustrade overlooking the garden where olive, orange and lemon trees fill the air with heavy scent. I take a few paces down the steps into the shadow of the villa and inhale the pine trees that, in the summer, provide welcome shade to the garden. I remember my first summer here and the swimming pool beyond the rocky wall where comfortable rattan sun loungers lay under windswept Tamarind trees. In the distance almond, fig and olive trees are dotted along the undulating hills branching out like Indian headdresses and I experience a sense of deep sadness. I cannot stay here. It's time for me to move on.

Sounds of a television from the villa next door and snatches of a broken conversation reach me in the solitude of the garden. A motorbike accelerates on the street and the crickets busy themselves clicking in the night air. The familiar sounds have a calming influence and my heart slows and I breathe more easily, stretching the taught tendons in my neck and yawning with satisfaction. It's time I found a place of my own with no more running but first I must be prepared. I can only brazen it out. The time has come.

***

The next morning I lay dozing and the neighbour's dog is yapping when the door to the street slowly opens.

The smell of paint, clay and varnish must tickle her nasal passages and she sneezes loudly. She wouldn't make a very good burglar.

I curl up in bed like a foetus but she pulls the duvet and raises her voice.

'Get up, Mikky! Put some clothes on, now.' Her American accent is stronger when she's angry.

Stretching lazily like a cat in warm sunshine I open my eyes and gaze up at her smiling with amusement, watching the horror and shock on her face as she scans my body.

'Oh my, God – get up!' Josephine says. 'Cover yourself.'

'Don't you want to see your baby naked?'

I want to upset her and I rise slowly to my feet watching her eyes travel over my body.

'Well?' I ask. 'You like?'

'You didn't invent tattoos. So don't think you did.' She picks up a pair of shorts and my creased T-shirt from the floor and shoves them into my chest. 'Get dressed!'

'This is *Peter's Betrayal*,' I say pointing to the image that covers the lower part of my stomach. 'And this is *The Supper at Emmaus*.' I point to my right thigh. 'I'm sure you'll recognise this one *The Last Supper?*' I hold out my left leg and her eyes remain fixed on the skilled artwork covering my body. I'm a walking religious icon.

'But this is my tour de force.'

She raises her eyes to my chest and breasts.

'It's the most perfect death scene, don't you think?'

Salome is gloating victoriously as she lifts St.

John the Baptist's bloody head with bulging eyes from a golden platter. Seven colourful veils wind around my waist and envelope my nipples. 'You should get one, Josephine. You said, we're alike, didn't you?'

I prowl naked toward the kitchen, leaving her to stare after me, enjoying her discomfort.

'Not at this present time, you're behaving like a spoilt and difficult child.'

'And you are like a wilful and angry mother.' I search the fridge, open a bottle of chilled water and drink thirstily. 'Why have you come back? If it's for the painting – I don't have it.'

'We have until six o'clock and then the Guardia Civil will be here.'

'Oh, so you've come to save my soul?'

She stands barely a metre away from me and tilts her head to one side. We're the same height and her overlarge mouth and broad nose resemble mine.

Why did I not see this before?

Her eyes rest on my forearm and *Scream;* swirling volcanic colours, symbolic of the horrors and insanity I went through. Her eyes darken and when she looks at me her face is pained and tired.

'Why did you have the Madonna tattooed on your finger?'

'Because she's the ultimate truth, she is what motherhood is all about; forgiveness, love, understanding and sacrifice…'

She takes a small icon of the Madonna from her pocket.

'Take it.' Josephine thrusts it into my hand.

I trail my nail across the icon's body and twirl it in my fingers before holding it to the light. The detail, the curves and the edges, her cheekbones and her shoulders are exquisite.

'It's beautiful,' I say. 'It's the one you showed me in Dresden.'

'I had believed the role was mine. I thought I was Tosca. It was the greatest role I ever played. Glorietta Bareldo gave it to me on the evening of my last performance and I believe this Madonna saved my life.'

I turn the icon in my hand.

'Afterward, she visited me in hospital and then she took me home to her villa. She cared for me and showed me what forgiveness, love and friendship truly are. She was my nurse and she became my friend and I began to heal. She was the first person I told about you and she helped me find a private detective. She gave me encouragement and hope. Finally, I had a purpose and a reason for living.'

'You didn't think to involve a professional? One who would offer counselling?' I place the small icon onto the worktop beside the scalpel, next to the marmalade.

'It's not too late to seek professional support. I can get help for you. There's a specialist in London who…'

'It must have been hard to see me for the first time and not to say anything. Why didn't you tell me sooner – in Dresden?'

'Because, I wanted you to like me for me, and not because I was once famous. People have always wanted to know me because I was an opera star and rarely for the person I really was – or am.'

'And Michael?'

'I loved your father. He was the only man who

ever understood me.'

'But he lied to you.'

'He believed in me.'

'He told you I was a boy! He betrayed you, as you have now betrayed me and when the police come, I will tell them you're wasting their time. There is no proof or a shred of evidence that the painting was the original or that I stole it.'

'I will fund your career. I will get the art critics to take note of your work. I will support you. I promise. I don't want you to spend the rest of your life incarcerated, beaten or abused in a prison. You are worth more than that. I believe in you–'

'Why?'

'I am an artist too. I sing – I sang – it was my passion and my life. It was my dream and I would have done anything but I was lucky, I met a very kind man who allowed me to discover myself and to explore my deepest desires. He gave me my life–'

'And just look where you are now.'

'I'm in the most important place in my life – right this minute. Here. Now. With you! I would not wish to be anywhere else.'

I laugh. 'You're very funny. You call the police then come and tell me that you are doing it all for me. You're fucking nuts.'

We both turn at the sound of the door creaking very slowly open.

My mouth dries. My body is taut. This is it.

'Get out,' I hiss at Josephine. 'Get out now…Get the fuck out!' I shout. 'You're not wanted. Go away. Piss off out of my life…'

The door opens and Maria's head appears with her

cheeky elfin grin. 'Mikky? Are you all right?' she says.

Wordlessly Josephine clutches her shawl, straightens her back and slides her body sideways past my nakedness and out of the door without a backwards glance.

'I have to be alone. Get out, Maria. Stay away from me. Don't come here any more!' I shout in the most angry and aggressive voice I can muster and I'm not proud of myself as shock registers on her face and tears well in her eyes and she scuttles away.

My carefully laid plan is unravelling but I must face what's coming. It's my only option and I must do it alone. I can hope for a miracle but as God hasn't looked after me so far in my life I can only assume that he will probably forget about me again.

***

By mid-afternoon I'm still waiting. What's taking him so long? My body is straining for each sound, each rev of a motorbike, every dog bark or squeal of a cat, even the whisper of a voice from the street. Then when the door eventually creaks open, I flinch and the muscles of my body are coiled tightly and my breathing is controlled.

Roy's beard is long and unkempt. His eyes are red and tired and his temple still carries the fading bruise from Annie's beating almost three weeks ago. His shirt is creased as if he has been sleeping rough but he moves lightly on his feet but with caution, his fists are clenched at his side.

'Hello, Mikky.' He closes the street door gently. 'There's no point in waking the neighbours from their siesta, is there?' He puts a finger to his lips and looks around scarcely believing his luck that I am alone and a vulnerable target.

I have a kitchen knife at my elbow but his stride is long and quick and he takes me by surprise grabbing my arm and shoving it behind me in an arm-lock. My left hand still clutches a paintbrush but he takes it gently from my hand and places it on the counter.

'We can make this as easy or as difficult as you like. First, I will tell you what's going to happen then I will give you some choices as to *how* it will happen. You see, I know you have the painting.' I wince in pain as he tightens his grip. His breath is stale and his eyes staring as if he hasn't slept. 'And, you're going to give it to me and the choice you have is *how* you are going to do it – the right or the wrong way? What do you think?'

'I don't have it.' I grit my teeth as a sharp pain shoots up my arm to my neck.

'Ah, I see, so it will be the hard way, so where is it?'

I swallow with difficulty. I think he will break my arm. He will never believe my story about Josephine. 'In London…'

He laughs and I scream.

'Now, now, now, there's no point in lying to me. It will only hurt you more in the long run. Let's do this amicably and get it over with, shall we?'

I'm like a rag doll in his arm, limp and ineffective but I nod. The pain is making my knees weak.

'Let's try again. Where's the painting?' He's like a father talking to a baby who's lost a toy: when did you last have it?

'In the studio.' I flick my eyes to the ceiling.

'Come on then. You lead the way.'

His grip is like cement and we walk like scuttling crabs up the stairs.

'Where?'

I gasp in pain.

'There.' I nod my head to a stack of canvasses propped against the wall.

'I haven't got all day, Mikky.' His tone is calm and casual as if he is a thoughtful friend.

'That wall – there.' I nod with my chin.

'Show me.' He could snap my right arm without any effort so I shuffle and when I bend forward he loosens his grip. I flick randomly through some of the paintings stacked against the wall, a Frampton and a Picasso then my hand reaches the Vermeer.

'You cut it from its frame,' he says.

'Couldn't bloody carry that too,' I hiss.

'You bought it over here?'

'Wrapped between two other canvasses.' I hold it out.

'Put it on the floor.'

I place it at his feet and as I stand up he spins me around and removes wire from his pocket but I grab a paintbrush from the easel and lunge toward him pushing the pointed end deep into his cheek narrowly missing his eye. He screams and holds his face but he sidesteps and balls his fist into my chest. The punch goes through the cavity of my lungs but as I double over I reach out and fling a jam jar it into his face, dirty water splashes into his eyes and his elbow deflects the glass. It shatters on the floor at my feet and as I bend, I snatch the canvas. Staggering away from him I reach out with my free hand and grab a silver candlestick.

'I'll break your fucking neck,' he growls then lunges for me but like a bullfighter I move deftly to one side and whack his head. He dodges the blow but his hand grips my throat and I knee him between his legs. He grunts, releases his grip and backs away, panting heavily. He is about to jump me but I shout.

'Wait!'

He pauses. Blood falling from his cheek and we stand a few metres apart.

I flick the lighter and hold the trembling blue flame to the corner of the painting.

'No.' He holds out his hands. 'Don't!'

'Don't make me,' I shout.

'You wouldn't.'

I'm winded and panting heavily. I can barely breathe. Pain ricochets across my chest. The room is spinning and I grip my stomach muscles forcing blood to my head to stop myself from fainting.

This is it. This is the end. My fate is sealed.

The flame licks the edge of the canvas. It sizzles slowly then a sudden flare and it begins to burn, glowing and crackling and I feel the heat on my fingers.

His mouth hangs open. Disbelief in his eyes and I think he is about to throw himself at me so I toss the burning canvas to the floor and prepare to take his body against mine but he checks his step and with slow control he lashes out and punches me in the face. I crumple to my knees and watch him dousing the flame stamping, cursing and swearing.

'She never owned the original. It's a fake,' I shout.

He picks up the charred painting and hot burning ash falls to the floor. He blows on his fingers and wipes blood from the gaping hole in his cheek. His eyes burn with anger. 'You bitch! You stupid fucking bitch.'

'She lied to you,' I shout. 'She wanted you to move in so she wouldn't have to go into a home. She knew it was a copy.' I shuffle away from him, backing against the wall, my knees hunched in front of me. My stomach heaves and pain causes green bile to spew from my mouth and I am sick.

He looks at my workbench and picks up a scalpel. It glistens in his hand and I scramble to my feet but he is faster and stronger than me. In two strides he's beside me. I push his fist away, thumping his arms, his face, his chest but he grabs my throat and the pain is excruciating. I cannot breathe and fear shoots though my veins as he holds the sharp, cold instrument to my cheek and then it all goes fuzzy and his slobbering breath covers me like an invisible fog and I slump, like a willing lover, in his arms and lose consciousness.

When I wake I'm lying on the cold cement floor. My head is burning and I cannot move. My eyes won't focus. Blood is trickling down my face seeping into my mouth. I cough. I choke. I spit.

I'm on fire.

My head is too heavy to lift. My world is silent filled only with my shallow breathing. My head is raw, open and vulnerable. Nothing makes sense. White noise fills my ears. Vibrant electricity. My lips are swollen with sticky tears.

My left cheek lays pressed against the floor and through my right eye it looks as if the studio has been raided; canvasses are slashed and torn, paint is dripping from overturned pots and easels lie broken. Swirling smoke drifts up the stairwell. I cough and try to move leaning shakily on my elbow but my legs are like dead anchors weighing me down. They refuse to move. My arms give way and my body collapses, the room swirls and I succumb to a world that welcomes me with darkness and the promise of sleep. It drags me deeper into its clutches and into obscurity that will last for eternity, a world without pain, without torture and without hurt. From behind my burning eyes and inside my throbbing head I see the familiar flashing red lights from a pinball machine:

Game Over. Game Over. Game Over.

Chapter Eleven

'On the floor I am more at ease. I feel nearer, more a part of
the painting, since this way I can walk around it, work from
the four sides and literally be in the painting.'
Jackson Pollock

A wet cloth goes over my face. Hands are under my
shoulders and I am dragged along the floor. My ankle
catches and a man curses. He kicks out. My chest is
exploding and I am bumped down stairs: choking,
bleeding, coughing and crying. Thick smoke fills my
nostrils and mouth, and a roaring heat intensifies
burning my face, it's the pain that makes me scream as
I'm pulled to my feet and he flings my arm over his
shoulder. The other arm dangles uselessly at my side.
He uses his hips to balance my weight and lifts my feet
from the floor but he's not strong nor fit and we
stumble against a chair and fall. My head is bursting,
hanging off, hanging loose as he grabs me in his arms
again and we stagger through the dense smoke and
finally we are outside. The air is fresh and the sun is
warm and I gasp for air, coughing and choking bile
from my throat and he lays me on the ground.

'Mikky? Where is it?'

My vision is blurred but it's still daylight and the
sky is deep blue. His face is only inches from me and
his eye is swollen and a graze on his cheek is bleeding
onto his chin.

'For God's sake, Mikky! I haven't come all this
bloody way to rescue you! Where is it?' He shakes my
shoulder. 'Where's the painting?' He shakes me harder

and a wave of nausea fills me and I turn on my side and heave.

'Crisisake!' His voice is angry and impatient. 'The Vermeer, is–it–in–there? What?' He leans forward putting his ear to my lips.

'Burnt…'

'Inside?' He staggers to his feet clutching his ribs.

'Gone…' I say but he doesn't hear me. My vision blurs and fades but not before I see Karl Blakey disappear into the burning building without a backward glance.

***

'Mikky?'

My head lolls to one side. I cannot lift it. My mouth is dry and my lips are on fire.

'Mikky!' Dolores' is wiping my cheeks with a wet towel. 'Graçias a dios, she's alive! What happened?'

I try to speak but I am wracked in pain.

'Tranquila!' She slides her hands under me and hoists me up so that I lean with my back propped against her chest. Her breath smells of tobacco but I welcome the strength of her body and her bony fingers that soothe my arms and pushes matted hair from my face.

'The ambulance is on its way–' *Josephine's voice?*

'Burnt?' I whisper. My voice is slurred. My tongue won't work and my eyes are heavy. They won't stay open.

A cool, damp cloth is pressed against my forehead. I want to drink it. 'Come on, Mikky. You'll be all right. Everything will be fine. Come on, my sweet girl. I'm here and I will never leave you again.'

Josephine?

'I told you to stay away…' I mumble.

'She's losing a lot of blood,' Dolores whispers.

'I won't let her die,' Josephine replies and presses water to my puffy lips and swollen eyes.

'Did …he …find it?' I slur but no one answers me.

'They're sending an air ambulance to get her to Palma quicker,' Josephine says.

'I hope they hurry,' replies Dolores.

The pain is too much and I pass out.

***

A smiling angel in a white tunic is beside me when I open my eyes. His fingers are cool, long and slim. He holds a plastic cup to my lips and places a hand gently behind my neck and this simple kindness reduces me to tears.

'It's shock, Mikky. But you're on the mend now.' His voice is soft and caring. His eyes are the colour of cinnamon and he has bleached blond hair.

The intensive care unit fades in and out of my consciousness but I watch him write something then he checks a tube in my arm. I don't remember much else apart from Josephine's hollow-eyes and vacant stare.

'Your mother has been here around the clock. She only went back to her hotel this morning after I insisted – she needed a shower.' His smile is broad and his teeth white against his smooth olive skin. I cannot take my eyes from him as he glides effortlessly like a silent, well-muscled ballet dancer and I am left with his image planted firmly on my retina when I drift back to sleep.

My angel.

When I open my eyes I'm in a private room. It's bright and white and light. My eyes hurt and there's a tight vice around my head that grips my skull. I fade in and out of sleep and when I open my eyes Josephine is sitting beside me in an upright leather chair. Her eyes are ringed black and she is pale and gaunt but her face breaks into a worried grin and she leans across the bed.

'Mikky!' She clasps my fingers.

I raise my hand to the gauze bandaged around my head as she plumps crispy cotton pillows behind me.

'How are you?' Her eyes are filled with tears.

'Terrible.'

'You're going to be all right.'

She follows my gaze as I look around the private room. 'I brought you flowers and grapes,' she says.

'Unoriginal.'

'They're supposed to cheer you up.'

'It worked – I'm happy.' I attempt a smile and hold my hand to my head.

'I can ask for some painkillers.'

'Please...'

'You will make a full recovery. No kidney needed.'

'I'll kick his arse next time.'

'Did Karl do this?'

I shake my head. 'Roy.'

'Roy?'

'I stabbed his cheek with a paintbrush.' Images come back to me and my eyes begin to close and I doze off, and this becomes the pattern, and each time I wake

Josephine is sitting beside me

The following day she is in her usual place, protectively, on the edge of my bed but this time a lanky, pale, bald-headed man is also standing at the window.

'This is Inspector Torres. He's with the art squad from Barcelona,' she explains quietly.

He moves around the room, stares out of the window then sits in the chair beside my bed.

'How are you feeling, Señorita?'

'So-so.'

'We want to catch the person who did this to you. Can you tell me what happened?'

I don't answer. It's too complicated.

'Who did this to you?' he insists.

'Roy…Green.'

'Why?'

I look at Josephine and she says. 'I told the Inspector what happened in London.'

'What did he want?' The Inspector moves closer to the bed. 'The painting?'

I don't answer so Josephine prompts me. 'Can you remember?'

'I stabbed him…'

The Inspector leans forward to hear me better.

'With a paint brush…'

'Did he come for the painting, Mikky?' he asks.

I nod.

'Was he alone?'

I nod.

'And he beat you?' says the Inspector. 'But you stabbed him with a paint brush?'

I motion my action with a loosely clenched fist.

'He was bleeding.' My voice is rasps and my throat is dry.

'Can you tell me what happened exactly?' When he leans forward his bald head catches the sunlight and it shines like polished marble. 'Did you give him the painting?'

'Burnt it.'

'Roy burnt it?'

'I – it was a fake,' I mumble.

Josephine and the Inspector swap glances.

'Was Karl Blakey there?'

I shake my head.

'When did Karl Blakey arrive?' he asks. 'Before Roy or after Roy?'

'After.'

'So Roy set fire to the studio, did he?'

I shrug and nod.

'But Karl dragged you out and saved you?' he says.

'The building was on fire.' I try to remember.

'He must have gone back in…' Josephine says to the Inspector.

'Did you see Karl Blakey go back in to the building?' he asks.

'I think so...'

'Why?' The inspector rubs his marble crown.

I'm trying to remember but my head hurts and I close my eyes.

'The painting,' Josephine says holding my hand. 'Did he go back inside to get the painting?'

I open my eyes. That's it. 'Yes.'

***

'You're lucky to be alive,' Josephine says to me later that evening. We are alone and I'm feeling more awake and stronger. I am recalling more of what happened but the details still evade me. I try to sit up and Josephine helps me get comfortable placing the pillows behind my neck.

'Roy beat you then set the building on fire and left you for dead,' she says.

'Karl Blakey was there– I think I told him I had burnt the painting.'

'But he went back inside. The Guardia Civil found his body,' she says.

Her nemesis is dead. How does she feel?

'He saved me. Why?'

'I think he wanted to be the hero – the one who found the painting and returned it to the Isabella Stewart museum.'

'But now he's dead?'

'Yes.' Josephine's eyes do not leave my face.

'I didn't like him – but I am sorry.'

'I know.' She takes my fingers and holds them tenderly.

'He saved my life.'

'I have to be grateful to him for that.' Josephine holds my fingers and we lock gazes then I close my eyes.

After a few moments I feel her prize open my fingers and she slides something cool into my hand. 'The Madonna saved you,' she whispers.

'Where did you find it?'

'In the pocket of your jeans.'

It seems surreal as if it all happened to someone else but the pains in my body tell me the truth.

'Karl is dead but I survived. The painting is gone,' I say.

'The Inspector and his team are going through the debris. It's difficult because it was an art studio but they're hoping that some chemical analysis of paint or canvas that was saved in the fire will give some indication that it was burnt.'

'But it wasn't the original…'

Josephine shrugs. 'We shall see. You were lucky.'

'Did they find Roy?'

'Not yet, he may need medical treatment if that paint brush hurt him like you think it did. He could still be on the island. There are police outside just in case he comes looking for you and they're keeping a watch on the airport and the ferries.'

'He won't come after me now. The painting is gone.'

'I can't believe you burnt Mrs Green's painting?'

'It was a fake.'

'You mean after all that trouble, you set it alight?'

'I know a fake when I see one and it wasn't a particularly good one either.'

'Why did you steal it?'

'I hoped it was the original but I knew as soon as I took it from the frame that it wasn't.'

'So why take it to Mallorca?'

'I didn't know what else to do with it. I had to get away after I went to see Angela Morris – you know – the nurse, and I was upset. I just had to get out. I needed to be on my own.'

Josephine sighs and I wonder if she believes me.

Does the private investigator still follow me?

'So, you broke into your neighbour's house and stole the painting. Then what?'

'I cut it out of the frame, rolled it up and posted it with some other canvasses to Mallorca but it was a forgery,' I say. 'Roy was trying to sell a fake. Mrs Green knew the painting was a forgery. She pretended it was real to get Roy to move back in and take care of her. She was a wily old woman. '

'How could she be so sure he would believe her?'

'He wanted to. He had lots of debts and she dropped enough hints that it was the original. It was like dangling a carrot in front of a starving donkey.' My head throbs and I reach for my forehead. 'What did he do to me?'

'He used a scalpel to cut into your forehead.'

I begin tugging the bandage, unwinding it and pulling in loose.

Josephine leans closer and holds my wrists trying to stop me and I smell her familiar lavender cologne.

'Get off! I want to see it. What did he do?'

She lets me go then helps me gently to remove the bloody bandage leaving it laying coiled on the sheet like an inert bloody white snake. I pull off the padded gauze.

'Mirror?' I demand.

She takes a cosmetic mirror from her handbag. 'Mikky, I have to tell you–'

I snatch it from her and hold it to my swollen face. There are five ragged letters scored across my forehead. I read them back to front in the mirror trying to make sense of what Roy did to me. 'Oh no.'

'It will be all right. I will get you cosmetic

surgery.'

I throw her small mirror onto the bed lean my head back and close my eyes squeezing the tears tightly inside. Silence envelops me. I will not sob aloud. She must not see me this way. I will not lose control.

'It will be okay, Mikky! I'll look after you.' She picks up my hand and I am too upset to pull away from her. My eyes and my trembling mouth are firmly closed and I try and block out the pain of the five scratched letters scored raggedly into my forehead: T-H-I-E-F.

***

'Javier called you again. He has phoned twice a day for the past three days,' Josephine says after my siesta.

'How is he?

'He wants to come over. He wants to see you.'

'He can't travel.'

'He can with a cast, although not easily.'

'What did he say about Karl?'

'He was shocked – upset.'

'I don't want to see him. I don't want to see anyone.' I turn away and gaze out at the turquoise blue sky where palm trees are bending in the gusty wind and I imagine my favourite beach near Tarifa, Spain's most southerly point, beyond Gibraltar and Algeciras with the Atlas mountain of Morocco across the Atlantic.

'I have organized a consultant to visit you about cosmetic surgery. He is the best.'

'I think I might leave it. It will remind me of who I am.'

'Don't be ridiculous. You're feeling sorry for

yourself. There are many people much worse off than you. We will get you sorted then we can carry on with our lives and it will be as if none of this has happened.'

I gaze at her and say nothing.

'In a year's time we won't even remember all this.' She affirms with a nod of her head. 'I will arrange some exhibitions for you and you'll be a recognized artist. Dolores told me that most of your artwork was in the art gallery. Was it a coincidence that you moved them in there?'

I shrug.

'Well, I'm pleased that my painting is not damaged. You will still finish it for me, won't you?'

'Have you always been so bloody optimistic?'

'Not until recently but when I saw you lying on the pavement in front of that burning building, I knew that I would do anything to make your life better. I said a prayer to the Madonna and she answered me. You have been saved. Now it's time to get well again and to live. We can get to know each other – if you will let me share your life?'

I am reluctant to push her away and I'm also curious. I wonder what it would be like to have a mother like her. She holds my hand and traces the contorted face of *Scream* with her finger.

'Do you like it?' I ask.

'It's excellent but I don't like the sentiment behind it. I don't want you to feel so angry and frightened – as if you are having a breakdown.'

'That was a long time ago.'

'We need to heal together, Mikky. Why don't we take some time out and spend a while getting to know each other. I could rent us a place to stay – anywhere in the world – so that you can get well again; feel the wind on your face and the sun on your skin. What do you think?'

'And what if the truth comes out about us?' I ask.

'Then we will deal with it together.'

'What if all your fans want to know who the father of your daughter is? What will you say?'

'We will think of something. Sometimes, like the Queen of England, it is best just to say nothing and to behave with dignity.'

'Will I tell, Javier?'

'That is up to you. The press have been waiting outside the hospital but I have managed to avoid them. Your story has been in the newspapers because a journalist saved you–'

'They will find out…'

'There are always rumours. The hospital staff know the truth because I told them I would give you anything. When we arrived here you were so badly beaten they thought you may need a kidney and I offered mine.'

'Thank you–'

She smiles and I am comforted by her presence. I'm getting used to her beside me and my eyes begin to close. 'Sleep, my darling. I will be here with you. I will protect you.'

Her fingers lightly caress my cheek and I'm aware that this is my mother's hand and this is how it feels to be loved. A flicker of tenderness is ignited in me and the sense of vulnerability is overwhelming. Although I know I shouldn't get used to it, I think it will be just until I'm better and a feeling of relief and contentment washes over me that is so strong it causes large tears to well up and when I fall asleep the pillow is damp against my cheek.

***

Javier phones my mobile I swing my legs over the edge of the bed but it makes me dizzy, nauseous and light headed.

'We're in the same boat,' he says cheerfully. 'Neither of us can move.'

'At least you are at home and Oscar is running around after you. He's probably treating you like a king.'

'All true – are you feeling bad?'

'More of a damaged ego – I got it wrong. I should never have got involved with the painting at all.'

'Why did you switch it?' he asks.

'I was hoping it was the original.'

'When did you realise it wasn't?'

'After I stole it but it was too late to put it back – and to be honest I thought the whole thing would blow over. I was sure Roy would realise his mother had said it deliberately so that she had company.'

'So what happened over there?'

I tell him how Roy came to the studio and how Karl rescued me from the burning building.

'You're lucky.'

'Yes – really lucky. I now have the letters T–H–I–E–F sliced into my forehead,' I sigh. 'Anyway, how's the commission coming on? Have you finished Josephine's portrait?'

'It will be shipped over to Italy in a few weeks.'

'Have they seen it?'

'I sent photographs and to Josephine.'

'Is she pleased?'

'You should ask her yourself.'

'I will.'

'She's been very good to you considering how rude you were to her. She will pay for cosmetic surgery – and she's paying for your private treatment. You're a very lucky girl. I honestly don't know why she's bothering with you.'

'She's kind.' I am not ready to tell him she is my biological mother. It's my secret.

'I still can't believe you set fire to the painting. Why?' he asks.

'It was a fake.'

'Are you sure you didn't paint a fake yourself? And substitute it?'

'Do you honestly think I could copy a Vermeer so easily?'

'You copied the one that you hung back up in Mrs Green's house.'

'Yes, and even Roy knew that it was rubbish.'

'Did Karl say anything to you, you know before…?'

'He wanted the painting, Javier. He saved me just to get the painting.'

'You know he was convinced Josephine is hiding something else – like she has a big secret. Do you know what it is?'

'No.'

'Why has she spent so much time over there with you? It is it because of the Vermeer?'

'You would have to ask.'

'She's obsessed with doing the right thing.

Perhaps she thinks you still have the painting? Have you thought about that?'

I've thought of nothing else but I reply.

'Well, Javier – I don't have it! Once the forensic evidence is complete and they find nothing to suggest that it was the original, all the fuss will die down and everyone will realise that Mrs Green was having a laugh at everyone's expense.'

'You are getting on well with Josephine – are you friends, now?'

'When we found you in Mrs Green's house we thought we'd lost you and I got to know her. We spoke for hours that morning. She's very fond of you, Javier.'

'So you like her now?'

'I respect her.'

'Umm. So what are your plans?' he asks.

'I'm having an operation on my shoulder tomorrow morning but when I leave here Josephine has asked me to stay with her in Dresden or she says we can go somewhere else – somewhere warm. She says she will look after me.'

'And will you go?'

'I can't fly at the moment. My head feels as though it has razors inside. I think I'll just stay on the island. The studio got trashed and burnt but the main structure of the building seems okay, luckily it's separate to the art gallery. Dolores said I can stay with her at the villa but I don't know yet...'

'So it's all over,' he says. 'When will you come home?'

'I don't feel right about going to England at the moment.'

'I was thinking the other day how you were so

keen to find somewhere to live in Strand-On-The-Green. You were like a woman possessed and it didn't take you long to make friends with Mrs Green either…'

'What are you trying to say?'

'Nothing, I'm just–'

'Don't, Javier. Don't start jumping to dangerous conclusions that could get us all into trouble. Mrs Green is dead. Annie is dead and so is Karl Blakey. Roy will be found – he can't hide forever. There's nothing left to discover. There is no secret. So, get well and go on holiday to South America with Oscar and live happily ever after. He suits you. It would never have worked out between you and Karl anyway. Take some time out, Javier. But please whatever you do forget about that bloody fake masterpiece.'

***

The following night I'm recovering from an operation on my shoulder, Josephine looked tired and worried and she needed to rest so I sent her back to the hotel.

I lay dozing still drowsy from the anaesthetic in that state of imagination and day dreaming before sleep takes its grip and I fall into dark oblivion.

I turn quickly, the footfall is soft but I'm suddenly alert. He looks vaguely familiar and self-consciously I pull my gown to cover the gruesome image on my chest of St. John the Baptists' severed head and Salome's gloating smile.

'You don't have to – I've seen all your tattoos.'

'You're the angel from my dreams,' I whisper.

'Er no, but I am your nurse from Intensive Care.

My name is Eduardo.' His laughter is light and teasing.

'I'd prefer an angel but you'll have to do if that's all God can spare.'

'I think you don't need an angel. You have someone far more important looking after you.'

'Like who?'

'A mother.'

'The Madonna?'

'Not that mother.'

He sits beside me on the bed. 'I wanted to make sure you are behaving yourself.'

'I can't do much else.'

'You will be better soon. You will be able to go next week.'

'Bliss.' I sigh dramatically.

'Where is home?'

'I haven't decided,' I reply.

He smiles. 'I'm from Cadiz.' Then he asks me about London and we talk for while and I'm surprised that he talks candidly about himself and I'm comfortable in his company. It is the end of his shift and he tells me he lives in Palma. He rides a motorbike to work and he says he is going home for a cold beer on his terrace.

'I could drink one now,' I say.

'When you are better I will invite you for a drink and we can watch the sunset together.'

My eyes are heavy and I fall asleep without saying goodnight and I dream of a brilliant orange sky and the lapping of the Atlantic and salt on my lips.

The next morning Eduardo pops in before his shift with the excuse that he wants to make sure I slept well. 'There's a guy hanging around outside who wants to talk to you. I think he's too old to be your boyfriend…'

'I don't have a boyfriend.'

'No?' Eduardo smiles.

'What does he look like?'

'Medium height, hair tied back in a ponytail, tattoos and silver rings on his fingers.'

'Oh!' I stare out of the window at the blue sky wishing I could run away.

'Do you have someone to take care of you?'

'You mean to cook and clean?'

'No, I mean someone who will keep you out of trouble and stop you from getting into more cuts and scrapes.'

My finger automatically traces the outline of the word on my head covered with gauze. 'It is quite unique.'

'Not a great character reference though if you are looking for a job.'

'I'm a freelance photographer.'

'Just as well, much better for you to be behind the lens.'

'I photograph nurses for magazines who have the potential to be male models– are you interested?'

'No.' His eyes do not leave my face and his smile widens. 'Besides I think that isn't true. It's just a ploy.'

'Ploy?' I smile, 'For what?'

'For you to flirt with me and to see my body.'

'I don't know how to flirt. Besides I'm not looking my best.'

'You can look better?'

'I've been known to make an effort. A little makeup and a hat.' I indicate the brim that would cover most of my face.

'A black pointy one?'

'I was thinking of something prettier – more feminine.'

'You'll never hide all that hair.'

'I'll use a balaclava.'

'Ah? And what about in the summer when it gets hot and we go to the beach?'

'Swimming cap?' I giggle.

'You like the beach?'

'I like to sunbathe.'

'I don't suppose you want to learn how to kite-surf, do you?' he asks.

'Can you teach me?'

'Yes.' He looks at his watch. 'I'll pop back later.'

'What about the man outside? Were you joking?'

'No.' He reaches out and gently touches the tips of my fingers. Then from the doorway he winks and blows me a playful kiss.

***

They have told me I'm on heavy painkillers and strong medication to combat the infection of my swollen organs. I'm drowsy but the first thing I notice is the faded *Iron Maiden* T-shirt and my senses are suddenly alert. It was a Christmas present I gave him eight years ago. There are sunburnt laughter lines around his scrunched up eyes and I wonder if he needs glasses. Chest hairs grow up to a scraggly beard and his long hair is tied back with a leather band.

'Hola.'

'Papa?'

'How are you?'

'Fine,' I lie. 'How are you?'

'Like you care?' He sits on my bed and reaches for my fingers.

'Why are you here?'

'Josephine called me.'

I stare at him wondering who we both are and how well we know each other.

'Did she tell you that I know?'

He rubs the back of his hand across his nose and won't look at me.

'I'm adopted,' I whisper. 'I'm not yours.'

'What happened to your forehead?'

'Tell me the truth, Papa.'

'Don't be ridiculous.'

'Why did you and Mama want a child? Why did you want me?'

There is silence while he thinks. 'Your Mama and I loved you very much. She would be very proud of you if she were alive today.'

'Are you proud of me? Have you ever taken an interest in my career?'

'You know I don't like London. I hate big cities.'

'I have proof that you're not my parents.'

'Don't be crazy, cariño. Our names are on your birth certificate.'

'You both lied.'

'Why would we do that?' He won't look me in the eye.

'Because you were paid well and it allowed you to live the life you both wanted. But I was an inconvenience. I was a burden to you. That's why you left me in churches and monasteries, and–'

'That's not true–'

'Mama never really wanted me. She was jealous when you spent time with me and then she would have an affair to punish you.'

'That's not true, cariño'

'You know it is.'

In the silence he lets out a sigh and his shoulders droop. 'Josephine said you would insist on knowing the truth and I have thought about it a lot.'

'She came looking for me. She hired a private investigator to find me.'

'I know, she phoned me. She thought it would be a good idea for me to visit you – I came as soon as I could but if you don't want me here…'

'I do.'

He settles himself into the chair beside me but I am uncomfortable turning sideways to look at him.

'It has been over eight years,' I say. 'But I've managed. I've done well. I'm a photographer now.'

'We brought you up to be independent – to be tough.'

'I can look after myself.'

'That's good.'

'I had to.'

'You're still angry.'

'I am far angrier now. Now, I know you're not my parents.'

'Your Mama and I *are* your parents. We brought you up. We raised you. We did the best we could.'

'Mama was jealous and angry. She hated me…'

'Only as you got older, when you grew taller and more beautiful and then she was frightened that I would take advantage of you. She didn't want anyone to know that you were not our daughter.'

'You wouldn't have taken advantage of me. You're not like that. You barely spoke to me.'

'She was very possessive. I had to be careful for both of us.'

'She hated us laughing together but you never stuck up for me.'

He doesn't raise his eyes to look at me so I continue speaking.

'I was fourteen when she died. We could have been friends afterwards.'

He shakes his head. 'I was filled with guilt, Mikky. We had argued about you and she was drunk. She took my motorcycle and I couldn't forgive myself – all the guilt – and after she died when we were on our own I couldn't comfort you. I was frightened her predictions would come true. It was like she was still taunting me even though she was dead. I loved you so much. We both needed comfort but I couldn't trust myself. I couldn't tell you the truth, so–'

'You didn't want me around.'

'I wanted you to be self-sufficient and not to need anyone. I wanted you to be strong emotionally – in here.' He thumps his chest with his bunched fist. 'But I did miss you.'

'I went looking for love from anyone who would give it to me,' I say.

'I couldn't stop you.'

'You didn't try.'

He strokes the edge of the sheet folding it over his calloused, oil ingrained fingers as if testing its softness.

'Did Michael send you money?'

'That's how I afforded to send you to University.' The irises of his eyes are pink and bloodshot as if he was drinking until late last night. 'We were young when we agreed to take you. Your Mama had an abortion before I met her and it had gone wrong. We were working in the same hotel and we needed money.'

'How much?'

'What?'

'How much did he pay you to take me?'

He pauses. 'Ten thousand pounds.'

I stare at him. 'I was sold.'

'It allowed us to start a new life and he paid each year until he died.'

'That was only last year.'

'Yes. Then the money stopped.'

'But I never saw any of the money.'

'No.'

'Did you know Josephine was my mother?'

'Not until two days ago – she phoned me. We guessed you were special because of all the secrecy but Michael never told us that you were his daughter. Michael was your Mama's cousin and when your Mama couldn't have children I was devastated but then Michael said that we could register you as our own and we jumped at the chance. We didn't ask questions, we took off to Spain and never looked back.'

'You never thought I looked like Michael?'

He shakes his head. 'She – we never noticed.'

'Mama wrote to the nurse who delivered me in London just after we arrived in Madrid. I went to see her.'

'I remember her writing to say we had arrived in Spain and we were happy. I found work in the Imperial Hotel near Los Cibeles. We were very excited. It was a new adventure for us.'

'Why didn't we stay there? Why did we live like gypsies – always moving around?'

'Because that's who I am cariño, your Mama and I – are – were free spirits, wandering through life. We wanted to have fun. We laughed a lot and made friends.'

'I hated it. I had no stability, no home life and no comfort. Look at this.' I hold out the hideous six–inch scar that runs on the back of my hand from my middle finger to my wrist. 'It could have been my face.'

'I'm sorry, Mikky.' He brushes away a tear with the back of his hand. 'I'm truly sorry. You have no idea how sad I am to see you like this. You're like an injured sparrow. You look so poorly. I wish I could help–'

'You never helped me when you had the opportunity.'

'I'm sorry,' he whispers and gazes down at his oil stained fingers wrapped in the sheet.

'You can go now.'

'Go?' He looks up.

'Yes.'

There are footsteps outside in the hallway and the trundle of trolley wheels. He waits until they pass and then he says:

'Will you forgive me?'

I don't answer him instead I look over his shoulder at the palm trees waving, bending and rustling in the breeze.

After a few minutes he stands up and hovers beside the bed, eventually shuffles pathetically to the door looking older than I remembered and I suddenly wish Josephine were with me.

'Papa,' I call.

He turns around with hope and half a smile on his face.

'I do forgive you.'

His face lightens into a small smile.

'But I will never forget her cruelty.'

'Take care of yourself, cariño. Let your mother look after you now as she should have done thirty-years ago.'

'Thirty-one, Papa. Thirty-one years ago.'

Chapter Twelve

'No longer shall I paint interiors with men reading and
women knitting. I will paint living people who breathe and
feel and suffer and love.'
Edvard Munch

You hardly think I would go through all this for
nothing – to plan so meticulously only to fail at the last
minute and, you hardly think that I will be affected by
a selfish, greedy and oafish man I have called Papa for
thirty-one years.

I gaze out of the window at the palm trees bending
and straining in the wind formulating my plan and
calculating my actions. I have been in hospital nine
days. It's time for me to go. I test my weight on my
feet and hold onto the bed. The pain is excruciating and
nausea invades me. I pause thinking I may be sick and
when it passes I begin inching my way slowly to the
cupboard. I take off my gown. The bruises around my
waist and my back have turned from blue and black to
yellow and brown giving a strange colour to the artistic
pictures tattooed across my body.

I'm pulling on a T-shirt when Eduardo appears in
the doorway.

'Por Dios, Mikky – que haces? You shouldn't be
out of bed. Here, let me help you.'

I let him guide me slowly back to bed and I'm
relieved and exhausted when I lay down. My swollen
face is perspiring and my throat is dry. I can't tell him
my plans or my fears.

'Mikky, you are severely bruised. Liver and

spleen injuries very often accompany traumatic kidney injuries. You must be careful. You've been very sick. You've suffered a serious assault and your body will take time to heal. You cannot go anywhere at the moment – perhaps in another day or two.'

'I need to move. I need to get out of here.'

'You can't leave just like that. You can't go – besides where would you go on your own?'

I allow him to settle me back onto the pillow and I bathe in his tender actions and kind words. His calming presence and genuine smile envelops me in warmth and I feel that he actually cares about me.

He's a professional. I chide myself. *He is a nurse. This is his job.*

'I have never experienced this before. When I was a child I was left to fend for myself. Tough love they called it. I – I wasn't allowed to be sick. I just had to get on with it.'

'Things change,' he replies, 'and you're not a child any more.'

'I'm not used to all this attention. There was never a doctor. Mama and Papa never had enough patience to wait in a clinic. They were always in a hurry; Papa had a bike to fix or money to collect and Mama was constantly harassed so she smoked cannabis to calm her nerves.'

'Mikky?'

I blink.

'Are you dreaming?' Eduardo perches on the bed beside me and takes my hand in his. 'You need looking after,' he whispers, bringing my fingers to his lips.

I want to smile but hot burning tears form behind my eyes and I wipe them on the back of my hand willing them to stop and cursing myself for being so weak.

'Shush, it will be all right. Josephine will be here soon. She loves you. She is determined to get you the best cosmetic surgeon.'

'T–H–I–E–F,' I spell out the letters. 'They haven't caught him yet.'

'Josephine told me about it. She said it was a huge misunderstanding and that you left London because you were in shock about some news she told you. They will catch him.'

'I'm not a thief,' I insist. 'I'm not a bad person.'

'I believe you.'

'I don't think he couldn't spell opportunist – either that or my forehead was too small.' I laugh, although tears continue to fall. 'If only I had more energy...'

'What do you want to do?'

I turn away and close my eyes.

'If you cannot tell me perhaps you can speak to Josephine?'

I ignore him.

'Mikky, you have to learn to trust. You have to learn to confide in those people around you – in the people who love you. Can you learn to trust me?'

***

Josephine leaves a trail of lavender scent in her wake as she glides around the room fussing over me. She regularly brings fresh flowers and fruit, and magazines and puzzles lay untouched and stacked in a pile on the cabinet beside me.

I sleep for a few hours forgetting that she is beside

me and I am comforted when I open my eyes to find her there. She leans across the bed to hold my hand.

'Are you ready to speak to my friend, Joachin?'

'Who?'

'Joachin, my friend in the Guardia Civil.'

'What for?'

'So we can get to the bottom of this mess about the painting. He wants to know about Roy and what happened in Arta.'

'I thought it was all over and forgotten. I spoke to Inspector Torres – isn't that enough?'

'Roy must be caught. He must face charges. He must learn that he cannot go around beating up young women and Joachin wants to speak to you.'

'I can't remember anything.'

'Nothing?'

'No.'

'But you must,' she insists.

'I don't.'

She regards me with intensity and I turn away. 'There's something you're not telling me. You're not being honest with me, Mikky. The art dealer was convinced–'

'I will be honest with you. I need you to help me. I've got to get out of here.'

'The doctors said in a week or so. Look at the pain you are in when you move around.'

'I have to leave today.'

'You can't.'

'Next week will be too late. Close the door. I want to tell you something and there's no one else I trust.'

She glances in the corridor before closing the door.

'Sit here,' I pat the same spot where Eduardo sits on the bed and she obeys me. 'I have to go to Malaga – urgently.'

'You can't. Why?'

'Then there is something you have to do for me. I'll never ask you for anything else but I have to be able to trust you.'

'Stop talking in riddles and tell me.'

'You're my mother. You owe me this or you will lose me forever.'

We stare at each other for a few heartbeats and I wait for her to speak. I will not be the first one to break our gaze.

'Okay.'

'Promise?'

'I promise,' she says.

***

The following day when I wake up from my late siesta Eduardo is beside me. He is out of his hospital clothes and he wears mustard coloured jeans and a tight navy T-shirt revealing well-toned muscles and tanned arms. He spends time making idle conversation, passing me pork and potatoes from a tray and encouraging me to eat.

'I want proper food,' I complain, 'and I didn't like the lunch either.'

'I'll invite you for dinner soon enough.'

'I don't recognise you in normal clothes.'

'I've had a day off. I'm still me.'

'I prefer my guardian angel in white.'

He turns his mouth down at the corners, which

make him endearing and I wonder if he has practiced this on many women before.

'Is there anyone else I have to protect you from?' he asks. 'Any other people with a grievance that you may have upset?'

I smile feebly. 'I'm a natural disaster. I have nothing to offer you. You should leave now while you can.'

'I can't walk away.'

'Why?'

'Because I am fascinated with your body art.'

I smile. 'Um. All done during my renaissance phase.'

'My Grandma is very religious.'

'Which would she like the most?' I eat another fork full. 'I could murder a paella.'

'Perhaps the *Last Supper* she is particularly fond of the Easter processions in Cadiz.'

'Not *Scream* then?' I offer him my arm.

'It's a brilliant tattoo but perhaps a little too depressing. But maybe we should find out one day – and ask her?'

'That's beginning to sound like a date.'

'Does that frighten you?'

'I'm not sure. I haven't got a great track record.'

'Maybe you've just never met the right person?'

'Maybe.' I grin at him and a warm feeling spreads though me.

'And, I make a great paella–'

There is a light tap on the door and we both turn. Josephine is dressed in a black leather jacket and beige chinos. Her hair is swept off her neck into a chignon and pearl earrings dangle from her ears. She looks tired but triumphant. She greets Eduardo with a warm smile and a kiss on both cheeks.

'Lavender?' I say referring to her perfume as she leans forward to kiss my cheek. It's warm and comforting.

'We've missed you today,' Eduardo says. 'Where were you?'

'I had to run an errand for my demanding daughter.' She maintains eye contact with me and then says icily. 'We need to talk.'

Eduardo looks at me and raises his eyebrows and I smile back at him and wink.

*****

Josephine waits until he is gone then she takes his place on the bed. She smells of outdoors, fresh air and wind and sunshine, and I want to drink in the smells that she has brought in on her clothes.

'Have you got it?' I ask.

She opens her bag and pulls out a cardboard cylindrical tube and places it on the bed.

'Are you going to lecture me?'

'Would it make a difference?' She keeps it slightly out of reach so I settle back against the pillow.

'I know how important this is to you.' She taps the cardboard with her fingernail teasing me. 'But I want you to think carefully about your future and the person you are or who you want to be–'

'I don't think you're in a position to give me a lecture on integrity so, let me have it.'

She tilts her head and when she holds it out I grip it tightly. The masterpiece is in my hand. It is finally mine.

I twist the roll to read the address written in my hurried scrawl. It's addressed to me, care of: Carmen Muñoz, Curator, Picasso Museum, Malaga.

I've done it! I sigh and lean back contentedly. I have all the time I need.

Josephine's stare is hot and my legs are trapped under the sheet. I try to tug it free but she doesn't move.

'How was Malaga?' I ask.

'It was sunny and warm. I'm pleased to get back in the same day.' Her gaze cuts me like a razor and I cannot meet her eye.

'How's Carmen?'

'She would like to see you. She was concerned. Dolores had told her about the fire.' When she pauses I look up. 'She remembers you were very kind to her when she spilt with Javier.'

'It was a long time ago.' Outside, palm trees illuminated in the streetlight bend with the breeze. I want to take the gauze off my head. I want to be normal, healthy and free. I want to run and laugh and live and go out for dinner.

'I also met Yolanda. We had tapas together near the airport. She told me that she has done most of your tattoos.'

'Aren't they inspirational?'

'There's nothing wrong in having friends who love you.'

'I'm fine.'

I trace the postmark very gently with my fingertip, remembering the morning Josephine had appeared in Arta and I took her to the art studio for the first time. After she left I had asked Maria to help me and I had sent her to the post office.

'You could have a very happy life, Mikky. You have good friends who care about you,' she insists.

'It's too late.'

'For what?'

'I don't know – everything.'

'Not everyone gets things right all the time. But you must give them the opportunity to put right what they have done wrong, and the one thing I have learned is that there's more pleasure in life if you share – especially with those you love.'

'I'm not sharing this. Not with you – not anyone.'

'I don't want it. It's not important to me. But I would like you to do the right thing, Mikky. You could get a reward from the Museum. You could pretend that you did it to recover it for them and then you wouldn't have to spend the rest of your life in hiding.'

'I'm going somewhere warm and far away.'

'It will be a hard and difficult life running, always looking over your shoulder, never knowing if you're being followed or that someone has found out. It would be like always dwelling on the past instead of looking forward to the future.'

'You're wasting your breath.'

'But if you return it, Mikky, if you give it back, then you will become the hero.'

'Like you and the Golden Icon?'

She ignores my sarcasm. 'If you like yes, but this time – with you – it's different. I'm lucky to be alive but my career is over and I lost Raffaelle. I wish I could change things or have done things differently – but I think everyone in the world feels like that about something in their lives. We would all like to rewrite some of our past, take back an action or even an unkind gesture or a word – but we can't. That is why it is called the past. But we can change the future, Mikky. The future is in our hands and there is no one else who is responsible or who will do it for us. We can make a difference to our own lives but we must stop blaming others.'

I look up at her sharply. 'I don't blame you.'

'It wouldn't make any difference, Mikky. I can't change what I did. I can't begin to imagine the girl I was at twenty-two or understand her actions. I can only give you all my love at this moment in time. I can only promise to give you all my support and I hope that one day you will love me, as I love you. You're my daughter. I would like you to do the right thing so that you can live with yourself because, believe me, living as a person who has done wrong, who has caused hurt to the person they love most in the world is the most awful thing to live with. I'm not proud of myself. I'm disappointed and ashamed that I let you down and that I wasn't there for you. But I cannot make excuses. I have to live with the consequence of my actions, my conscience and my guilt but I will tell you this – I have learned my lesson and I will not repeat it again. I will never abandon you, Mikky.'

It is the longest dialogue she has ever said and when she continues speaking her eyes are glassy with tears.

'You will make a full recovery but you must live with yourself after you leave the security and safety of this hospital. If you return the painting, people will feel sympathy for you knowing that you did it to help the Museum and you have done the right thing. People love a hero–'

'I don't want to be anyone's hero.'

'Aren't you sick of being alone? Fending everyone off with your coldness and hostility?' her voice rises.

'Do you think it's *that* important to be loved?' I retort.

'Remember, I have been ostracized and I have also been embraced – publicly. Once the fuss dies down, after you give the painting back, you will have enough money to live a reasonable life. We can hire a publicist and then you can have your own painting exhibition anywhere in the world. You are an amazing artist with a serious talent.'

'And if I don't?'

'What do you want out of life, Mikky?' She sounds exasperated but I see love, tenderness, and genuine concern reflected in her eyes as she searches for the right words. 'You can have any life you please. You are young and beautiful, and filled with energy and youth. You're at a crossroads in your life. You have a mother who wants to get to know you and form a proper loving friendship. You have Javier in London who has been a good friend to you for the past eight or ten years – he has his faults – I know, and he got carried away with the fame and recognition and the promises that Karl made him but we all make mistakes. We all need forgiveness.'

'He betrayed me.'

'He lost sight of what he wanted and he had no idea what you were after. Your paths diverged for a while but it doesn't mean you can't be friends. It doesn't mean that you don't love each other.'

I grunt and rub my stinging eyes.

'Carmen and Yolanda want to see you again. They tell me how funny, witty and intelligent you are…'

'I don't need this,' I reply, kicking my legs under the sheet but she refuses to move and persists in speaking.

'And, you have met a kind and handsome man who wants to get to know you. What will you tell Eduardo? That you really are a thief? And you deserve the name that has been scored into your forehead? Or that you are honourable and can be trusted and would one day like a family of your own?'

'The path to darkness is an easy one…' I reply.

'Maybe it is–'

'It suits me.'

Her smile is wide and loving. 'But Mikky, the path to light will fill you with warmth, security and love and you won't be alone. Eduardo and I will be with you, as will Javier and Oscar, Carmen and Yolanda, and Dolores and Maria. Perhaps you may even have a family of your own – and a daughter you will love more than life itself – and you will give her advice as I am trying to do now with you. You have a full life ahead of you. Fill it with love and happiness. All you have to do is to reach out and take it. This–' She taps the cylinder. 'Is only money and that means nothing if you are all alone with no one to share it with.'

I swallow hard. My throat itches and I bite my lip and concentrate on Carmen's address in my handwriting willing this moment to pass. It seems an age ago since I sent it, so much has happened. I sent Josephine away to Bruges and now she has been to

Malaga and collected the painting. She has spent hours at my bedside and will even pay for cosmetic surgery.

I sigh. 'Would you verify my story?'

'Of course.'

'You would lie?'

'If you were doing the right thing and I had to protect you.'

'You really would do anything for me, wouldn't you? You would risk your reputation to repair mine.' I tap the plastic lid.

'I'm your mother,' she replies. 'Before we met I imagined you wouldn't speak to me – I will not let you go.'

'But you expect me to give this back – after all my planning and hard work?'

'Planning?'

'Two years ago I did some restoration work in Bruges. I was there when Mrs Green bought the painting from the art dealer – the guy you met –Theo Brinkmann acted as a go–between for the IRA. He was coerced into selling it and Mrs Green agreed that when she died it would be returned to him and he or his son could legitimately claim it as the original masterpiece and receive a reward from the Museum.'

'And you followed her?'

'She was ninety and I guessed at her age she wouldn't live for long.'

'You went to London?'

'When the flat beside hers came up for rent I knew it was too good an opportunity to pass up. It was an opportunity some people would call fate–'

'But you didn't – kill her?'

'Don't be ridiculous, Josephine. I'm a thief not a

murderer. Can't you read?' I point at my forehead.
'Besides I became really fond of the old lady. She was
lovely. She was more like the Grandma I never had…'

Josephine reaches for my fingers but I move my
hand away and continue speaking. 'I painted the
forgery at Christmas after we came back from Dresden
and the night Mrs Green died, I went into her house
and switched it. No one else had seen the painting –
only Roy and I guessed he wouldn't know the
difference and if he did then it was only his word. But
then Javier spoke to Mrs Green and then Karl Blakey
got involved and Roy was convinced he had been
duped.'

'So, after you stole the painting why didn't you
just disappear?'

'I was going to but then,' I pause and decide to tell
the truth. 'You arrived in London.'

'You wanted to see me?'

'I wanted to support Javier.'

'Oh.' Her head drops.

'You had a bond with him. You were important
and he asked me to be kind to you.'

'You kept the painting in your flat?'

'I was worried that Javier might guess.'

'And you…?'

'I posted it to Mallorca. And then you came to
Arta and then Karl appeared and I thought it would
only be a matter of time before Roy showed up so I
made the decision to wait and face him. I decided to
brazen it out.'

'That's why you got rid of me…'

'I knew he was angry.'

'And the hurry to get to Malaga?'

'If the press wrote about a stolen painting Carmen would suspect me and I didn't want her to open it.' I tap the tube with my finger then peel the tape away and flick open the lid. As I pull the painting from the cylinder I glance at Josephine and when I unfurl it, she gasps. 'Oh my goodness.'

I'm holding a canvas measuring 69cm by 63cm – exactly the same size as the Vermeer but it's a Cubist water colour painting. I am holding a picture that appears fragmented and abstract.

We both stare at it.

'That's not *The Concert*.' Her eyes are wide in disbelief and her mouth is open.

'No, it isn't,' I agree.

'I – I – I haven't substituted it, Mikky. I promise you. I did as you said and I didn't even open it.'

'You haven't?'

'No – I promise.'

I laugh. 'Don't worry, Josephine. I believe you. This is it – this is the Vermeer.'

'This? It can't be–'

'I painted over it.'

'But – you can't do that. It's a – it's a masterpiece.'

'I can restore it.'

'You've ruined it.'

'No one will ever know. I'm a professional.'

'But you can't keep it.'

'Why not?'

'It's stealing.'

'It's in my possession. It belongs to me.'

'You're not clever, Mikky. Someone will find out.'

'Like who? This is our secret Josephine – no one else knows – just like the fact that you are my mother.'

'And what if I don't like your secret? What if I don't agree, Mikky? Then what?'

'There are lots of rich Eastern Europeans who will jump at buying it.'

'It's not yours to sell. It belongs to the Isabella Stewart Museum,' she says.

'It belongs to me.'

'You're not thief. You're better than that.'

'Come on, Josephine. Think of it as an adventure. Come with me and let's have some fun,' I smile.

'Please, Mikky. I beg you – don't...'

I place it on the bed and it lies between us, semi-curled up like an ordinary painting.

There's a risk I could get caught. Maybe Inspector Torres will follow me. Roy hasn't been found and they're still investigating Karl's death. I will have to deny everything and keep lying for the rest of my life. Who would I trust?

I sigh and lean back against the pillow suddenly feeling very weary. The thought of being a hero is beginning to seem a lot easier and a lot more enticing.

'Give it back,' she says. 'Please.'

Through the open window palm trees rustle and sway beckoning me and I'm reminded of the outdoors: long sandy beaches, the sun on my skin, and the promise of a paella and cold beer. I want my freedom and in a moment of complete clarity, my mind is suddenly made up and a sense of calmness fills me.

'It's worth a fortune,' I reply.

'But you're worth far more, Mikky. I don't want to see you go to prison.' She takes hold of my hand.

'I have no intention of it.'

'A daughter is worth more than any masterpiece,' she whispers. 'My daughter is priceless.'

'Well, thank goodness for that, Josephine. We finally agree on something.'

I lean forward and for the first time in my life I feel my mother's arms around me and I am overwhelmed with tenderness and love; relief, joy, comfort and happiness flood through me – a tsunami of emotion – and when we pull apart my mother's cheeks are as wet as my own.

THE END

Other books available on Amazon & Kindle by Janet Pywell

The Golden Icon

Josephine Lavelle a once–famous opera singer and international outcast has one last opportunity to resurrect her career. She was born to sing Puccini's *Tosca*. But her fight for the future she craves is derailed when her ex-husband embroils her in a cynical blackmail plot. She is forced to take possession of a solid gold icon, part of a secret hoard of art treasures stolen by the Nazis. Josephine must come to terms with her past and fight for her own life.

If only her choices were simple…

Red Shoes and Other Short Stories

RED SHOES and Other Short Stories is an entertaining mix of unusual and absorbing tales, set in Ireland, Portugal, Bosnia, England and Spain with themes of humor, crime and mystery to stir your passion and pique your interest.

Ellie Bravo

Ellie Bravo is more than just another love story. She becomes the marketing manager for an ailing IT company and deals with prejudice, violence, jealousy and a computer virus that threatens the travel industry. Ellie has chosen a difficult path but after falling for her colleague she has a harder choice to make…

www.janetpywell.com

Reading Group Guide

One of the central themes to this novel is honesty. Where does it come into play? Is there an over–arching message in *Masterpiece* about the consequences of telling the truth?

Could you relate to the characters? Did your feelings toward the characters change during the novel? Why?

As in real life not all character are wholly 'good' or wholly 'bad.' Do you think the main characters in this novel had a reasonable balance to evoke emotion? What feelings were they? Did you find the distinction between their right and wrong actions conflicting or satisfying?

Which character do you feel is the most betrayed?

The structure of the novel is based on Mikky's point of view and written in the first person. Did you find her a truthful narrator? Did you find this structure made an impact on the twists of the novel and how the plot was revealed?

Transformation of or evolvement with a character can create emotional conflict for the reader. Did you identify with Josephine's developing character from *The Golden Icon* and her quest to find her adopted child?

The important themes of *Masterpiece* are family and relationships. What does it highlight about how we behave with regard to family and the lengths we will go to protect them. What effect do the secrets have when revealed?